One Baker's Dozen

By

Jay Dubya

One Baker's Dozen

By

Jay Dubya

Published by
Jay Dubya
Hammonton, NJ 08037
2175_7

ISBN 978-1-58909-477-2

Printed in the United States of America

Other Books by Jay Dubya

Adult Fiction

Black Leather and Blue Denim, A '50s Novel
The Great Teen Fruit War, A 1960' Novel
Ron Coyote, Man of La Mangia
Frat' Brats, A '60s Novel
Pieces of Eight
Pieces of Eight, Part II
Pieces of Eight, Part III
Pieces of Eight, Part IV
The Wholly Book of Genesis
The Wholly Book of Exodus
The Wholly Book of Doo-Doo-Rot-on-Me
Thirteen Sick Tasteless Classics
Thirteen Sick Tasteless Classics, Part II
Thirteen Sick Tasteless Classics, Part III
Thirteen Sick Tasteless Classics, Part IV
Thirteen Sick Tasteless Classics, Part V
So Ya' Wanna' Be A Teacher!
Mauled Maimed Mangled Mutilated Mythology
Fractured Frazzled Folk Fables & Fairy Farces
FFFF & FF, Part II
Nine New Novellas
Nine New Novellas, Part II
Nine New Novellas, Part III
Nine New Novellas, Part IV
Two Baker's Dozen
RAM: Random Articles and Manuscripts
Modern Mythology
Time Travel Tales
UFO: Utterly Fantastic Occurrences
Prime-Time Crime Time
Snake Eyes and Boxcars
Snake Eyes and Boxcars, Part II
The Psychic Dimension
The Psychic Dimension, Part II
Shakespeare: Slammed, Smeared, Savaged and Slaughtered
Shakespeare: S, S, S & S, Part II
First Person Stories
The Arcane Arcade

Thirteen Tantalizing Tales
PLOTS
PLOTS, Part II
THEMES
Hawthorne: Hacked, Shakespeare: Sacked, & Thurber: Thwacked
Hawthorne: Hazed, Hooked, Hammered and Hijacked
Suite 16
The FBI Inspector
Poe: Pelted, Pounded, Pummeled and Pulverized
Twain: Tattered, Trounced, Tortured and Traumatized
London: Lashed, Lacerated, Lampooned and Lambasted
O. Henry: Obscenely and Outrageously Obliterated
Homer's Odd Sea Odyssey
HOMER'S ILL ILIAD
Homer's Ill Iliad and Odd Sea Odyssey
The Timeless Time Machine
War of the Worlds
The Invisible Man
Parody Paradise
Parody Paradise, Part II
Parody Paradise, Part III
Parody Paradise, Part IV
A Christmas Carol
Bee 17, Short Stories
Bee 17, Part II, Short Stories
Bee 17, Part III, Short Stories
Bee 17, Part IV, Short Stories
Bee 17, Part V, Short Stories
Bee 17, Part VI, Short Stories

Young Adult Fantasy Novels and Stories

Pot of Gold
Enchanta
Space Bugs, Earth Invasion
The Eighteen Story Gingerbread House

Contents

“Luck and Love”

The first Sunday in July marks the “Annual Blueberry Festival” on the grounds of the Hammonton Middle School at the intersection of Fairview Avenue and Liberty Street. The event attracts an enthusiastic crowd of over twenty-thousand visitors to the somnolent, southern New Jersey agricultural community, which proudly advertises itself as “The Blueberry Capital of the World”. The Hammonton Lions Club sells blueberry pies, muffins, strudel, and turnovers as a fundraiser at the popular event, and other town service clubs and organizations offer visitors freshly picked twelve-pint flats of blueberries; blueberry jam; blueberry custard, and other assorted blueberry products with various enterprising town merchants hawking boardwalk-type food, children’s amusement rides, and carnival-style balloons and souvenirs.

On that sultry 2007 summer afternoon, Mark Varga sauntered around the festival grounds, eating a large pretzel that he had purchased at the Kiwanis booth. The paint store co-owner always had enjoyed attending carnivals, county fairs, and circuses, which generally made him reminisce about his childhood memories at such similar recreational affairs. ‘I don’t have to stop and buy any junk food at the corner WaWa convenience store today,’ Mark philosophically mused. ‘I have all of these high-calorie temptations right here, and only a dollar away!’

A fortune-telling machine, featuring a tawdry-dressed, manikin gypsy woman positioned inside soon caught the casual stroller’s attention, so Mark fumbled inside his pocket with his loose left hand for a quarter to insert into the alluring slot. ‘I remember when these things used to be a penny,’ Varga cynically recollected. ‘I’ve always been a sucker for such silly devices, whether they’re on the Atlantic City, Ocean City, or Wildwood boardwalks, or right here at the annual Blueberry Festival,’ the fascinated attendee acknowledged. ‘I’ll just insert two bits into this ancient mechanism, and see what either fate or destiny has in store for me. My mediocre life could use an infusion of good luck and excitement. Out of curiosity, let’s just see what materializes.’

Ten-seconds later, a small printed card exited the obsolete-looking, slow-operating machine, and the prognostic language read: “You’ll have success based on your upcoming skill. By all means, show your confidence! Don't be humble! Learn to be assertive! And finally, love will eventually come your way!"

'Such a general evaluation could pertain to anyone ambling around these crowded festival grounds,' Mark Varga reckoned. 'The statement was a little too vague for my liking. Serves me right for throwing a quarter away for the same type of information I could've easily gotten in the horoscope section of the *Atlantic City Press.* So much for astrological predictions! Oh well,' the normally shy and laconic fellow reasoned, 'at least I still have three bites remaining from this absolutely delicious pretzel. Now, all I need is an ice-cold *Coke* to wash-down this non-healthy junk food.'

After purchasing his refreshing soft drink at the nearby Rotary Club concession stand, Mark whimsically contemplated a recent pursuit he had been considering. The fortune-telling device had given the Bellevue Avenue businessman a certain idea. 'I know what I'll do!' Mark persuaded his often-doubting mind. 'I'll try out for the local theatrical company's upcoming play 'Autumn Frolic'. I don't care if my old high school nemesis Cliff Arnold is also trying-out for the lead part, even though the bully's landed several supporting actor roles at the prestigious Walnut Street Theater over in 'Philly. The newly-constructed Eagle Theater on Vine Street has just been completed, thanks to the contributions and efforts of the Hammonton Arts League, and now, I'm more than determined to show the world my undiscovered, amateur acting talent,' the suddenly inspired paint merchant decided. 'I'll not let Cliff Arnold intimidate me, even though the jerk beat me out when we were seniors at Hammonton High for the lead in *West Side Story*. I understand that Cliff's seeking the male lead role in 'Autumn Frolic', but now he's in for some unexpected stiff competition. This play tryout rivalry will not be high school revisited, that's for sure!'

On Wednesday, July 11th, 2007 inspired Mark Varga followed his impulse to escape depressing monotony. His paint-retailing partner Chuck Hafter would be running the Bellevue Avenue store on Mark's regular day off, so Varga decided to abandon his reclusive conservative lifestyle and drive thirty-miles east to Atlantic City and explore the Showboat Casino, situated on the north end of the world-famous boardwalk. 'When I was a wandering teenager, I used to love traveling with friends to boardwalks, especially those in Wildwood, Ocean City, Seaside Heights, Coney Island, Asbury Park, and of course Atlantic City. And now that A.C. is such a phenomenal gambling attraction,' Mark considered, 'I figure I should mingle with some exclusive adult companions also seeking entertainment, and temporarily escape from everyday reality. Harrah's now owns the Showboat, Caesar's World, and Bally's Hotel and Casino, but for some reason, I feel an urge to exclusively visit the Showboat. I suppose I like the gaudy décor and the rowdy New Orleans Mardi Gras theme.'

The Blueberry Festival's fortune-telling booth had had a remote impact on Varga and had given the bashful paint merchant incentive to deviate from his ordinarily very predictable behavior pattern. 'I seldom take risks, but I'll gladly lose five-hundred dollars if that's what's required to shake my mind out of its present lethargy,' Mark concluded as the driver maneuvered his mist-green *Nissan Altima* off of Pacific Avenue and into the Showboat's high-rise garage. 'I need to get this wicked depression out of my system, and today is as good an opportunity as any to do a little unique experimentation with my all-too-boring life. Oh well, okay Showboat! Get ready for another foolish sucker, willfully entering your alluring trap!'

Inside the glittering casino Mark tried his luck at a nickel slot machine "Jackpot Party", and the player boldly thought after inserting a crisp fifty-dollar bill into the money chute, 'To win anything decent, I gotta' play the maximum seventy-five coins. Now that's three-dollars and seventy-five cents of hard-earned cash for a single spin, according to my simple mathematics. But I suppose as the old wheel-of-chance barkers used to yell on the resort boardwalks all along the coast, I have to 'spin to win'.'

Much to Mark's surprise and satisfaction, on his fourth attempt, he had hit the machine's exciting "Bonus Round", where Varga could keep selecting coin accumulation mini-jackpots until the exhilarated player finally chose two "Bloopers" after randomly touching available choices provided on the video screen. Amazingly, the lucky gambler had amassed a bonus total of seven- hundred-and-fifty-dollars when his good fortune finally expired. 'This is the best I've ever done at any casino. Usually, I have the luck of the Biblical Job, and even the most minimal success eludes me. Now, I have the house's money to fool-around with. I'll quit the slot machines while I'm ahead, and see what damage I can do at the blackjack tables.'

The day-tripping bachelor anxiously meandered his way through the crowded casino from the nickel slot area to the more sophisticated and ever-tantalizing blackjack tables. 'All I have to remember is to hold my hand on seventeen against the house, or hope to get an ace accompanied by a face card or a ten,' the happy "Jackpot Party" slot machine winner imagined. 'If my luck at chance continues, who knows what'll happen after that?'

Contrary to his characteristic, frugal nature, the maverick-for-a-day felt compelled to sit-down at a ten-dollar minimum table and bravely acquire fifty chips in exchange for legal tender. 'I'll wager my original total dollar amount I had budgeted to lose, and if I do just that, I'll still be over two-hundred-dollars ahead when I exit the doors, and then drive back to Hammonton,' the anxious bettor figured. As Mark glanced around the table to evaluate the other preoccupied casino poker patrons, Varga quickly determined from the grim expressions exhibited upon their countenances that the other four seated men were 'serious casino customers and dedicated gamblers'.

After two hours of impressive luck (evident in ace and face card combinations), Mark had vanquished both his four opponents and also the house at the green felt blackjack table. His successful efforts had accumulated a remarkable bonanza of seven-thousand- three-hundred-and-fifty-dollars. One of the other zealous players temporarily abandoned his stone-cold frown and reluctantly congratulated Varga on *his* rather splendid achievement.

"My name's Clint McGuire," the stranger sitting next to the jubilant card victor introduced himself. "And I've won over a hundred blackjack tournaments out in Vegas and Reno. But I gotta' admit that this afternoon, you demonstrated perhaps the greatest good luck streak I've ever had the privilege of viewing. Are you a professional gambler, or an expert card counter? You certainly showed me great skill and savvy!"

"No, Sir," Mark modestly answered, shaking his head in sheer, humble astonishment. "I'm just a regular guy who came here to the Showboat out of pure boredom while seeking a little gambling adventure. Usually, on the average Wednesday,

I'm home trimming the bushes on my property, mowing my lawn, or watching old vintage movies on cable television. Today, you caught me strangely deviating from my mid-week routine. I assure you, Clint, that my success today was an extraordinary aberration!"

"To tell you the truth, I was about to report you to the management," the pit boss interrupted before the perspiring blackjack dealer could render an opinion or additional comment. "But now, I believe that you were just a typical guy involved in a fantastic win skein. I gotta' commend you on having a really impressive win streak that must've had the camera surveillance guys upstairs shaking their heads. You could've conducted a gambling seminar today! I gotta' confess, you really gave us a gambling clinic!"

"Again, nice going, and I'm very envious of your prowess at the table," the renowned Las Vegas blackjack champion Clint McGuire acknowledged and praised. "I'm never seen anyone have such tremendous luck holding on seventeen against the house. Whenever I tried duplicating your standard method, I was nailed with the dealer landing himself' a three or a four card. The angels were definitely on your side from the moment you sat-down at the table. If not the angels, then the Devil himself! Again, nice going!"

"Thank you, Mr. McGuire!" Mark modestly replied. "I don't believe I'll ever be able to perform so marvelously again if I live to be a thousand. It was just a once in a lifetime miracle, and I'm glad that you were here to witness it happening. Now to redeem my chips and convert them into cold cash! It was a distinct pleasure making your acquaintance!"

On the pleasant *Route 30* westward drive back to Hammonton, the jubilant winner reviewed recent developments in his very active mind. 'Not only did I triumph against the odds at the nickel slot machine, but I also defeated perhaps the world's greatest blackjack player. If I had known the man's identity as the notorious Clint McGuire, I could've never had the wherewithal to do what I had done. Perhaps I should've gotten a room and stayed overnight at the Showboat, but I didn't want to press my luck at the tables!'

Then, the contented motorist reflected some more on current events. 'Could that silly quarter card I had gotten at the Blueberry Festival have caused all this to happen? Perhaps that damned paper object isn't that ridiculous after all! Oh well, after the income taxes have been withheld from my Showboat exploit, I'm still five-thousand bucks out in front of Uncle Sam! Maybe next Wednesday, I'll take a casual excursion over to Caesar's World!' the man behind the wheel chuckled and then smiled into his rear-view mirror. 'If I'm in a wild mood, I'll even wear a Roman toga and sandals!'

In early August, Mark gained the courage to bid on a sheriff sale property on Valley Avenue, his offer going up against Chad Ingram, a local real estate mogul that seldom lost a bid. Incredibly, Mark had offered a hundred-and-three-thousand-dollars for a two-lot property, beating out Ingram's bid by a mere fifteen-hundred-bucks. A week later, the very scrupulous and confident Mr. Ingram purchased the prime building lots from Mark for a quarter of a million. The wheeler-dealer hesitantly commended Varga for *his* "great audacity" in cleverly overbidding his bid.

"That was quite unbelievable, Mark, the way you coolly obtained those lots over on Valley Avenue," Chad Ingram stated. "I never suspected that you would've gone over a hundred-thousand. But I had promised Lou Cappuccio, the builder, that I would sell those prime locations to him to construct two luxury homes, so now I had to put up another hundred-thousand to go partners with Lou on the dual projects! Thanks to your recent out-of-character audacity, I'll be lucky to break even on the deal. I never thought that you would be so aggressive! I'll certainly be more alert and wary of how you operate at a sealed-bid land auction next time!"

"Thanks for the nifty kudos, Chad!" the equally-shocked paint-store retailer returned. "I can't exactly explain what had gotten into me! I simply decided to use some recent winnings at Showboat Casino, along with my life's savings, to make the settlement. And the next thing I know, you come along and more than double my investment. God Chad! I'm beginning to absolutely love American capitalism! Free enterprise is a really wonderful thing! It involves much more intriguing aspects than merely buying and selling gallons of paint! Perhaps I'll soon be doing some more profitable real estate dabbling."

"I hope some of your terrific magic rubs-off on me!" Chad respectfully replied with a degree of admiration apparent in his tone of voice. "I just want you to know that your audacious wizardry has not gone unnoticed throughout the town!"

'Holy cow!' Mark marveled and considered. 'Under ordinary circumstances, I could've never outbid or outsmarted Chad Ingram at a sheriff's sale! The developer even agreed to paying-off the properties' back taxes if I cooperated with him! Perhaps that cheap gypsy card from the fortune-telling booth does possess some supernatural ability after all! I guess time will tell!'

September soon rolled-around on the 2007 calendar, and Mark Varga was determined to follow through on his long-contemplated ambition of challenging his high school nemesis, arrogant Cliff Arnold, in the Eagle Playhouse Theater's upcoming production of "Autumn Frolic". 'Okay, first I had inadvertently won big at the Showboat Casino, not knowing that I was going up against Clint McGuire, one of the premier blackjack players in the United States. Then, I shrewdly out-bid that wily Chad Ingram, although I gotta' admit that the real estate guru had entirely underestimated me, based on my past performance as a feckless business wimp,' Mark considered and reviewed. 'But in the final analysis, I still greatly profited from my initiative. Now, my next difficult obstacle is to defeat golden-throat Cliff Arnold, my old high school play contender, who had coyly stolen my former sweethear,t Jennifer Reynolds, away from me, and then flamboyantly escorted the blonde beauty to the Hammonton High senior prom.'

At the grueling tryouts for the lead role in "Autumn Frolic", the long-shot underdog Mark Varga astounded everyone (including the casting manager, the producer, and the director) by convincingly outperforming a perplexed and overconfident Cliff Arnold, who then shook his head in despair at hearing and interpreting the stunning (and to *his* huge disbelief), disappointing announcement. And the rejuvenated, late-blooming stage talent calmly received all of the exaggerated accolades in stride, as the incredulous and despondent nemesis, Cliff Arnold, dejectedly accepted a supporting character role with his head crestfallen, barely making eye contact with either Mark Varga, or the Eagle Theater play officials.

* * * * * * * * * * * * * *

In early October, Mark encountered his high school heartthrob inside a franchised pharmacy at the intersection of *Route 206* and *Route 30,* the White Horse Pike. Initially, the general conversation between the pair was stilted and cordial, but then the twice married Jennifer (Baker, Harper) Reynolds made a rather startling personal admission that astonished her former, rejected, Hammonton High beau.

"You know, Mark," the forty-year-old attractive blonde said and emphasized, "I thought that your performance last week at the Eagle Theater was totally magnificent. Your elocution on stage was near perfect! And I had no idea that you possessed such a powerful, dynamic singing voice."

"Thanks a million, Jen!" the blushing recipient of the laudatory remark replied as Mark's mind searched for the correct words to appropriately express himself. "I guess that all those years pretending to be a tenor in the shower has finally paid off. Humans can accomplish great feats, once they put their minds down to it. Please pardon the raunchy, Shakespearean pun, but I suppose I've finally got my act together!"

"And I also understand from town gossip that you've more than adequately conquered an international blackjack champion over in Atlantic City, not to mention you cunningly outsmarting that devious rogue, Chad Ingram, over a couple of valuable Valley Avenue building lots. And Mark," Jennifer proceeded with her abundant compliments, "your local reputation is really thriving around town with you earning the lead role in that hilarious play 'Autumn Frolic', easily beating-out that sanctimonious, snot-nosed creep, Clifford Anderson Arnold!"

"Well, Jen, I do believe that my depressed ego had really received big boosts when I had hit it big in Atlantic City, and then when I parlayed my success into the lucrative real estate investment involving that lousy cad-speculator, Chad Ingram," Varga explicitly indicated, showing a rare degree of braggadocio. "Now that I've gotten the leading role over my formerly invincible old rival, Cliff Arnold, in the town play, I guess I've successfully attained most of my personal goals. Quite frankly, the Showboat Casino escapade seemed to be the catalyst that sent all the other dominoes into a terrific chain reaction," Mark sincerely explained. "But gratefully, I've now completed all of my recently set objectives. Thanks again for your encouraging words, Jennifer! I really appreciate your kindness and encouragement!"

But then the gorgeous Jennifer (Baker, Harper) Reynolds had a most-staggering revelation to divulge to her old boyfriend, standing in the center of the mammoth box-store pharmacy's main aisle. "Well anyway, Mark. I gotta' confess that I had once dated both Cliff Arnold and Chad Ingram back in high school, at separate times of course," the flirtatious Jennifer Reynolds confidentially emphasized certain past truths that Varga had already known. "But ever since *our* junior year at Hammonton High, I've had an ongoing crush on you, Mark, that absolutely wouldn't quit. That being said," the still-attractive woman continued, "how would you like to take me to the Showboat to demonstrate exactly how you had won that handsome payoff at the blackjack table? Perhaps you could even enter a card-playing tournament before we enjoy a delicious dinner together."

Mark Varga was positively flabbergasted upon learning of his former girlfriend's ongoing fondness for him over the past twenty-two years. For a long interval, the normally reticent fellow was at a loss for words. Then, the fortunate paint store proprietor finally gathered together his scruples. "Gee, Jen. I had no idea that you've kept a warm spot in your heart for me over the past two decades. Honestly, I'm both flattered and thrilled! What actually motivated you to finally tell me how you've truly felt? I hope not either guilt or greed!"

"To be perfectly sincere about this confession, Mark, I really feel quite silly telling you my true motivation, so please promise to keep it a secret," Jennifer prefaced her honest response. "I had always lacked the emotional strength to approach you after I had gone to the senior prom with Cliff, and left your sensitive feelings in shambles. I've been pretty ashamed at my selfish actions and have had to live with my negligence and insensitivity all these years! Incidentally, Mark," Jennifer continued her admission. "In addition to regretting abusing you, I had a really lousy time on that particular prom date with abominable Cliff Arnold. It certainly was less than mediocre! But it's all water over the proverbial dam, now! I'm sure that *we've* both greatly matured over the years! I feel relieved getting this heavy burden off my conscience! Perhaps now, we can start at square one again!"

"But what finally prompted you to tell me your true feelings?" Mark insisted on learning as several pharmacy shoppers pushed their carts around the reminiscing pair. "To quote infamous Long John Silver, your expression sort of *shivered my timbers* when I heard your warm words, which were a kind of poetic music to my ears! In fact, I still feel a trifle weak-in-the-knees!"

Mark Varga was in for more than a coincidence as the former loser attentively listened to Jennifer's next shocking statement, with his mouth agape. The bachelor's vulnerable mind had trouble processing the extraordinary information.

"Okay, here's my full explanation, plain and simple, Mark. But please don't laugh at what your ears are about to hear!" Jennifer requested in an embarrassed tone of voice. "The whole matter will sound entirely absurd to you, that I'm quite sure. Excuse me for sounding a trifle superstitious!"

"Alright, now that you've captured my wholehearted interest, I cross my heart and hope to die!" Varga replied with a wry smile evident on his facial features. "I'm ready for just about anything except death, bankruptcy, and cancer!"

"As you are aware, Mark, every summer I religiously attend the 16th of July carnival celebrating the feast of Our Lady of Mt. Carmel," Jennifer rambled and revealed. "That Sunday afternoon, I noticed a lackluster-looking fortune-telling machine with an ancient-looking gypsy woman dummy inside. Her face appeared as if it needed a new coat of paint. Anyway, I inserted a quarter in the slot, and a card was dispensed reading: 'Be more assertive in the future! Marry for love and not money! Just pretend it's Sadie Hawkins Day, and approach the one you really love, and let him or her know your true feelings!' Well Mark, I suppose the rest is now all history! What do you think about all that craziness?"

Mark Varga's head became a tad dizzy as the former boyfriend abruptly cleared his throat and rapidly blinked his eyes. "Oh my God, Jen! My mind's spinning like an out-of-control top. It's all quite an amazing coincidence! Now please brace yourself. I have a fantastically similar fortune-telling story to disclose!"

"Galaxy Gambol"

"Galaxy Gambol"The celestial Milky Way Galaxy is home to planet Earth and its solar system, with the Sun representing just a small orange star situated among billions of other hot gas masses, ranging in size from white dwarfs to immense giants. "The Galaxy," although mediocre in size compared to others in *our* remote neck of the Universe, is around 100,000 light years across, a rather massive diametrical distance when considering that light travels at a mind-boggling speed of 186,282 miles per second. The Milky Way is actually spiral-shaped and flat like a pancake, with *our* puny solar system being located approximately thirty-to-thirty-five thousand light years from the center. Our commonplace "Galaxy" has a bulge at its middle, giving the distinct appearance of being lens-shaped.

Star clusters, dust clouds, swirling nebulous-like gases, and a variety of planets and moons are held together by the force of gravity, as the billions of stars rotate around the center of the Milky Way. And naturally, the dependent planets revolve around the myriad stars. A million earths could fit inside the Sun, and the Earth's star obediently moves once around the center of the galaxy every 200 million years. And it is quite well-known to astronomers that a million stars the size of our Sun could easily fit inside the most gigantic stars populating our rather ordinary-sized Galaxy. Although the Earth has existed for four-to-five billion years, the Milky Way (along with the Universe) is estimated at being around thirteen billion years old.

The Milky Way is pin-wheeled in shape, featuring four spiral arms extending out from its center, one of which includes our relatively tiny solar system along with our quite diminutive Earth. The interesting reference "Milky" pertains to the hazy band of dull light readily visible to observers on Earth on a clear evening. "The Galaxy" and our corresponding Universe hardly experience change over the centuries, as man in the year 2,397 AD boldly attempts exploring the vastness of outer space in search of other intelligent life forms, and also finding solutions to the Universe's great cosmic mysteries. Two such daring astronauts are Americans Richard Mitchell and Gary Dobbs of the United States Space Coalition.

* * * * * * * * * * * * * *

"Here we are Gary, many billions of miles away from Earth, searching for intelligent life, when we aren't preoccupied mapping-out the exact dimensions of the Milky Way," Astronaut Richard Mitchell said to Astronaut Gary Dobbs. "It's a lonely existence out here in deep space, so please by all means, stay healthy and mentally alert. Believe it or not, I even miss my wife and kids, and if something fatal should ever happen to you, I'll be several thousand light years away from the nearest Coalition outpost on Alpha 7. Now, I know exactly how awed the advance scouts used to feel, heading towards the Pacific in the old Wild, Wild West!"

"Sure thing, Rich!" Astronaut Gary Dobbs casually concurred. "Earth's around four-billion-years-old, and if the planet's history were a twenty-four-hour-day, man's tenure would be represented in just the last three seconds before midnight. Ya' wanna' know something, Rich? I even miss my wife's home cooking and listening to Julia and Jimmy arguing over what non-educational telescreen 3-D shows to watch," Dobbs elaborated. "But I do agree with you that the human race really discovered and developed a lot of knowledge in the last fifteen-thousand-years. Only fifteen millennia ago, our primitive, scavenging ancestors were still living in caves, wishing that they had the ability and tools to build sturdy huts on mountainsides. Just look at all the terrific inventions man has created since the time of Edison. I mean, it's been one heck of a quantum leap forward."

"And thanks to organ and cell regeneration technology, along with matter-anti-matter thrust accelerators, and the use of wormhole shortcuts existing between star systems," Astronaut Richard Mitchell casually pointed-out to his colleague, "you and I can confidently voyage from constellation to constellation without the worry of physical or mental aging. And needless to say, our well-preserved wives can enjoy the benefits of their anti-aging serums, and will look just about as beautiful as the girls had appeared in the past, when we finally return home. Who in their right mind would've ever imagined three-centuries-ago that the average life expectancy of an adult male or female would be three-hundred-years? And the best part of the scenario is that we won't show our age by becoming geriatrics until we're two-hundred-and-eighty. That is," Astronaut Richard Mitchell objectively qualified, "unless of course accidental death interrupts the delayed aging process."

"Very eloquent speech!" Astronaut Gary Dobbs commended his garrulous companion. "Now Rich, if you hadn't joined the space program after saucer training school, you could've been an excellent Congressman, or maybe even a famous Senator. But getting back on topic," Dobbs said and paused while seeking the best words to explain his lucid thoughts, "I gotta' admit that I'm becoming a bit sentimental while we're jabbering-away, trying to evade the inevitable front porch rocking chair. In the meantime, I know that I can't wait to see Carla, Jimmy, and Julia, and that you can't wait to reunite with Jackie and your daughter Denise."

The astronauts were diligently charting new interstellar territory for the Coalition, finally leaving the spiral arm in the Milky Way that was home to Earth, Venus, and Mars, and now becoming the first humans to navigate through unknown space, while the voyagers were investigating "the second spiral" in the expansive Galaxy. Everything seemed copacetic and was proceeding according to schedule without a noticeable problem or hitch. Mitchell and Dobbs intended (with great anticipation) to be back home in another twelve-months, upon satisfactorily completing their scheduled three-year expedition.

"As long as our trusty instruments know where Polaris is," Rich chuckled while glancing in Dobbs direction, "we shouldn't get lost anywhere this side of Pluto. Say, Gary. Do you suppose kids will someday be studying about our spectacular accomplishments along with the achievements of Columbus, Balboa, Neil Armstrong, and Harold V. Clements?"

"By the time we finally get back to Earth, I predict that schools and reading will have become obsolete," Astronaut Gary Dobbs politely joked to his fellow journeyman. "Although this has been a pleasant and uneventful cruise so far, I just hope, Rich, that we aren't history before we *are* history, if ya' know what I mean! I have a weird feeling about this particular space trek, if ya' grasp my gist! If we both die on this adventurous mission, neither of us will ever be buried back on good old Terra Firma!"

"Forget about me becoming a Congressman, Senator, or even President of the United Federation Coalition!" Rich Mitchell quipped with an element of anxiety evident in his tone of voice. "I do believe that I'm traveling through this sector of the Galaxy with none-other than Socrates resurrected! I must admit that your abundant wisdom eclipses my limited empirical knowledge!"

The jovial astronauts were then ready to enter a twenty-four-hour period of suspended animation in separate "life conditions' simulation chambers" in order to replenish their bodies. Just then, Astronaut Dobbs astutely indicated an observation on the overhead screen and mentioned the sighting to his normally calm-and-collected companion. Soon, the merry conversation transitioned to a more conservative verbal exchange. "Now, we're definitely speeding ahead where no man has ever before ventured!" Gary Dobbs described to Rich Mitchell. "We're now entering deeper into the second spiral arm of the Milky Way!"

"And if my weary eyes are accurately interpreting our new environment," Astronaut Mitchell marveled and commented, "this second arm incredibly seems to be a facsimile of the first. Look in the distance, Gary! In the background, there're almost carbon copy duplicates of Capricorn, Sagittarius, Scorpio, and Libra! We can't be re-entering our corner of the Galaxy!" the now-excited mission commander stated. "But contrary to reason, certain familiar patterns of the first arm appear to be replicated in this second spiral! This is all pretty damned phenomenal! I think I'm beginning to require the services of a skilled psychiatrist!"

"And look over there to our right, Rich!" Astronaut Dobbs anxiously exclaimed. "Carbon copies of Taurus, Aries, Pisces, and Aquarius. Now confirm my thinking, but could we have just discovered a new constant or axiom of the Universe? Could this second Galaxy arm have the identical twelve zodiac constellations as those star-groupings seen from Earth in the first arm?"

"If this bewildering truth we're witnessing is present throughout the whole Galaxy, then perhaps it's also redundant throughout the entire Universe!" bewildered Astronaut Mitchell speculated and articulated in amazement as sweat-beads began appearing upon his brow. "Let's get all our ducks in a row, Gary, before we prematurely begin formulating any outrageous generalizations or wild theories! But now that I also recognize Leo, Cancer, Gemini, and Taurus," Mitchell perceptively uttered, "I can only conclude…"

"That we could possibly be in the vicinity of a parallel Earth!" Astronaut Gary Dobbs finished Mitchell's oral conjecture. "We could possibly run into…"

"Ourselves exploring deep space!" Richard Mitchell presumed and stated. "I suppose there's still room for astounding surprises, even in the year 2,397 AD! Let's establish a heading in the direction of what ought to be the Sun! That'll be easy, once we locate Polaris! Who had ever hypothesized that space travel wasn't as absolutely fascinating as science fiction? This exceptional exploratory trip might just be too controversial to ever make its way into grammar or high school space history textbooks!"

* * * * * * * * * * * * *

A month of intense apprehension passed, and Mitchell and Dobbs finally visually located Polaris (or a star that was a replica of Polaris), and then meticulously set their coordinates to speed in the direction of what they imagined to be *their* "sister solar system". Much to the space adventurers' consternation, the overhead 3-D screen soon reflected magnified images of Pluto, Uranus, Neptune, and Saturn, a showing as a lustrous sphere with its very distinguishable rings and physical markings. Next, the totally "star-struck" astronauts viewed spectacular Jupiter, with its enormous red spot, and then magnificent Mars, along with the familiar asteroid belt situated between the two very identifiable heavenly objects. Everything was in the exact same pattern, with the odd exception that the familiar planets belonged to a "counterpart solar system", definitely other than the one that Mitchell and Dobbs had left.

"Are you sure we're zipping through space in the Galaxy's second arm?" Astronaut Commander Mitchell incredulously asked his similarly confused navigator. "My rattled mind is both befuddled and perplexed! I'd be afraid to report these findings to Base, out of fear of being placed in an asylum ward, upon our eventual return home!"

"Yes, Commander, without a doubt. according to the new maps our computers have charted and verified, our incredible observations are valid!" Dobbs formally confirmed. "I strongly suggest that we revert to stealth concealment technology mode, so that no alien spacecraft, telescopes, or advanced radar system can detect our imminent presence. Thank God the *Lewis and Clark* possesses that new futuristic technology. You never know what kind of peculiar intelligent life might be in the vicinity. I mean Rich," Astronaut Gary Dobbs said before rubbing his eyes, symbolically indicating his total bewilderment. "We can't be too careful in this situation! Hostile beings could be inhabiting that majestic blue sphere appearing on the overhead. Could it be that oxygen-breathing, carbon-based humans are living on *that* beautiful Earth? And Commander, do you think that…"

"That the members of that hypothetical human species are exact models of the same people we had left behind when we confidently initiated this Coalition-sanctioned mission?" Astronaut Mitchell worriedly finished Astronaut Dobbs' hypothesis. "And just look at another extraordinary parallel, Gary! The planet's continents and its oceans are identical to the ones we recollect from memory! And they're all in the exact same geographic positions, too! North America is directly above South and Central America! And look; there's Europe, and Asia, and Africa, Antarctica, and Australia, and also the Atlantic and the Pacific, and oh my God, there's the good old…."

"United Federation Coalition of America, with the sprawling Los Angeles and San Francisco metropolitan areas on the West Coast, and the great megalopolis stretching all the way from Boston down to Charleston on the East Coast," Astronaut Dobbs gasped in exhilaration.

"I think, Commander, that we should hide the ship behind the far side of the moon, despite our implementation of advanced cloaking technology. Perhaps during our absence, breakthrough progress has been made, along the lines of military surveillance, that could recognize our arrival, or should I say intrusion? You never know what kind of welcoming committee will greet us. I'm not in the mood for any vitriolic interrogation sessions."

"Good idea, Gary!" Commander Mitchell immediately agreed. "Things might not be exactly as the reality now appear. I volunteer to take the shuttle down early tomorrow morning and check things out. I'll pay a little visit in the *Einstein* to 458 Bremen Avenue, Egg Harbor City, New Jersey."

"That's your home address!" Astronaut Dobbs realized and exclaimed. "You're going to visit your residence and see if your wife Jackie is there?"

"Well, I'll first determine if my house is where it should be found, and then I'll surreptitiously knock on the door under the pretense of seeking directions. And if someone who looks like Jackie answers, I'll reunite with my facsimile wife. And of course, Gary, my daughter Denise will have…"

"Will have just left for high school, and you'll have a friendly uninterrupted reunion and relationship with your surprised and unsuspecting wife! It's too bad you out-rank me, or else I could be taking the *Einstein* down to Ellicott City, Maryland and possibly visiting *my* wife, too."

* * * * * * * * * * * * *

The next evening, Commander Richard Mitchell returned the reliable *Einstein* to the *Lewis and Clark,* and upon exiting the craft's pressure equalization chamber, the space commuter was immediately confronted by his very curious co-journeyman, Astronaut Gary Dobbs, who was extremely anxious to learn about prevailing social and cultural conditions down on the "replica Planet Earth".

"Rich, I've been closely monitoring communications, radio and television transmissions, and high frequency chatter, and everything is the same except *the place* we're now sharing in the Galaxy," Astronaut Dobbs stated. "I hope you can bring me up-to-speed without doing any serious back-pedaling. Is this all some sort of exotic grand illusion, or what?"

"I can definitely assure you, Gary, that it most certainly isn't an illusion!" Commander Mitchell emphatically replied. "It's much more than a mere dual coincidence', I can honestly attest to *that* fact. I had taken the *Einstein* down through the atmosphere and landed in a familiar field surrounded by woods, just behind my Bremen Avenue home. I soon approached Jackie, or who I believe was an identical twin to Jackie, hanging clothes in the backyard. She was absolutely thrilled to see me, and her voice, eyes, and facial expressions were so exceptionally similar to my wife's back on Earth in Spiral One of the Milky Way! I mean, everything I experienced defied scientific logic. It was most uncanny, to say the least."

"Did she invite you into your, how should I say, invite you into your reciprocal home?" Astronaut Dobbs nervously inquired. "I mean Jules Verne, Isaac Asimov, Ray Bradbury, and H.G. Wells could never have invented fantastic fiction like this! What happened next? Romance, I presume!"

"We did engage in casual conversation, with me explaining that I had been involved in a secret government project and was committed to not divulging classified information, not even to my wife," Mitchell disclosed to his thoroughly fascinated co-pilot. "Then, after discussing recent family news, mutual concerns, and current events, we did have an interlude, so to speak, in the master bedroom. And I have to confess, Jackie seemed to be, and reacted, just like my passionate spouse had often done in the past. Let me tell you, it was all so surreal, yet all so natural!"

"Rich, we've been close friends for over seven-years now, going back to our memorable Academy days, and there's something pertinent I just have to mention, if you'll excuse my audacity!" Dobbs declared. "I gotta' preface my remarks, so that you don't think I'm playing Devil's Advocate here and looking for the proverbial fly in the ointment. This is more than everyday rhetoric, I have to say."

"Speak your mind and express your heart!" Commander Mitchell insisted. "Tell me exactly what you're thinking. I believe that candor is an important part of any solid friendship."

Gary Dobbs stared meaningfully into his superior's eyes. "Rich, if you were down in Egg Harbor City, New Jersey making love to your attractive wife, then obviously, that possible means that there's another fellow astronaut named…."

"Named Richard Stephen Mitchell visiting Planet Earth in Spiral Arm One of the Milky Way Galaxy, telling another astronaut named Gary Thomas Dobbs about him making love to *his* beautiful wife Jackie," the astonished speaker communicated. "What an ugly can of worms this whole mess is! Now, right this minute, I suspect that Jackie is inadvertently cheating on me…."

"Just like you had recently been deliberately cheating on her," Gary Dobbs truthfully responded. "This is such heavy stuff that I feel like we're have a conversation on Jupiter, or on some more habitable people-friendly planet with a mass a thousand times that of Earth! That about summarizes the *gravity* of the situation! What do you make out of all this? Are you jealous? Is this a mass hallucination, a dream, a contrived artificial reality?"

"I can't rightly determine that," Commander Mitchell bluntly acknowledged. "Everything is so weird, so bizarre, and basically inverted, completely topsy-turvy! It's a totally warped dilemma of unfathomable proportions. I now wish I had never taken the shuttle down there. I feel guilty that I've selfishly violated Jackie's trust and marital vows. My conscience is deluged with remorse and regret. This is the most shame I've felt in a long time. Conquering the mind's inner space is sometimes a much more formidable challenge than figuring-out basic outer space."

"That wasn't Jackie down there!" Dobbs endeavored convincing Mitchell. "That woman was another Jackie in another place in the same time, if that peculiar explanation makes any sense or logic. And I guess that your now teenage daughter Denise was already away at her' high school."

"Next time, it'll be *your* turn," Commander Mitchell sternly ordered. "At our next stop, we'll explore Spiral Arm #3 and see if another parallel development occurs. Let's see if we could reunite you with Carla, along with Jimmy and Julia. If my theory is correct, we should be arriving at destination Earth 3 in ninety days, if we travel at maximum speed."

"Okay, Nostradamus!" Dobbs answered, amenably nodding his head in full agreement. "I'll bravely subscribe to your proposition-one-hundred percent!"

* * * * * * * * * * * * *

Thirteen weeks later, the *Lewis and Clark* spacecraft was zooming ten times as fast as lightning across Milky Way Spiral #3 at "Enhanced Interstellar Warp Speed". After finding a third Polaris, much to the astronauts' intrigue, the pilots discovered that the composition of Galaxy Arm #3 was consistent with the dimensions and characteristics of Arm 1 and Arm 2. According to their mutually agreed-upon arrangement, Gary Dobbs ventured from behind "the third moon" in the *Einstein* shuttle craft to visit his wife at 77 Waters Avenue, just off Frederick Road, in Ellicott City, Maryland, while Commander Rich

Mitchell stayed aboard the main ship, which was shielded in the spacecraft's super-classified "Clandestine Mode".

Upon returning from *his* personal excursion seven-hours-later, an enthusiastic Gary Dobbs had similar familiar circumstances to report about his escapades to his very attentive Commander, who now took his subordinate's descriptive narrative in stride without ever questioning the eyewitness's basic outlandish premise, let alone Dobbs' perception of reality.

"I'll tell you Rich, I had landed in an open field not far from my home," Dobbs dramatically recollected and related. "Julia was away after staying overnight at a friend's house, and my son Jimmy was away at summer camp, so *that* afforded me the chance of spending quality time with Carla, or with my convenient Carla substitute," the animated Earth 3 visitor conveyed to his all-too-patient commanding officer. "Aside from the home's den being redecorated with a new rug and soft cranberry-color leather furniture, the place looked exactly like the one I had left behind in Ellicott City."

"What about your wife?" Mitchell demanded knowing. "I mean were her teeth and eyes the same? How about moles and birthmarks? Was she the same woman you remembered both in mannerisms, tone of voice, and general behavior?"

"Carla was precisely as I recall her being back on Earth 1, faithful like the mythological Penelope had been while waiting for Odysseus to triumphantly return home to Ithaca after the Trojan War," Dobbs maintained with a serious expression upon his face. "I never realized until this moment how much I actually missed her company and her warm embrace, not to mention her genuine sense of humor. Carla was positively sensational! In many respects I would like to zip back down there and do it all over again."

"You've become ensnared in the same type of wicked spider's web that had entrapped me," Commander Mitchell informed his idealistic space-flight co-pilot. "You intentionally had an affair with a woman that was a duplicate of your wife, without considering that she was voluntarily submitting to and instinctively surrendering to your aggressive advances out of marital necessity. You're guilty, Gary, of the same kind of pernicious evil that had tricked and enveloped me! You've had an illicit and immoral affair out of wedlock while persuading a vulnerable woman that looked like Carla to go to bed with you. Don't you see what I'm alluding to here? Malice has twice vanquished goodness, all with *our* full cooperation and consent!"

"Yes, Commander," Dobbs reluctantly admitted before his teeth bit his lower lip. "Your words do project a certain moral clarity! Another rogue Astronaut Gary Dobbs has just taken advantage of and raped my real wife Carla back in Ellicott City, Maryland in Spiral Arm #1 of this unbelievably complicated Milky Way Galaxy. I now jealously find *that* bizarre concept to be both reprehensible and repulsive!"

* * * * * * * * * * * * * *

Four additional Earth months gradually elapsed, and Commander Richard Mitchell and Captain Gary Dobbs expertly and nonchalantly guided the *Lewis and Clark* through the galaxy's gaseous outer perimeter and into the dark, mysterious regions of the Milky Way's nebulous 4th Spiral Arm. Since the pair had decided to alternate in navigating *Einstein* down to Earth, and since Mitchell outranked Dobbs, the former repeatedly reminded the latter of the pre-established "rank privilege accommodation". Upon finally reaching their pre-determined destination, Dobbs obediently manned the Mother Ship stationed behind the moon, and the Commander cruised down to Earth 4's surface in the *Einstein* to successfully reunite with another rendition of Jackie Mitchell.

Seven hours later, Astronaut Gary Dobbs had been leisurely listening to classical music when Beethoven's Fifth Symphony was rudely interrupted with the appearance of an angry Commander Richard Mitchell emerging from the air equalization chamber, wildly wielding his matter-disintegrating gun in his right hand.

"What's this strange charade all about?" Dobbs wondered and then curiously asked. "Are you futilely impersonating Al Capone or Pancho Villa?"

"This is no time for juvenile childish jesting!" Commander Mitchell nastily rankled. "I've just returned from what I believe was Egg Harbor City #4 and found Jackie in bed with another man. I think I've stretched my sanity to the max! I'm about to explode from fury!"

"Well, Rich, don't take your angst and your frustration out on me!" Astronaut Dobbs argued as the co-pilot gingerly lowered the volume on the ship's stereo intercom. "And besides, you gotta' remember that the woman you had caught in the act of infidelity was not your devoted spouse Jackie, but only a Spiral Arm #4 version of *her* masquerading as Jackie."

"You must be a real ignoramus!" Mitchell loudly and disgustedly answered as his right hand holding the ray gun began to tremble. "The person that Jackie was in bed with was a rendition of you, Gary Dobbs! You've been all along having an affair with my wife behind my back, while pretending to be my best friend!"

"You're absolutely crazy!" Dobbs loudly volleyed back. "You've gone totally bonkers! How could I be having an affair with Jackie when the real Jackie Mitchell is back on Planet Earth in Spiral Arm #1, and I was up here in the spaceship concealed behind the moon in Spiral #4? Quite honestly, I think you're becoming a little paranoid and psychotic too, Commander!"

"Enough of your lame-brained garrulous equivocating!" Mitchell vehemently yelled. "Regardless of where you were or where you are, the same damned thing is evolving back on *our* Earth! Either you, or your clone, or whatever the hell it happens to be, is licentiously sleeping with my wife!"

"Well, Rich, what did you do with *that* arrogant, amorous impostor you've been describing?" Dobbs worriedly asked.

"I killed him on the spot with my matter/flesh blaster and sent his sinful soul directly into oblivion!" Mitchell shouted in an out-of-control rage. "I've murdered the rogue, just like I'm now compelled to eliminate you! And I always wrongly believed that *you* were my trustworthy friend!"

"Hold on just a precious minute, before attempting anything rash or drastic! Don't do anything foolish or hasty!" Dobbs begged. "Maybe a powerful tranquilizer will help calm you down!"

"It's too damned late to plead for mercy, or for me to swallow-down a miracle relaxation pill!" Mitchell hollered under extreme emotional duress. "Now, you too must die, and then I'll surreptitiously hunt-down and destroy the other two malicious Gary Dobbs that are causing plenty of unnecessary amorous havoc throughout the Galaxy!"

Commander Richard Mitchell then violently pulled the trigger and instantaneously, the defenseless Captain Gary Dobbs' body and skeleton disintegrated into dust. The livid perpetrator then reflected for a moment on his very egregious deed.

'My soul won't rest until I annihilate the remaining two dangerous Gary Dobbs roaming around the Galaxy!' Mitchell rationalized. 'Perhaps they're currently on the prowl, looking to kill me right now! I wonder how many vile vigilantes are now searching for *my* hide, with perverted designs of obliterating me from existence? Is my hunter another Gary Dobbs or perhaps the vile predators are dual Gary Dobbs? Oh well, I'll be a desperate fugitive from justice, on-the-lam, scrambling all throughout the immense Galaxy! Who's going to catch me? I have enough food aboard to last a whole decade!' Astronaut Richard Mitchell crazily reckoned. 'I suppose I'm now my own worst enemy, destined to live a lonely life as a wanton renegade on the loose! Maybe I'll even escape the Milky Way and explore for intelligent life forms over in Andromeda, not the constellation, but the galaxy! Yes, good old M-31, that's where I'll spend the rest of my pathetic days! Pride and jealousy can eventually warp a decent man's immortal soul! It's all so very, very simple! Vengeance is now the name of the game!' Astronaut Richard Mitchell rationalized. 'I'm self-exiling myself from the remainder of my species! Yes, that's exactly what I'm desperately doing! But now that I'm entirely alone and exploring on my own, cruising the vast, infinite Universe, who actually really cares about anything?'

“The Indestructible Teapot”

Ben Siscone loved being a bachelor and never gave the idea of marriage (to even the most beautiful available woman in town) a second thought. The Hammonton, New Jersey resident loved going deer hunting with pals inside Wharton State Forest; having lunch at the Maplewood Inn on the White Horse Pike; enjoying sumptuous dinners at Rocco’s Town House on North Third Street, and attending Philadelphia Phillies baseball games at Citizens Bank Park with longtime friends Marty Ingemi and Sam Perone, not to mention bi-weekly automobile pleasure excursions to Showboat, Harrah’s, Bally’s and Caesar’s World casinos in Atlantic City. Dating attractive women was not out of the question for Benjamin Anthony Siscone, but for all intents and purposes, the 323 Maple Street resident preferred solitude when the “Italian Stallion Sicilian” wasn’t busy industriously selling car and home insurance.

On Saturday July 14th, 2007 Ben Siscone received a phone call from his garrulous buddy, Marty Ingemi, who wanted to make arrangements to attend the annual July carnival that commemorated the Feast of Our Lady of Mount Carmel, traditionally celebrated in Hammonton the week of the 16th of July.

“Ben,” Marty began his narrative, sounding a little like a circus midway barker. “What do ya’ say we go to the feast like we do every year. I mean, I’m not too hot-to-trot about the gravel carnival grounds, or the gaudy amusements or games,” Ingemi clarified and elaborated. “Every year this week I just gotta’ have…”

“A delicious peppers and sausage sandwich on Italian roll at the Our Lady of Assumption Concession,” Ben finished Marty’s very predictable statement. “I understand that this year the food stand’s been moved from the convent’s lawn to across Third Street, next to the church, because the nuns objected to all the outside noise and activity while they were trying to pray in their chapel,” Siscone informed Ingemi. “But be careful of the raw clams and oysters the religious group serve there. Sammy Perone claims he had contracted a bad case of parasites, *giardia* (giardiasis) I believe, two summers ago, and spent a week in Kessler Hospital recovering from severe digestive problems. Sam’s abdominal tract was rather abominable! Ha, ha, ha!”

“Well then, Ben, let’s plan on strolling over to the food and beverage stands next to St. Joseph Church. I’m no priest or minister, but we’ll congregate and leave from my place on French Street,” Marty persuasively suggested. “I’ll contact Sammy, and we’ll meet in my kitchen at around 7 tomorrow night. Remember, tomorrow's Sunday, and not Monday night!"

"Okay, sounds like a plan to me!" Ben promptly confirmed. "I'm pretty tied-up tomorrow going to Mass; mowing my lawn; trimming some bushes, and pulling bothersome weeds growing in the garden and sprouting among the shrubs. That's my standard routine every Sunday from May to October."

"Well, what are ya' doing this afternoon?" Marty inquired. "Watching *Bonanza* or *Ozzie and Harriet* on cable TV? I'm taking my twelve-year-old nephew to Six Flags Great Adventure up in Jackson. Do ya' wanna' tag along? You're hereby officially invited to help me baby-sit!"

"No thanks!" Ben apologetically laughed. "I have a certain aversion about riding on roller coasters; giant spinning on Ferris Wheels, and speeding-around corners in runaway trains. The local carnival is about all I can tolerate in *that* kind of dangerous venue. You know that I collect antiques, Marty, especially colonial era items. This afternoon, I'm going-over to where Frank Mazza's Furniture used to be on 12th Street and check-out the new Antiques Dealers' Market that's just opened. The place has something like twenty-five small-time merchants occupying the building."

"Yeah, Mazza's Furniture moved out to *Route 322* in Egg Harbor Township and is now called Mazza's Bassett Furniture," Marty Ingemi recollected and then academically lectured. "Everything's changing in this town! But honestly, antiques and I don't get along too well! I'll see you at my place tomorrow night! And don't forget where French Street is located!" Marty Ingemi joked to Ben Siscone. "My house is only two blocks north of the carnival grounds! Write it down on a piece of paper and stuff it in your wallet in case you get a mild attack of amnesia."

"Tell Sammy I said 'Hi' when you contact him about us trekking over to the carnival and swallowing some peppers and sausage on Italian rolls and washing it all down with some ice-cold beer," Ben reminded his best chum. "So long, Marty!" Click.

That Saturday afternoon, Ben Siscone drove his Ford Expedition SUV down Bellevue Avenue through downtown Hammonton over to the newly opened Antique World on 12th Street. After browsing the merchants' extensive inventory, a salesperson approached Ben and inquired whether he could be of assistance in helping the customer peruse household items from the American past.

“Hi, my name's Frank Bartolone,” the tall gentleman cordially introduced himself. “I think I can put your mind in the right direction here. How may I help you?”

“I’m especially interested in the colonial era,” Siscone politely answered. “I already have a cherry-wood chair; an oak hutch; a fine spinning wheel, and an authentic cranberry scoop dating back to the late 1700s. What do you have, Mr. Bartolone, in your merchandise line that suits my’ particular interest? I’m not in the market for anything large, like a piece of furniture for instance, because quite frankly, I just don’t have the room to accommodate another chair or desk in my bungalow. But I could use something, let’s say, like a conversation-piece knickknack for the kitchen.”

The on-commission salesman considered Ben’s purchasing criteria and then provided an appropriate recommendation. “How about this almost mint-condition teakettle, er I mean copper-colored teapot, that I believe still works and gives-off a steam whistle!” the salesman suggested. “The thing’s still functional, and can serve as a useful teapot. It’s definitely from the colonial era, and I’m sure it has its own rich history, being gradually passed-down from generation to generation.”

“I suppose it was probably once owned up in Massachusetts by Samuel Adams or Paul Revere, just prior to the Boston Tea Party!” Ben cynically joked. “Do you know anything about its origin, or about its recent ownership?” Siscone asked as the colonial wares collector casually examined the exquisite item in his hands.

“The metal kettle, pardon the dumb rhyme, since I meant to say ‘teapot’, had been acquired from the estate of a wealthy bachelor up in Princeton,” the suave-sounding antiques’ salesman informed. “It’s my understanding that the gentleman who had owned the delightful-looking object was an eccentric fellow, who one day, a full century ago, just vanished, and was never heard from again.”

“Well, what an odd coincidence! I’m also a happy bachelor, but have no intention of disappearing from the face of the Earth, let alone leaving modern Hammonton without sufficient notice,” Siscone skeptically jested as the prospective customer continued scrutinizing the copper-colored, tea-pouring device, while inspecting for any defects. “How much is this rare treasure? Think hard and give me a good figure, because my antique acquisition budget is presently in a bit of a shambles.”

Frank Bartolone contemplated Ben’s remark and then succinctly uttered, “Two-hundred-and-fifty-dollars, tax included! The cost is non-negotiable.”

“Sold!” Ben Siscone jubilantly exclaimed. “That modest price is indeed within my buying parameters!”

“Great! I just have to clear the sale with my boss, Mr. Robert Ruberton standing over there behind the cash register, and then this magnificent, still-functioning colonial kitchen item will be all yours,” Bartolone courteously disclosed. “Will you be paying by cash or by credit card?”

“Cash!” Siscone replied. “But Mr. Bartolone; you’ll have to give me *credit* for shrewdly making a fine addition to my impressive colonial era antique collection,” Ben finished and punned, with a wink of his right eye accompanied by a sparkle in his left one.

* * * * * * * * * * * * * *

Right on schedule, Ben Siscone joined-up with Marty Ingemi and Sam Perone, and the trio trekked the several blocks from Ingemi’s French Street home to the carnival’s Third Street concession stands, recently erected next to St. Joseph Church. The friends occupied a picnic table placed on the church parking lot’s asphalt, and over the course of the next forty-five minutes, ravenously consumed two delicious pepper and sausage sandwiches each, along with slices of pepperoni pizza, and three prodigious pitchers of beer.

The jovial triumvirate was reminiscing old girlfriends the men had dated back at Hammonton High, and reviewing various pranks and high-jinks that had been mischievously played on teachers and class trip chaperones. After another hour of idle chatter, the loyal chums did their standard annual rotation of the gravel carnival grounds; met and conversed with several old acquaintances; tried their luck at a dart game of chance, and then again at a basketball skill shooting booth, and finally, the middle-age sages returned to Marty’s comfortable domicile on French Street to watch (on Ingemi’s new 39” plasma flat-screen TV) several innings of the Phillies and Florida Marlins baseball game.

By ten p.m., Ben Siscone had returned home with a minor headache, and also a queasy feeling in his stomach. After taking several popular over-the-counter antacid tablets, the beleaguered, independent insurance salesman took a quick hot shower, entered his summer pajamas, and then hopped into his electric-controlled adjustable bed. ‘I bet I ate too much peppers and sausage,’ the distressed fellow thought. ‘I gotta’ learn not to overindulge. I’m not as young or as virile as I used to be! And tomorrow morning, I have back-to-back appointments with Mr. Roberts and with Mrs. Dugan, two of my most demanding clients. Oh well, I'd better get some shuteye while the moon's still governing over the night sky. Maybe sunrise will bring about a much-improved change in my alimentary canal's condition.'

At three a.m. the sufferer woke-up with nagging gas pains in his intestines. 'I might be coming down with some summer virus symptoms,' Ben conjectured. 'I probably caught the bug from an infected person at the carnival concessions. I'll down a few aspirins and then prepare myself a cup of green tea. I know,' Siscone pondered. 'I'll put my new colonial teapot on the stove and see if it still functions. That'll cause a little diversion to get my mind off of these lousy gas pains that are plaguing my upper and lower digestive tract. This better not be *giardia!"*

Five minutes later, the water inside the newly acquired stove item started boiling, and soon thereafter, steam began exiting the metal teapot, being accompanied by a singular shrill whistling sound. And then, much to Ben Siscone's utter amazement, a figure the size of an Arabian lamp genie filtered-out of the magical antique, the unexpected apparition completely startling and then mesmerizing the ailing teapot owner. The hazy figure's spectral appearance soon came more into focus, and Ben apprehensively perceived what appeared to be an early twentieth-century businessman dressed in a dark-gray, three-piece pinstriped suit, with a gold watch and fob chain suspended from his vest. The peculiar-looking phantom sported a mustache and thick bushy sideburns.

"Where did you come from?" Ben asked the former occupant of the extraordinary teapot, all the while thinking that his upset stomach had significantly contributed to the unearthly manifestation that his eyes were witnessing.

"Obviously. Sir, I've come from inside the teakettle, er, I meant to say *teapot!"* the strange-looking anachronism matter-of-factly stated. "And I'm here precisely because you had summoned me by wondrously making the water inside the marvelous teapot boil and whistle upon the stove. In fact, I surmise *that* that's the first time the metal antique has been utilized in the last ten decades or so. Unfortunately, my erratic memory is a bit fuzzy, and I tend to lose track of time."

"Well then, what is your name, if I may ask?" Siscone queried in a shaky voice, with his lips quivering and his buckling knees knocking. "Are you human? Tell me, what is the purpose of your intrusion, er, I mean visitation?"

"One predictable question at a time!" the now three-dimensional figure declared and admonished. "Are you some sort of local court prosecutor?" the little man quipped. "I just can't stand obnoxious, inquisitive interrogators! All I can tell you at the moment, Sir, is that my name is Hiram Jackson, and I've been commissioned by potent beings much more dynamic than myself to grant you three wishes of your choosing, which incidentally, will not be reversible. Now then, Mr. Siscone, I believe *that* is your appellation, have I made the reason for my presence perfectly clear?"

"Is this some sort of weird spontaneous miracle? I still think you're some sort of hallucination or apparition! What if I refuse to participate?" the sometimes-stubborn owner of the newly-obtained magic teapot wanted to know.

"Then Sir, you risk incurring much greater punishments and consequences than those that someone of my low caliber is capable of administering," the strange-but-neurotic, weirdly arcane character revealed. "I urge you to fully cooperate with my proposal, and I don't want to be associated in any way, shape, or form with what your detrimental defiance may ultimately generate. Now then, Mr. Siscone, I can only account for and be responsible for my own abilities and duties, let alone have to needlessly worry about *your* annoying recalcitrance!" Hiram Jackson effectively chided his incredulous host. "My personal advice is for you to accept the three wishes I'll confer, or else, face definite retribution from powers much greater than either of us possess. Is that perfectly understood?"

Ben then asked the 'steam-generated-wizard' if there was a time frame for *him* to make the three wishes, but was abruptly told that *the requests* had to be uttered right away, otherwise, drastic supernatural events would afflict and torment Siscone's normally-tranquil life and peaceful existence. "You have a five-minute time-window in which to favorably respond!" the strange genie, dressed in early turn-of-the-last-century haberdashery, instructed.

"Well then, since I have no other alternative in this most-peculiar matter," Ben stated while assessing his unprecedented predicament, "I hereby wish for a long life; I wish to enjoy continual good health throughout my longevity, and finally, I wish to be the richest man in all of Hammonton, which incidentally has more than 100 multimillionaires among its prosperous population. But in the final analysis," the still-stunned Maple Street resident articulated, "I definitely think, Mr. Jackson, that you're some sort of undigested piece of sausage affecting my mind's cerebral activity, making my affected brain conjure-up oddball illusions and mirages!"

Hiram Jackson was not-too-pleased or impressed with Ben Siscone's already-cited, all-too-selfish magical aspirations. "Are you sure, Sir, that you don't wish to improve the lot of your struggling neighbors? How about benefiting the poor, the needy, and the less fortunate?" the out-of-place-and-time 3-D image suggested to the now somewhat-settled teapot owner, hinting at the prospect of moral redemption (or perhaps even an opportunity for eternal salvation).

"I've always believed that charity begins at home," Siscone defensively answered in justification of his earlier self-indulgent responses. "I'm basically an American capitalist at heart, and once I thoroughly help myself to an extravagant lifestyle and swiftly advance into the upper echelons of local affluence, then during my spare time, I'll engage in some basic philanthropy, just like the Rockefellers and the Vanderbilts had done for the huddling masses over a century ago! That is, Mr. Jackson, after I spend part of my fortune building my opulent mansion in Newport, Rhode Island!"

Mystical and completely disgusted Hiram Jackson instantly realized that Ben Siscone was very adamant and serious about *his* greedy wishes, and was not about to change his arrogant mind. "Very well then," the seemingly supernatural being declared in a disappointed tone of voice, "I see that you're quite obdurate and set in your habits, Mr. Siscone. I hereby acknowledge and authorize that you can have your all-too-typical three wishes, if you solemnly promise not to leave your house until *a full day* after your third wish has been granted and fulfilled. Is that specific condition agreeable to you, Sir?"

"Er, yes," Siscone cautiously acceded. "It all seems quite fair and reasonable. I find your stipulation to be quite…"

And before the captivated, self-centered resident could fully utter his acceptance statement, Mr. Hiram Jackson abruptly turned-around quickly, and stridently stepped toward the kitchen stove, and then the cantankerous fellow swiftly leaped and filtered through the dense kitchen wall, thus amazingly exiting the Maple Street red brick bungalow.

* * * * * * * * * * * * * *

Being very fatigued from his recent emotional ordeal, Ben Siscone was able to fall asleep, but soon chirping robins woke him up at precisely 6:30 a.m. the next morning. 'I have more than enough time to dress and to get ready for my scheduled appointments with Mr. Roberts and Mrs. Dugan,' the lucky, newly transformed fellow evaluated. 'I think I have all my bases covered. I'll live a long life; I'll have excellent health all throughout, and I'll have lots of amassed wealth! I'll be the most desirable eligible bachelor in all of Hammonton!' the then-jolly gent concluded. 'Let me check my online Merrill Lynch account to see if I've gotten any richer than I had been yesterday. Could it be that mysterious Mr. Hiram Jackson was some sort of colossal hoax?'

Much to the good luck recipient's overall joy, the incredible sum of two-billion-thirty-seven-million-dollars had been generously and anonymously deposited into the quite elated insurance agent's now-burgeoning "Cash Management Account". 'I'll have to spend at least an hour calculating how much interest I'll earn a day, just at regular money market rates. Won't my account executive be astounded by this sudden tremendous accumulation of assets! He's gonna' probably call me at my place of business as soon as the bean counter arrives at his office over in Northfield. Who needs an office? Mr. Roberts and Mrs. Dugan can be damned! And physically and mentally speaking, I must confess that I feel almost invincible! I'll call my secretary at nine o'clock and tell her to cancel all my idiotic office appointments!'

Then, the egocentric teapot owner considered exactly how he had become such a noteworthy beneficiary of such a fortuitous destiny. The good-fortune receiver thought about important events that had occurred during the early 1900s, and about the historic San Francisco Earthquake of April 18, 1906 came to mind. 'I remember reading a Jack London eyewitness account in a college English journalism class describing the catastrophe. But today is July 17th 2007, and it's been over a hundred-years since the San Andreas fault caused the spectacular California disaster,' Siscone anxiously recollected. 'But I gotta' admit that good old Hiram Jackson looked like he had lived during *that* terrible pre-World War I event.'

Suddenly, the man's reverie was broken with the sound of glass being shattered. 'Oh my God! Someone's breaking into my car!' Ben instinctively imagined as the startled resident quickly put on his bathrobe and slippers. 'I gotta' go outside and investigate the source of the noise! It's probably some early morning teen vandals on the prowl, either looking for a convenient car to have a joyride, or searching for drug money or things to fence! I knew I should've parked my auto' inside my garage last night, and not have left it in the driveway! Who says this is a safe neighborhood?'

The perplexed teapot owner spontaneously grabbed a baseball bat and rushed out of his bungalow. No one was running or walking around. Maple Street was deserted, and Ben's vehicle was unscathed and looked as good as new. 'That's strange! I'll go back inside, get my keys, and take a ride around town to see if I can detect anything suspicious! I'll appoint and assign myself to be on citizen's patrol!'

The perplexed and jittery fellow started-up his late-model white *Toyota Avalon,* rapidly backed out of his driveway, and then drove down Maple to Third Street. Making a left from Third Street onto Central Avenue, a half-mile later, a stunning realization entered the almost obsessed driver's mind. 'This is totally absurd! There's absolutely no one walking or driving-around in the entire town! No pedestrians; no policemen on the beat or inside squad cars; no tractor-trailers; no cars honking horns; no buses; no pollution; no anything! It's as if the entire community has been suddenly abandoned, deserted, and downtown Hammonton has become a veritable ghost town.'

Upon returning to his Maple Street abode, and then entering his home, Ben Siscone was in for another supernatural phenomenon that obviously transcended everyday reality. Miniature Hiram Jackson was standing in the kitchen with his arms folded, and featuring an enormous smile upon his countenance.

"Greetings again, Mr. Siscone! I thought you'd never get back to your splendid little dwelling," the odd-looking man sarcastically stated. "And yes, it's true that I had lived through the great San Francisco Earthquake of 1906 as you had imagined, and after surviving *that* horrible calamity, I then came east and eventually settled-down in Princeton, just forty-miles or so up what is now *Route 206,* but way back then, the trail was called Trenton Road!"

"But you've intentionally deceived me!" Siscone vehemently protested. "You tricked me into leaving the house! You deliberately made that sound of glass shattering to get me to violate our oral contract by me leaving my kitchen door!"

"All's fair in love and war, as the saying goes, but that's all water over the proverbial dam now," Hiram Jackson matter-of-factly maintained, while implementing several hackneyed clichés to support his point. "Your penalty, Mr. Benjamin Anthony Siscone, will be that you'll have to become my replacement trapped inside that copper teapot for the next hundred-years, just like I had been in horrible isolation since the year 1907. I guarantee that you won't age a single day while residing inside. And as for me, I'll gradually get used to this new exciting age with all of its fabulous inventions and technology. In the meantime, you'll be humbly incarcerated in solitary confinement inside that despicable, colonial pouring-device for at least a full century, just as I had been. And I very cleverly and magically had the teapot…."

"Conveniently and magically situated right inside the antique merchant's store a full hundred-years later!" Ben Siscone finished Hiram Jackson's depiction of recent events. "You're quite an accomplished conniver and manipulator Mr. Jackson, I must admit!"

"Now then, Mr. Siscone. I can, with a clear conscience, live-out the remainder of my biological life in your most splendid twenty-first century reality!" the effervescent magical trickster aptly chuckled. "But I tend to quickly adapt to new surroundings. And I sincerely hope that you adequately savor your hundred year tenure inside that very confining antique, where a full-century from now, you'll finally be able to let-off a little steam and live-out the balance of your days! Ha, ha, ha!" the inimitable Hiram Jackson loudly laughed. "All you have to do is pray that someone gullible and greedy such as yourself will try boiling water in the teapot on a stove-top to finally be set free. Ha, ha, ha! But I guarantee you, Mr. Siscone. That'll never happen in a hundred-years! Ha, ha, ha! But during your last year of totally boring imprisonment, you'll manage to acquire certain magical powers so that you'll be able to dupe someone else, who is just as basically avaricious and fundamentally flawed as yourself!"

"But you can't do this horrendous curse to me, just because you deceptively fooled me into leaving the house during a contrived crisis!" Siscone squawked and balked. "You had unfairly tricked me when I least suspected it!"

Hiram Jackson simply smiled, turned his back to Ben Siscone, and then slowly sauntered-out of the bungalow liked a happy, liberated citizen. The mentally-disheveled fellow was so distraught at *his* doomed disposition that the angry teapot owner swiftly dashed into his workshop; retrieved and lifted a heavy sledgehammer, and then approached the metal teapot. Siscone quickly grabbed the delicately-designed colonial object; placed it upon the beige tile floor, and then savagely and violently smashed the water-boiler with his heavy sledgehammer. Immediately, the crazed maniac was vacuumed directly into the indestructible teapot's spout, becoming a lost prisoner of fate, futilely and monotonously trapped inside until the glorious year 2107.

"Foreshadowing and Flashback"

In novels, in short stories, and in Hollywood movie screenplays, foreshadowing gives the reader or viewer a hint of what is to come, and flashback is the opposite, where the past is analyzed and reviewed. The daily hustle and bustle of people's lives make humans reflect about the future, while often contemplating the past. Such was the case of Marcus and Portia Italiano, and their friends, Jerry and Irene Tanner and Len and Andrea Bennett, who always reminisced about shared vacations *they* had enjoyed together, while also often discussing the prospect of touring Italy in the summer of 2007. Finally, after much anticipation, the dream of visiting Milan, Venice, Florence, Rome, Naples, Pompeii, and Messina became a splendid reality for the six adventurous, optimistic Americans in early August of 2007.

The three couples had just boarded a shiny new tour bus to convey them from enchanting Venice to the magnificent tourist-friendly Grand Hotel Baglioni, on the Piazza Unita Italiana in resplendent Florence. Portia and Marcus Italiano were marveling about how scenic the sights of their sensational European hiatus had been, as the enthralled couple periodically took turns staring-out of the luxury bus's huge side window.

"I wish we had a month to spend staying here in Italy instead of just two weeks," Portia shared with her equally-impressed husband. "I think the high point of our vacation will be visiting Messina, and I say *this* Marcus because of sentimental reasons. My mother's family had come to America from Sicily and landed at Ellis Island in 1902 to start new lives in a new land."

"Yes, your mother's folks were from Gesso, just outside Messina," Marcus remembered from studying family photo' albums, and then eloquently stating the fact to his spouse. "I looked on a map and the town is about eleven-miles away from the seaport. I can't wait to make that last stop on our Italian itinerary," the husband declared. "The harbor is beautiful, I understand, and there're many medieval forts and towers in the vicinity for us to visit and explore."

"Let's not jump too far ahead of ourselves!" Portia laughed and related. "You know, I was named after the wife of Brutus in the Shakespearean play Julius Caesar. Portia was worried about forthcoming tragic events that she feared would happen, and Caesar's psychic wife Calphurnia was quite apprehensive, too."

"I thought you were named after Portia, the charming rich heroine in Shakespeare's classic play 'The Merchant of Venice'," Marcus alertly answered. "Well anyway, at least I got the William Shakespeare part of your name correct. Right name 'Portia', but obviously, the wrong Elizabethan-era play!"

"Anyway Marcus, the Tanners and the Bennetts are also interested in visiting Messina," Portia indicated. "Hammonton, as you know, is one of the most Italian towns, not only in New Jersey, but also in the entire USA. Over fifty-percent of our community's residents had ancestors that originated from Italy, especially from Sicily. Most farming families in our hometown can trace their ancestry back to this part of Europe."

"Yes, the migrants went from growing olives and grapes in the Old World to harvesting blueberries and peaches in South Jersey," Marcus smiled and laughed, as the brand-new tour bus moved up a ramp and then proceeded onto a dual highway. "Let's show some patience! Messina will be the last stop on this terrific trip, and we'll get there right after seeing the ruins of Pompeii, and hopefully an inactive Mt. Vesuvius."

"Well, there're two special sights in Sicily I'm looking forward to seeing," Portia informed her rather jovial-mood husband. "One is the historic Cathedral in Messina, where I believe crusader King Richard the Lion-Heart stopped to worship on his way to the Holy Lands, and the other is the quaint Capucin Church in Gesso. My parents showed me photographs of the building many times when I was growing-up. But as we've said, let's not get too far ahead of ourselves dear, Husband. The best is yet to come."

"You're right," Marcus Italiano concurred with wife Portia's assessment and prediction. "We'll experience one city and one vacation destination at a time. Milan was a modern metropolis that still possesses many aspects of the Old World to combine with its attractive modern skyscrapers. And I have to admit that the fantastic La Scala Opera House was equal to a full week in Las Vegas, any time. And Leonardo's *Last Supper* was quite magnificent, too!"

"And the Tanners and the Bennetts absolutely loved Venice as much as we did," Portia reminded her well-mannered, good-natured travel mate. "The romantic gondola ride under the bridges was a little more realistic than the one we had taken at the *Venetian* on our last Vegas trip. And we got to see the real Campanile, along with thousands of pigeons in St. Mark's Square, and not just a Nevada-type model of the famous bell-tower," the wife gushed. "I just know that Florence will be equally as exciting when we'll appreciate the wealthy merchant Medici family history, alog with the glory of the Italian Renaissance taking place right there back in the 1400s. The museums, churches, and palaces have many treasures on exhibit for tourists like us to relish and savor."

"You're right, again Lady Portia," Marcus amiably dittoed. "I've read where Florence is the capital of the Tuscany region. The Ponte Vecchio over the *Arno River* and the famous Piazza Del Duomo are now only several hours away. I can't wait to take a few pictures of the colossal orange dome. Michelangelo, Donatello, and Leonardo da Vinci, here we come, ready or not!"

"I read where Ponte Vecchio means 'Old Bridge' in English," Portia academically pointed-out.

"Old Bridge, isn't that a small city in North Jersey, just outside New Brunswick," Marcus joked to his non-amused wife in typical American, cynical, sense-of-humor fashion. "It seems that you're becoming an expert on trivia, not to mention minutia!"

"I was meaning to tell you before you had rudely interrupted me with your ridiculous pun that the Ponte Vecchio was the only bridge in Florence that was not bombed by the Germans in *World War II!"* the high school librarian informed her happy-go-lucky architect husband.

* * * * * * * * * * * * * * *

Their first day touring Florence, the six energized vacationers strolled through the glorious Medici palaces and the incomparable Piazza Del Duomo, with Marcus and Portia easily filling two computer/camera disks with "captured memories". After partaking of a delicious American-style breakfast at the Grand Hotel Baglioni, the Italianos, the Tanners, and the Bennetts walked the short distance from the Piazza Unita Italiana to the majestic and classical Ponte Vecchio, which nobly spanned the scenic *Arno*. Many expensive retail shops flaunting high-end items were on display on the "Old Bridge", so Marcus and Portia, in quest of reasonably priced souvenirs, left the company of their friends and sauntered-over to an outdoor marketplace several blocks away. Their first stop was at an elderly, toothless woman's stall.

After browsing around and inspecting the merchandise on display, Marcus noticed that his wife was interested in an attractive gold chain necklace. "How much for the necklace inside the glass case?" the husband asked the wrinkle-faced old lady. "Quantos?"

"Four-hundred-and-ninety-nine Euros!" the aged woman quoted with a very distinct accent. "As you Americans say, it's a good bargain! A real steal!"

"Are you kidding!" the always-frugal inquirer loudly replied. "Even in New York, where the dollar's value is depressed compared to the Euro, *that* necklace would be selling for only around two-hundred-and-fifty bucks!"

"You shouldn't hassle the woman while you're supposed to be politely haggling with her," Portia criticized, in what constituted little more than a whisper. "Perhaps the vendor doesn't want to negotiate a lower price. Stop trying to dicker with her! Just remember, Marcus. You're in a foreign country and not kibitzing with hawkers on South Street in 'Philly."

Wanting to re-establish courteous tranquility between the aged female vendor and *her* rude-and-parsimonious husband, Portia then diplomatically asked, "How much for this beautiful soft leather shoulder-strap pocketbook! It's quite exquisite!"

"Two-hundred-and-fifty Euros!" the hoary-old woman bluntly answered. "Yes, two-hundred-fifty Euros!" she reiterated.

"Are you crazy!" Marcus strenuously objected. "That's around three-hundred U.S. dollars! Your asking prices are more than they're charging at swanky stores on the Ponte Vecchio, and *their* rents are probably five-times what you're paying over here! Are you sure you don't mean two-hundred-and-fifty Liras instead of two-hundred-and-fifty Euros?"

Seeing that her marital partner was becoming quite perturbed to the point of becoming belligerent, Portia desired to quell the disagreement by making a safe purchase, thus smoothing things over. "Well, what about this soft leather man's belt?" Portia calmly requested, while looking directly into the old woman's bloodshot, dark brown eyes.

"It's made from the finest Tuscan leather!" the old wench prefaced her reply. "It's only forty-nine Euros, tax included!" she added in broken English.

"I can buy the same damned thing on the boardwalk in Atlantic City for less than half that inflated price!" Marcus angrily insisted. "Come on, Honey!" the spouse implored, grabbing his wife's left arm. "Let's head back to the Grand Baglioni where we could probably get the same item for twenty-five Euros! I hope the Tanners and the Bennetts have had better luck finding and purchasing memorable souvenirs than we're had!"

As the dissatisfied couple slowly ambled back in the direction of their hotel, the toothless street merchant removed an ancient pentagram from under her cash register's counter, and pointed the object at the unwary distant walkers. "May Satan curse thee, you ungrateful Americans! May hell's fury fully-consume both of you!"

* * * * * * * * * * * * * *

The following day of their whirlwind two-week Italian vacation, the enterprising American tourists were transported by charter bus from the Hotel Grand Baglioni in Florence to the regal Hotel Mediterrano on the Via Cavour in Rome. Marcus had finally gotten over his intense verbal altercation with the old hag Florence street vendor after emphatically sharing his bad buying experience over morning breakfast with the sympathetic Tanners and the very tolerant Bennetts.

After a relaxing night's sleep, the six friends gathered in the hotel's dining hall at 7 a.m. "Three wonderful days in Rome!" Irene Tanner exclaimed at morning breakfast. "Our first stop will be the site of the great Circus Maximus. It's now just an oval area of open ground, and according to a brochure I read last night, it's not far from the Colosseum, which of course we'll certainly be visiting tomorrow morning."

"It's too bad we won't have time to take a stroll over to the archeological ruins of the Roman Forum," Andrea Bennett complained to her companions. "But I suppose lunch will seem more important then, that is, after we women do some grueling walking with our out-of-shape husbands. Our empty stomachs will be growling like those of famished Alaskan grizzly bears."

"But we'll be able to see the Forum columns while traveling on the bus to the Circus Maximus and the Colosseum, and then again while riding back to the hotel," Portia astutely reminded her fellow travelers. "And please don't forget, on the third day here in Rome, we'll be..."

"Touring the Vatican Museum and St. Peter's Basilica," Marcus perceptively chimed-in. "I'm an architect as you all well know, but it's rather incredible how ambitious men centuries ago were able to design and construct such colossal edifices."

"Well, I'm an interior decorator, and I'm anxious to see the superb mosaics inside the Pope's gigantic cathedral, along with the various statues and artifacts on exhibit inside the Vatican Museum,"

Jerry Tanner added to the upbeat conversation. "Rome is certainly living-up to expectations as the 'Eternal City'."

"Let's finish-up our bacon, toast, coffee and eggs," Len Bennett advised his fellow epicures. "The tour bus over to the Circus Maximus leaves in just twenty-minutes."

On the south side of the *Tiber River* is where most of the ancient Roman ruins are located. After the traveling entourage finally stepped-off their tour bus and observed the current open-space spectacle, their fertile imaginations pictured what had actually occupied the immense site nearly two-thousand-years before, as the knowledgeable tour guide explained the magnitude and the recreational purpose of the aforementioned ancient Circus Maximus.

Suddenly, Portia and Marcus felt that the pair was entering a powerful supernatural portal, leading into a strange past dimension of space and time. Their addled minds immediately comprehended an enthusiastic crowd that was wildly shouting encouragement, along with loud cheers and jeers, directed at various chariot racers that were standing and speeding on wheeled platforms behind swift horses, galloping inside a mammoth oval inside of an ancient, jammed-packed, outdoor stadium. Alarmed Portia and Marcus stared incredulously at each other while sitting upon hard stone slabs, both witnesses being shocked and awed by their unforeseen flashback, and also by their abnormal physical surroundings.

"Don't say a word!" Portia cautioned and whispered to her totally exasperated husband. "If these fanatical people around us hear us speaking a foreign language, the mob might become suspicious and have us arrested, if not assaulted!"

"But you're wearing a Roman tunic and I'm wearing a white toga," Marcus observed and uttered. "We're probably upper-classed citizens, and not slaves or servants. Yes, Portia. I think we're actually patricians!"

"Be quiet and just pretend you're watching the chariot race in progress!" Portia commanded. "I think I could use a large bottle of aspirins right this second, along with a strong antacid formula!"

As the driver of a red chariot (pulled by four fabulous black horses) approached the finish line, Portia and Marcus perceived a dull blue haze enveloping their presence, and before either could express another word, the couple was mysteriously transported ahead to the exact same spot in the year 2007.

"Where have you two been?" Andrea Bennett asked the newly arrived time voyagers. "We were beginning to worry about you two meandering wanderers!"

"Yes, we thought that maybe you middle-aged lovebirds had left our illustrious company to buy some antiquated-looking sandals, togas, and tunics," Len Bennett jested. "I'm quite disappointed, seeing the both of you in fancy Adidas sneakers and decked-out in designer blue jeans."

"We'll tell you all about our little ramble after we get back to the States," an out-of-breath Marcus Italiano promised his curious friends, as *his* puzzled mind reversed a scene and vividly visualized the villain/antagonist Messala winning the spectacular chariot race (over the protagonist hero) in the 1955 movie *Ben Hur*. "Portia and I decided we needed a few moments to ourselves to resolve a confidential, personal issue."

"Playing Cupid on your second honeymoon, huh?" Jerry Tanner laughed. "Oh well, I suppose that there's a time and place for everything."

"I can't wait to visit the Colosseum tomorrow!" Irene Tanner piped-in. "Could you imagine what it was like living in ancient Rome with all of the military victory parades and thrilling chariot races? I would love to spend a day in the age of Julius Caesar or Emperor Nero, and get a true feel for what our competent male tour-guide had been graphically describing!"

The Italianos' second day in Rome was quite similar in nature to their rather extraordinary first. After arriving at the very impressive Colosseum on their red and white tour bus, a second paranormal manifestation had occurred. Marcus and Portia were again being mystically transported back to ancient Rome, finding themselves' cast as involuntary spectators, but this time, witnessing a brutal, bloody, gruesome gladiatorial contest.

Portia had to cover her eyes upon viewing all of the excessive gore and savagery amidst the wild Latin chants and cheers being generated by the boisterous Roman audience. Just as Portia was about to faint from extreme emotional duress, she and Marcus were again inexplicably and magically conveyed to their duplicate position in the year 2007, safely inside the famous monumental structure's ruins. Again, the befuddled husband had to contend with the not-too-humorous banter of Jerry Tanner and Len Bennett concerning *his* mysterious departure, and then later *his* "uncanny rendezvous" with his now thoroughly-amused friends.

The next morning, Marcus and Portia accompanied their four merry companions to the remarkable Vatican Museum, which (according to the itinerary) was followed several hours later by a "preferred admission tour" of awesome St. Peter's Basilica. The assigned guide was lecturing the Hotel Mediterrano group about how Vatican Hill had once been the site of "Emperor Nero's inspiring gardens", and that many early Christians had become martyrs of their faith at *that* location, thus, the original basilica being erected over what was believed to be St. Peter's tomb. "The first Christian Emperor, Constantine, had the initial church constructed on this exact same location," the female guide disclosed to her receptive listeners. "The Vatican Palace along with the other familiar buildings you've seen all around the square were, over time, erected around the first basilica."

Without any overt indication, Marcus and Portia were quickly drawn into a blue mist, and before either of the recipients could pronounce a single syllable, the awestruck time trekkers were instantaneously conducted to a hillside overlooking Emperor Nero's public gardens. Several first century Christians were being cruelly crucified upside down, much to the amusement, elation, and satisfaction of callous Roman soldiers, wearing long red capes, accompanied by red-plumed, solid bronze helmets. The heartless tormentors took pleasure in torturing their victims by viciously scourging and hitting the prospective martyrs (tethered to *their* inverted crosses) with barbed whips.

"Oh my God!" Portia sobbed to her equally-distressed husband. "This ugly carnage is horrendous! I think that's venerable St. Peter over there hanging upside-down from that cross. We're incredibly witnessing religious history in the making!"

"When did St. Peter die?" the now-distraught husband asked.

"I read in a hotel lobby pamphlet that it was in either 64 or 67 AD. Biblical scholars and historians are uncertain about the exact date. But it all seems to make chronological sense now!" Portia related. "You heard the tour-guide's lecture. St. Peter was buried on the site of the Vatican, which was, back then, Nero's personal property. I know for an encyclopedia fact that Nero had died in 68 AD, a year or so after St. Peter had been executed. I had once researched that information in the high school library."

"I think that *that* witch vendor over in Florence had put a wicked curse on us!" the wholly-perturbed husband speculated and shared. But before Marcus could speak another discouraging word about his hypothesis, several Roman soldiers spotted the frightened time intruders and hastened in *their* direction, dashing up the steep rocky incline while brandishing raised bronze swords. And when the hostile guards were within twenty-feet of capturing the totally petrified time visitors, Marcus and Portia were mystically transported from the grassy hilltop back into St. Peter's Basilica, where upon being recognized, the couple had to contend with the annoying jokes and not-too-funny quips from both amused Jerry Tanner and Len Bennett.

"Say Marcus, the six of us should go back to the Colosseum and have our pictures taken outside on the cobblestones, with those three Roman soldiers that were dressed-up like ancient guards!" Jerry Tanner suggested.

"Great idea!" Len Bennett agreed and chuckled. "Maybe we'll be able to enlist our pal Marcus into Emperor Nero's service!"

* * * * * * * * * * * * *

Two mornings later, the Italianos were engaged in an impromptu conference inside their second-floor accommodations in Naples' Best Western Hotel Paradiso, conveniently located on the city's Via Catullo. Portia was especially unnerved upon her contemplation of certain recent, bizarre events.

"I wish that we could cancel Naples, Pompeii, and Messina, and fly directly to Philadelphia International Airport," the wife seriously maintained, speaking to her equally-perturbed husband. "I don't want to die during any violent volcanic eruption! Mt. Vesuvius could be ten-times as lethal to people than Mt. St. Helens had been to West Coast Americans a couple of decades ago, at least that's my honest opinion."

"Yes, Honey, but when we were somehow teleported to the actual Circus Maximus, and later to the real Colosseum in Roman times, and then to Nero's Gardens, we were merely observers witnessing history in the making. I mean, we weren't being run-over by wild horses; we weren't being violently maimed in the arena, or being fiercely mauled by hungry lions. And we weren't being evilly crucified like St. Peter. In each particular instance, Portia, we were passive eyewitnesses and not active participants."

"Maybe so, but I don't like the prospect of going to Pompeii and risking death one iota," the under-duress wife argued. "As you might know, Marcus, school librarians now have to teach instructional classes in addition to monitoring book issuances and returns, not to mention having to supervise scheduled study halls in our little academic domains. Last year, I remember reading with a totally bored sophomore class a very graphic story about the destruction of Pompeii that had been written by Robert Silverberg."

"Did it mention anything about the sexual graffiti scribbled on the walls, which incidentally, had been featured in a *Philadelphia Inquirer* article last month!" the husband foolishly and irrelevantly asked. "Those ancient Romans must've been sex perverts, besides being bloodthirsty maniacs!"

"Don't be so ridiculous when our lives might be in immediate jeopardy!" the wife scolded her sometimes-facetious mate. "Pompeii was obliterated on one hot August day in 79 AD, when Vesuvius blew its crown into the atmosphere. Don't you get it! It's now a bright sunny August day here in downtown Naples, only several miles away from Pompeii!"

"Okay, Hon. I'll buy into your extraordinary stranger-than-fiction coincidence theory!" Marcus remarked. "But what else was in the story you had read with the disinterested sophomore library class?"

"Well, Pompeii was a thriving city of 25,000 citizens, most of whom lost their lives during the terrible catastrophe," Portia divulged. "Hollow rock called lapilli blasted-out of the mountain's summit and rained-down on the entire city. Many villas' stone roofs collapsed from the excessive weight. Thousands had died that way! Other roofs belonging to the poorer citizens were made of wood, and the buildings instantly caught on fire."

"How did other people perish? Were there any survivors?" the grim-faced husband inquired.

"Some that left after the first explosion managed to safely get to boats in the harbor, and the survivors luckily made it to other distant towns and cities," Portia informed her fascinated, but pallid-looking spouse. "You see, Marcus. Pompeii was sort of like a seashore resort, where many wealthy patricians from Rome owned summer villas. The Roman historian Pliny recorded and described *their* dramatic escape in a manuscript that the scholar had written. But others that unfortunately remained in the doomed city eventually died from carbon monoxide poisoning, with the colorless, deadly gas being emitted from inside the Earth, and then being expelled from Mt. Vesuvius into the already-contaminated atmosphere. So, when the lava finally exited the volcano's crater," Portia authoritatively lectured, "it rolled down the mountainside and covered the city but…."

"But most everyone had already been dead!" Marcus logically concluded and summarized. "But we'll still have to go on the Pompeii tour, regardless of our very real personal concerns."

"Why?" Portia apprehensively challenged. "It's too potentially lethal! We could accidentally become missing persons' statistics, never to again surface in the year 2007!"

"Peer pressure!" Marcus candidly replied. "Our dubious friends would never believe our lame excuse for not going, and will pester us for the rest of our lives about our unwarranted phobia of inactive Italian volcanoes!"

The following morning, the familiar red and white tour bus picked-up the Hotel Paradiso's mostly-eager American guests, and an effervescent tour-guide, who announced herself as "Monica", described various sights of interest along the way. Jerry and Irene Tanner, along with Len and Andrea Bennett, were unaware of any immediate volcanic threat, and were conscientiously listening to Monica's scripted-but-informative presentation.

"You'll have plenty of time to visit the famous cameo shop, just outside the walls of Pompeii, after your memorable visit," the young college student suavely articulated to her mostly-receptive, seated passengers. "And while you're exploring Pompeii, be sure to visit the gladiator barracks; the temple remains; the tavern graffiti; a wealthy citizens' villa, and also the amphitheater ruins. Now, I'll be quiet and allow you to enjoy the panoramic views over there to your right. That's the scenic Isle of Ischia you see out there. It's not Capri as many tourists falsely believe!"

Upon entering Pompeii forty-minutes later, Marcus and Portia Italiano were carefully climbing the steps of the demolished city's amphitheater and cautiously walking behind the Tanners and the Bennetts, when suddenly, *they* were drawn into a powerful blue haze, and soon emerged inside a rather chaotic scene; the duo being pelted with hot pumice rocks descending from the darkened sky. Toxic Mt. Vesuvius was noisily exploding and spewing lava in the background. Now, the alarmed couple was frantically fleeing to save their lives, and the two terrified sprinters were not being mere spectators as the Italianos had been at the Circus Maximus, inside the Colosseum, and later at Emperor Nero's Gardens.

Amidst all of the hectic turmoil that was wildly transpiring, Marcus and Portia passionately embraced, and then the disconsolate pair slowly collapsed to the stone street, just before a tall pillar snapped, fell, and crumbled directly on top of their fragile bodies.

* * * * * * * * * * * * * *

“Where are Marcus and Portia?” Irene Tanner curiously asked her three equally-dismayed companions. “It appears that the easily distracted wanderlusts have gone-off on their own again!”

“You’d think that they’d tell us of their intentions before the loners simply radically detour off the beaten path!” Jerry Tanner criticized. “That would only be the polite thing to do. I guess appropriate social protocol has become obsolete.”

“Just look at those two pathetic-looking figures inside that airtight display case!” Andrea Bennett pointed-out. “They’re locked in an embrace after being covered by volcanic ash, almost two-thousand years ago. The last tour speaker said that after the bodies decayed inside the sealed ash cover, scientists poured plaster inside the remains, and as a result, formed these unbelievable casts that clearly outline the poor victims’ forms. I’m certainly glad I wasn’t residing in Pompeii when that horrible tragedy happened on August 24, 79 AD!”

“Where are Marcus and Portia?” Andrea Bennett worriedly asked *her* three chatty friends. “The lovebirds honestly don’t know what they’re missing during *their* absence!”

"An Erroneous Coincidence"

Flying saucer (UFO) investigations have been conducted since the latter stages of *World War II*. Much of the original speculation about UFOs had to do with Russia developing the atomic bomb, and U.S. and Soviet secret military projects being initiated and implemented during the decades-long *Cold War*. But generally speaking, UFOs refer to unusual lights or shapes appearing in the sky that escape practical scientific explanation.

Some UFOs have been depicted as circular, while others have been described as cigar-shaped. The strange objects zoom across the sky at unbelievable speeds, and some have been attributed to have left behind defined physical markings, while others are reputed to have caused severe electrical interference. But most rational analysis, done by objective investigators, has maintained that the UFO mystery has to do with people's minds conjuring-up "copycat observations", since the individuals are nervous about certain science-fiction movies that *they* might have seen in the past, or in the present.

Many government researchers agree that most UFO incidents can be dismissed as atmospheric reflections, or as sunlight or moonlight being mis-perceived. In addition to common high-altitude reflections, most government spokesmen and skilled scientists state that UFOs might also be the juxtaposition of stars and planets; or simple mirages; or traces of meteors and rockets; or the extraordinary perceptions might be experimental weather balloons, or perhaps even the orbiting of man-made satellites.

Project Blue Book, an authoritative Air Force Inquiry had concluded that over twelve-thousand individual UFO investigations, conducted between 1949 and 1969, suggest that most "flying saucer encounters" can be legitimately explained as natural phenomena. Nevertheless, there still remain thousands of dubious earthlings who argue that the government has been engaged in a monumental massive cover-up. Needless to say, the complicated UFO matter represents a huge, unresolved controversy in standard, contemporary American culture.

* * * * * * * * * * * * * *

Rick Fredericks and Tom Fagan were seated at their favorite downtown Atlanta, Georgia bar discussing current events on the front-page newspapers, and also recent developments within the lackluster

National League baseball pennant race. The general conversation was both amiable and informal.

"I'll tell you something, Tom," Rick Fredericks said before imbibing another gulp of delicious cold beer from his frosted mug. "The *Braves* will never catch the *Mets* and the *Phillies* in the National League playoff race. We'll have to write this season off as a major disaster. And it's too bad that dear old Uncle Sam won't allow us to write-off our great disappointments as sizable deductions on our federal income tax returns!"

"Our favorite team obviously lacks the right combination of dominant pitching, timely clutch hitting, and a solid batting lineup, all staying free of injuries," Tom Fagan evaluated and related. "And the abominable *Braves* could have a stronger array of bench performers contributing to the overall team effort. I mean to say that their defense is adequate, but their offense remains suspect! Oh well, Rick. There's always spring training next year! It's goin' to be a mighty long winter!"

"Harry, kindly give us two more draughts of *Budweiser* with accompanying new frosted mugs," Rick commanded the always-alert, friendly bartender. "Tom and I can gulp our baseball woes away in the comfort of this familiar drinking hole. Help us share our excessive misery!"

Before the two dedicated-but-frustrated baseball enthusiasts could continue their casual discussion, the *Braves* appalling four to nothing deficit was mercifully interrupted by a television flash news bulletin. All eyes at the bar focused on Robin Walsh, a popular Atlanta news reporter standing erect with a microphone held in her right hand. Harry turned the volume up on the overhead flat screen television, so that everyone present could hear the special announcement.

"That luscious doll used to be a reporter for Fox 5 WAGA," Rick Fredericks whispered to Tom Fagan. "Now she's on the local NBC affiliate. Wonder what important information Robin has to convey during this unusual interruption of the baseball game. Maybe Elvis's ghost has been discovered working at a Memphis Burger King!"

"Quiet, Rick!" Tom politely insisted. "Let's give a listen to what emergency that luscious blonde babe has to report. Anything's better than watching the pathetic *Braves* debacle!"

"Flying saucers have been witnessed hovering over northern Atlanta," Robin Walsh began her introductory story line. "The aerial formations are in the shapes reminiscent of various crop circle patterns that have been widely-filmed and documented. Ralph," the reporter melodramatically indicated to her astute cameraman. "See if you can zoom-in on the weird phenomenon we're now recording, just north of the city."

The veteran cameraman adjusted his lens and effectively captured twenty-five UFOs, dancing around the pitch-black night sky in five associated, distinct but very sensational formations. Everyone at the bar sat mesmerized with their' mouths agape, each patron awaiting more particular details about the fantastic maneuvers that their curious eyes and minds were interpreting. The extraordinary occurrence had definitely merited the bar customers' undivided attention. The crowd simply remained quiet and stationary as Robin Walsh briefly paused, and then professionally continued with her dissertation.

"Our NBC sister station in San Diego is now reporting a similar celestial phenomenon that is happening over Carlsbad, California, approximately thirty-miles north of that city," Robin Walsh shared with her intrigued viewers. "It is perfectly reasonable to speculate that these two instances are more than a mere coincidence. Our Washington news bureau is now reporting that the Air Force has dispatched several F-16 fighter squadrons to investigate and intercept these strange objects that are cluttering the night sky. But right now," the attractive on-the-scene reporter stated with a glum expression upon her beautiful face, "I'll not speculate about the origin of these' presumed extraterrestrial spacecraft. Right now, our only alternative is to simply observe and marvel at this fascinating mystery dancing, or should I say 'occurring' right before our disbelieving eyes," Robin Walsh proceeded. "And may I add that Atlanta is nearly three-thousand-miles away from famous secret Area 54, located just north of Las Vegas, Nevada. But what we're seeing is not an aberration! It's the real deal folks!"

For three consecutive nights, the fantastic non-hostile, atmospheric anomaly repeated itself with myriad astronomers, scientists, and UFO enthusiasts hypothesizing a plethora of amazing theories ranging from abnormal atmospheric plasma activity to the advent of Armageddon and Judgment Day. The press was in a feeding frenzy, attempting to account for and explain the bizarre nightlights that prevailed above Atlanta, Georgia, and also above Carlsbad, California, on the evenings of July 8th to July 10th, 2007.

* * * * * * * * * * * * *

On the evening of July 11th Rick Fredericks and Tom Fagan were again present, commiserating at the downtown Peachtree Plaza bar, and the pair was thoroughly reviewing the inexplicable flying saucer "meteorological manifestation". Other anxious patrons milling-around at the popular lounge were also conversing about the rather peculiar and predictable nocturnal wonders that had been recently witnessed on the busy establishment's 43-inch overhead television screen.

"Tom, as you know, I'm normally a very skeptical and cynical person," Rick prefaced his remarks while endeavoring to sound somewhat objective. "But I'm not buying into the government's shallow answers about these flying saucer incidents having simple rational explanations. Atmospheric conditions are definitely not causing what our pupils are acutely perceiving."

"Are you afraid of being abducted by space aliens lacking official green card documentation?" Tom awkwardly and nervously joked. "The next thing I know, you'll be interviewed on the Sci-Fi Channel, elaborating on your exotic theory that the twenty-five UFOs over Atlanta, and the twenty-five saucers buzzing over Carlsbad, California represent the fifty States of the Union, and that each one is carrying a new interstellar governor to replace the irresponsible duly-elected American ones! Harry, bring two more cold beers over here, please!"

"Now Tom, you're being absolutely ludicrous and absurd on this important subject!" Rick Fredericks countered in a rather perturbed tone of voice. "The military brass is baffled beyond belief, and our most sophisticated technology has been rendered completely useless. These enigmatic UFOs are making a total mockery out of our science and technology, and you're quite content doing amateur sit-down comedy on your wobbly bar-stool. Tom, I hereby insist that you just have to take this obvious space alien threat more seriously than you are! I mean, ya' gotta' read a quality dictionary and thoroughly research the meaning of the word 'extinction'!"

"Rick, I tell ya' that the *Falcons* football season can't begin too soon! Oh no!" Tom Fagan exclaimed with a degree of apprehension evident in his tone of voice. "Look up at the TV screen! The beginning of the *Braves* game is again being preempted. Robin Walsh is making another dramatic appearance! Let's listen in to what the gorgeous doll has to communicate this time!"

"Two strange sets of twenty-five UFOs have again simultaneously appeared, the first north of Atlanta, and the second over Carlsbad, California for the fourth straight night! Although the President has directly stated in his press conference this morning that the flying saucers are being caused by a collaboration of unique environmental circumstances in the Earth's stratosphere, many Americans, including myself, are becoming doubtful of the shallow logic and the vague explanations being generated out of Washington. As you can plainly determine, this evening, in the clear night sky above," the excited reporter maintained and stressed, "what we're witnessing seems to transcend both reason and everyday common sense. According to our reliable NBC sources, some of the top brass at the Pentagon have confidentially mentioned that our fastest supersonic jet fighter planes can't even get close to the UFO formations, because of a remarkable force field being employed, which apparently defies scientific understanding. Of course, as usual, those dependable sources at the Pentagon wish to remain anonymous!"

Rick Fredericks and Tom Fagan (along with the two-dozen other shocked bar patrons assembled at the downtown Atlanta tavern) stared incredulously at the large overhead flat-screen, plasma television. Before anyone present could utter a syllable, the very competent on-the-scene reporter Robin Walsh made a pertinent but rather stunning articulation.

"The UFOs are now maneuvering about and scattering," the female news correspondent announced. "They're most certainly dispersing! And my producer is informing me that the same incredible development is now also occurring above Carlsbad, California! The Carlsbad saucers are now heading east, and the ones over Georgia are presently traveling at a high rate of speed westward. It seems that the threat of an impending alien invasion is no longer imminent with the UFOs not remaining stationary! My producer has related to me that the hundred-thousand citizens of Carlsbad are currently in the streets, celebrating the saucers' departure! We now return you to our regularly scheduled program, that is to say, until more relevant details develop!"

"Harry, give everyone at the bar, including my buddy Tom, a free drink of their choice!" a jubilant Rick Fredericks declared and emphasized to the equally-ecstatic bartender. "This special moment in American history is indeed cause for recognition and celebration! It's quite apparent that the Earth has been gratefully spared from almost certain devastation. And to add to the overall glory, the lowly *Braves* have taken a two-to-nothing lead!" Rick emphasized to Tom. "And for those of you at the bar drinking straight whiskey," Fredericks jubilantly yelled, "don't hesitate to order a double!"

* * * * * * * * * * * * * *

On the majestic evening of July 11th at precisely 7:45 p.m., Admiral Zarg of the Andromeda Interstellar Fleet Command had been adroitly passing through the asteroid belt, situated between Jupiter and Mars. The perceptive alien officer noticed something irregular appearing on his spacecraft's ultra-advanced control panel. Admiral

Zarg immediately transmitted an emergency verbal/video message to two dignified, memorial, funeral processions, that had recently descended toward planet Earth. The distinguished Space Admiral was not-too-thrilled or complimentary.

"You blundering, incompetent Idiots!" Admiral Zarg vehemently chastised. "Sixty-years ago, two of our spacecraft had accidentally collided over Roswell, New Mexico. The historic Earth date was July 8th, 1947. You totally irresponsible Participants in the two memorial processions commemorating the anniversary of that tragic incident involving your dear friends have grossly misinterpreted my original instructions, and now, I must inform *you* knuckle-headed interstellar Fools that your present coordinates are indeed in error. This embarrassing mistake must be corrected immediately!"

"Where are we supposed to be, Admiral?" a distinct distant squeaky paranoid-sounding voice sincerely asked in the space aliens' native tongue. "You did say Roswell, didn't you? I'm certain that you had said with clarity the name 'Roswell'! That was your explicit direction!"

"Yes, Colonel Drak!" the aggravated Admiral angrily blustered from midway across the solar system. "But unfortunately, you're scheduled to be hovering over Roswell, New Mexico, a desert community of around forty-thousand residents, and not over Roswell, Georgia, a small residential town of about ten-thousand-inhabitants, situated ten-miles or so above the city of Atlanta!"

"But Admiral, didn't you mention that Roswell was not far from Carlsbad!" a second voice meekly challenged from the lead spaceship, flying in the vicinity of Carlsbad, California! "Our procession is presently hovering over Carlsbad right now!"

"You foolish, doltish Clown!" a very enraged Admiral Zarg vociferously reprimanded his error-prone subordinate. "Listen, Captain Sargo! Carlsbad, California is a flourishing city of around a hundred-thousand-humans that can be found thirty-miles above the metropolis commonly known as San Diego. On the other hand," the irritated Space Admiral loudly bellowed to Captain Sargo, "Carlsbad Caverns, a popular United States geological landmark, is remotely located near the White and the Sacramento Mountains, just west of Roswell, New Mexico. Obviously, Captain Sargo. You need to have a, pardon the ironic expression, you evidently need to have a 'crash course' in Earth geography!"

"It's my foolish mistake, and I'll accept full responsibility for the blatant miscalculation! We'll abandon our present position, and our procession will strategically head east, and then favorably rendezvous with Colonel Drak's memorial service contingent that's heading west toward Roswell, New Mexico," Captain Sargo promised the flustered and very animated Admiral Zarg. "Sorry about the ugly mix-up, Admiral! I assure you that we're on our way to the realigned coordinates right this very second!"

"And we'll be readily heading due west from our present location over Roswell, Georgia, and soon be meeting-up with the other delegation originating from Carlsbad, California," Colonel Drak prudently apologized to his very annoyed and agitated commanding officer. "Unfortunately, Eminent Admiral, Captain Sargo had gotten Carlsbad, California mixed-up with Carlsbad Caverns, located near Roswell, New Mexico. And conversely, I had gotten Roswell, Georgia confused with Roswell, New Mexico! Nobody's perfect you know!"

"You two doltish interplanetary Imbeciles better get your scruples together before you're both relegated to slave status, and shipped-out to Zenno V for rehabilitation!" the Fleet Commander threatened his not-too-astute, worried, piloting officers. "Such dereliction of standard operating procedures cannot be condoned or tolerated! Do you two embarrassing Buffoons fathom my words!"

"Admiral Zarg! Thanks for giving us the essential heads-up! We had no intention of insulting your enviable integrity, or sullying your impeccable reputation!" Captain Sargo respectfully answered. "Now, both dedicated funeral processions can promptly congregate over the correct site coordinates of the terrible 1948 Roswell tragedy, so that the families of the deceased riding aboard our ships can conduct their solemn memorial vigil! Thanks again for your sage insight, Admiral!"

"Now obviously, you extremely inept Dunderheads, the inferior earthlings should know that the brilliant illuminations in their night skies aren't exactly being piloted by the brightest members of *our* planet's Illuminati!" Admiral Zarg communicated and rankled at his occasionally-dysfunctional subordinates.

"Figurines"

Mrs. Joan Butler entered the family's Grape Street ranch home's laundry room from the garage and announced to her husband, "Mike, I just dropped-off the kids at my sister's place. She's throwing a pool party in her back yard, and Johnny and Karli will be having some fun spending six-hours of quality time over on Pratt Street with their cousins and with some of their other school friends. That gives us free time the rest of the morning, and most of the afternoon, to get some exercise by strolling-around the mall. I still haven't bought a new dress for our nephew's wedding over in North Philly' next month, so there's a method to my madness."

"Okay, Dear. But just don't become rambunctious and launch into one of your notorious, extravagant shopping sprees. Which mall do you want to go to?" Mike Butler asked before stretching his arms over his head and yawning. "There're four main ones to choose from. What about the one in Deptford? We could eat lunch at the nearby Adelphia, or we could catch a meal at the Lone Star Steak House over on *Route 322,"* the independent tile and marble installer constructively suggested. "The only problem is the traffic congestion as we go west closer to Philly', or travel east in the direction of Atlantic City."

"Or we could zip-over to the Echelon Mall in Voorhees and have lunch not far from there at your favorite eatery, Cap N' Cat's Seafood Restaurant in the Eagle Plaza," Joan Butler answered. "Or we could drive-up to the Burlington Mall and eat at Charlie Brown's on *541,* or enjoy a decent meal at the Gallery on High Street overlooking the *Delaware.* You always talk about watching the huge cargo ships and the sleek pleasure boats going up and down the river. You don't see that sort of thing here in Hammonton."

"I have an even better idea," the husband offered. "We can drive to the Hamilton Mall over in Mays Landing, and after you purchase your fancy dress, we could...."

"Buzz over to Harrah's Casino in Atlantic City, use the comps on your Diamond Card, and have lunch in the Reflections Restaurant," Joan Butler accurately interpreted her spouse's inspiration. "And then, after you have your usual personal-size brick oven pizza, and I have my delicious turkey club sandwich, we could spend an hour or so playing the slots. I really like those new nickel machines, Jade Monkey and Pegasus."

"That sounds great!" Mike agreed. "I like Harrah's a lot. And then, while we're in the Reflections, I could easily swallow-down a massive hot fudge sundae for dessert."

"Just remember, Sweetie, that tomorrow morning you have your annual physical over at Dr. Cramer's office," Joan reminded Mike. "You're supposed to be watching your cholesterol and sugar levels. The Doc thinks you're a prime candidate for diabetes, and that you have to exercise more, too. If *that* ugly health reality ever happens," Joan Butler paused and emphasized, "then brick oven pizzas and hot fudge sundaes will be absolutely taboo!"

"Okay. Honey," Mike conceded in recognition of his immense appetite. "Maybe I'll nix the hot fudge sundae idea and just order a plain old fudge brownie, instead. And I gotta' stress that I do get enough exercise mixing cement for wet-bed foundations; applying grout to floors and counters, and kneeling-down on my pads for hours-on-end while expertly laying tile in kitchens and bathrooms," the husband defensively maintained. "I can't wait until Johnny graduates from high school. I'll make him a junior partner in the firm, and have our athletic son do most of the strenuous labor."

"Forget that brilliant notion!" Joan laughed, shaking her head in disapproval. "Your intellectually-oriented son has ambitions of becoming either a trial lawyer or a banking executive, once the honor roll scholar gets over his impractical whim of becoming a professional baseball player. I'm afraid that you'll just have to become a trifle more versa*tile* in choosing your junior business associate," the wife cleverly quipped. "And forget about employing Karli, even though she's still sort of a tom-boy!" the wife joked. "Your daughter likes working with her mind, too, and wants to attend college outside of New Jersey! She's even talking about living and working in California. Not too bad for an eight-year-old!"

On the way to the *Route 322* Hamilton Mall, Mike drove his white *Infiniti* sedan east on Egg Harbor Road, and then turned *right* onto Weymouth. In another five-minutes, the luxury auto' was speeding past the expansive Atlantic Blueberry Company Farm, the largest cultivated blueberry plantation in the world.

"Here we are in Hammonton, New Jersey, Mike, the undisputed Blueberry Capital of the World. I wish it were late June and not a Saturday in early September," Joan Butler regretted and mentioned. "It's too bad that the fresh-picked blueberry season only lasts eight short weeks."

"You can buy frozen ones all winter long," the sometimes-argumentative husband reminded his fussy wife. "Atlantic Blueberry keeps tons of frozen berries in cold storage over in Vineland for distribution, all year round."

"I know," Joan Butler acknowledged. "But frozen berries just don't taste the same as the fresh-picked fruit. I guess we'll just have to eat supermarket California and Chile blueberries until next summer arrives. I especially like the Duke and Blue Crop varieties. They're without a doubt the very best."

When the Butlers finally reached the Hamilton Mall, Joan gave Mike some specific last-minute instructions. "I'm going to try Macy's, and if I can't find a dress to my liking, I'll have to splurge and buy something fairly fancy from Sak's Fifth Avenue. I figure I'll be about an hour-and-a half shopping, so while you're killing time, you can…"

"Check-out the bookstore, the music shop, and a gift shop or two," the husband declared. "Say Joan, why didn't we just stop at Ideal Manufacturing in Hammonton up on *Route 30?"*

"They're now specializing in selling high school and college prom dresses," the wife replied with a look of frustration on her face. "And the Ideal's formal adult wedding attire selection is not nearly as good as the ones here at the mall. Don't get too bored, Mike, and I'll meet you in front of the fountain near the main entrance in about ninety-minutes. Don't get lost wandering around the Food Court! Remember, we'll be eating at Reflections in about two-and-a-half hours!"

Michael Franklin Butler synchronized his wristwatch to match the exact time on his wife's, and then entered the mall's Walden Bookstore and perused various items in the history and in the current bestsellers' sections; scanned several sports' magazines, and then checked-out the discounted bargains occupying the modern lit' paperback aisle.

Not finding anything unique that captured his general interest, the browser abandoned his bookstore patrol and trekked to a neighboring shop, lethargically repeating the same sort of routine, but this time inspecting various compact disks in the pop and rock music areas, again without getting excited about any of the youth-oriented featured products. 'I can't stand rap rhythms, and I believe that most of the good music was over by the 1980s,' the mall visitor pessimistically thought. 'Thank God for nostalgic Frank Sinatra, Tony Bennett, and Elvis recordings! I've already made the transition from cassettes to compact disks for my favorite songs and artists, so I guess there's little selection here that can motivate me to make a purchase. I still have another hour to burn before meeting Joan in front of the fountain. There's a gift shop on the other side of the Food Court where I'll pay a visit. This next hour is probably going to be the longest sixty-minutes of my lackluster life!'

The first thing that the skilled tile installer noticed inside the Heavenly Gift Shop was the common square tile floor pattern. 'Whatever happened to professional pride and competency? Whoever put this mediocre job together had to be rank amateurs,' Mike negatively noted. 'Quite apparently, the workmen started with full tiles on one side of the store, and ended-up with half-tiles on the other. It's obvious that the guys didn't measure from the center and start there, and then working their way to each sidewall and making everything on the floor match evenly as rookies should have done. Craftsmen taking pride in their work, *those incompetent clowns* certainly were not!'

Then, the all-too-critical 'tile perfectionist' began examining the various pieces of retail shelf merchandise that were available for sale. The first item that Butler scrutinized was a figurine of a Dutch boy and girl holding hands. Automatically, the novelty object reminded the man of his teenage romance with the former Joan Mildred Davis, who ten-years later, became Mrs. Joan Butler.

Feeling self-conscious standing alone inside the almost-empty gift shop, Mike's mind fast-forwarded from his 1993 memory back to 2007, when the mall visitor's eyes observed an alabaster statue of a Roman' girl pouring water out of a jug. The statue's face seemed to be a duplicate of that of Butler's daughter, Karli, and the basic similarity brought a broad smile to the man's lips. 'I'll go over to the Christmas display counter,' the wandering browser thought. 'As far as the seasons are concerned, this gift shop is even ahead of the clothing sections of the large department stores that are still only showing fall apparel lines,' the fellow evaluated.

'These colorful Dickens figures presumably singing Christmas carols remind me of when my brothers, cousins, and I would go around Hammonton to friends and acquaintances' houses and sing our own off-key versions of traditional carols,' Butler fondly recollected. 'Our motivation was to get a shot of liquor at each stop, and by the end of the evening, all seven of us would become so inebriated that we had to cease our merry activity, and then go home and sleep-off our intoxicated state.'

Across the aisle from the grim-faced Dickens people display were several expensive figurines. Another arrangement with a Norman Rockwell theme seemed awfully familiar to Butler. Three boys (standing in a huddle) were vying for the honor of choosing-up sides while placing their hands near the knob of a baseball bat. 'I've seen *this* piece someplace before, but I can't remember where!' Mike seriously recollected.

Near a side shelf Butler's eyes keenly studied the form of a young doll wearing a white dress, sitting in a diminutive rocking chair, while innocently holding a small puppy. 'This figure makes me think of my younger sister, Barbara's First Holy Communion,' Mike recollected. 'My grandparents had a picture of it on the fireplace mantel in their living room.'

Then, a powerful realization dominated Mike Butler's formerly lazy state of mind. 'These exceptional strange similarities are rather unbelievable!' the browser shockingly reckoned. 'All of the objects I've just viewed were things that were present in my grandparents' place inside the old homestead on First Road,' Butler marveled. 'The Dutch boy and girl holding hands was in the kitchen hutch; the Roman girl statue pouring water from a jug was in one corner of the house's dining room; the Dickens caroling figures were usually displayed on a ledge next to the Christmas tree; the boys with their hands on the baseball bat was on a bureau in one of the upstairs bedrooms, and the photo' of my sister Barbara's First Holy Communion was indeed on the living room's fireplace mantel. How uncanny and remarkable could an odd set of coincidences be?'

Michael Butler's meditation was interrupted upon him hearing the courteous voice of a saleswoman. "Sir, may I help you?"

"No thank you!" the suddenly embarrassed store visitor answered as his face instantly turned florid. "My wife's spending a small fortune buying-up the rest of the mall, so I thought I'd spend a few spare minutes just browsing-around and inspecting your terrific inventory. I hope you don't mind."

"No, Sir, not at all!" the conscientious saleslady cheerfully replied. "Your situation is quite familiar to me. I hope your wife finds her way into this store, because for some reason, business has been exceptionally slow this morning," the pleasant woman casually explained. "But if you need any assistance or recommendations, just let me know. Everything is twenty-percent off today!"

Aware that he was the only non-employee ambling around inside the Heavenly Gift Shop, Mike Butler gradually proceeded to the rear of the business to squander ten more minutes of idle time before meeting Joan in front of the mall's main entrance water fountain. Tiny ceramic representations of Mickey and Minnie Mouse had been exhibited on a glass counter, and the mall trekker recalled two pleasurable family vacation trips to *Disney World* in Orlando,

Florida, and one very special transcontinental family flight to sunny Los Angeles, featuring a wonderful week-long stay at a motor lodge near *Disneyland* in Anaheim.

On a shelf adjacent to the miniature-sized Disney characters were appealing Raggedy-Ann and Andy dolls, which immediately had Butler's psyche reflecting about Karli's favorite early childhood possessions. 'Everything in this place seems to bring back warm nostalgic memories. I'm feeling a little uneasy about becoming so sentimental. I can't wait to climb back into the car, visit Harrah's, and then driving back to Hammonton!'

Hanging from a nearby wall was a pair of two-dimensional Chinese dancers dressed in ceremonial garb. The figures were exhibited inside a plain, silver-painted wooden picture frame, and the artistic print reproduction made Mike Butler's imagination think about the Orient trip to Beijing and to Tokyo that he and Joan had desired to take, but that had been twice postponed because of past family responsibilities and business commitments, which had unexpectedly arisen. 'I've seen those Chinese dancers somewhere before, but I can't remember exactly where?' Butler's overwhelmed mind languished in confusion.

And to add to his mounting consternation, hanging on an opposite wall was a painting of an old bearded Chinese farmer, which eerily complemented the pair of Oriental dancers. But then another set of small six-inch-high figurines brought everything (that already had Mike Butler's dis*oriented* mind in a quandary) into perfect perspective. Now, at last, the extremely anxious man fully comprehended everything that his eyes had perceived in the formerly nondescript Heavenly Gift Shop.

"It's a boy clad in a blue cap and robe, and a girl in a white cap and gown standing at a high school graduation," Mike inadvertently mumbled to himself. "The life-size statues can't be Johnny and Karli, because many school grades separate the kids. It must be Joan and me. Yes, it all makes logical sense now, in a strange sort of way. Those two statues, or ones just like them, were in my parents' home standing on the family room shelf,' Mike nervously recalled. 'And all of these exhibits are quite incredible! The Mickey and Minnie Mouse figurines; the Raggedy Ann and Andy dolls; the graceful Oriental dancers, and the old Chinese farmer carrying water buckets on a shoulder pole, along with the represented high school graduates, were all treasured keepsakes that *also* were in my parent's home. But the items all had been inherited by my older brother upon my dear mother's death in 1974. This heavenly Gift

Shop is rapidly becoming a hellish nightmare!' Mike Butler apprehensively thought. 'My grandparents and my parents are all dead, and for some remote mysterious reason, everything inside this haunted shop is making me think about my past associations with them. God how I miss *them* all!'

Sweat beads began accumulating on Mike Butler's forehead, and feeling terribly awkward and out of place, the spooked, bewildered man decided to swiftly evacuate the ominous Heavenly Gift Shop. Upon speedily passing by the cash register counter, and then exiting the premises, the beleaguered husband felt compelled to stop next to a pair of human-sized angels holding brass horns, both forms looking as if they belonged as part of the gift shop's quite extraordinary display. But yet, the rosy-faced celestial beings had not (up until that moment) been observed standing in *that* particular strategic location, especially at the very second that Mike had made his nonchalant entrance into the attractive retail establishment. The perplexed man's mind needed some plausible explanation to account for the rather bizarre chain of events he had been experiencing.

"Am I dreaming?" Mike Butler said out loud to the two divine-looking winged creatures. "My addled mind's entered some sort of weird alien dimension! My brain's commanding my feet to move, but my legs are paralyzed and will not cooperate! To tell *you* the honest-to-God truth, I'm quite spellbound by all that's happening! What's going on here? Who are you two, Gentlemen?"

"Hello, Mike!" the first angelic figure replied with a prodigious smile evident upon his handsome visage. "I'm Gabriel, and this is my colleague and constant companion, Michael, who incidentally *you* were named after, and had been baptized in honor of. Don't be overly alarmed with all the excited people frantically screaming and gasping, while staring-down at *that* limp figure lying there on the tile floor! Try and keep a tranquil spirit! For you see, you've just died a minute ago of a massive cardiac arrest. Please don't feel victimized! And so, Mr. Michael Franklin Butler," Gabriel continued articulating his rather morbid exposition, "kindly heed this important announcement. It's my expressed duty and distinct privilege to inform you that my associate, Michael, and I have been dispatched down to Earth to expertly escort your immortal soul to the Place of Final Judgment!"

"Butterton Woods"

Dave Anderson owned a four-hundred-acre blueberry and peach farm, principally situated at and behind the intersection of Walker Road and *Route 30,* the White Horse Pike in Elm, New Jersey, just outside the Hammonton town border, and a little west of the Atlantic/Camden County Line. Dave and Jill Anderson's comfortable residence was a seventy-year-old white Dutch colonial home located at the junction of the busy highway and serene Walker Road. In the late 1970s, blueberries became the dominant fruit crop in Hammonton and vicinity, and like many other area growers, Anderson followed the money and began removing his Blake and Red Haven variety peach orchards and replacing them with fields of Duke and Blue Crop variety blueberries.

The original fifty-acre homestead had been "grubbed" in 1902 by Dave Anderson's grandfather, who like most enterprising British and Italian immigrant farmers, planted peach and apple trees, popular regional crops that were then sold locally. But soon after the invention of the automobile, and just prior to World War I, trucks began hauling fresh "Hammonton fruit" to Philadelphia, New York, and other metropolitan markets situated along the Eastern Seaboard. After Dave Anderson's grandfather died during the height of the Great Depression, his father (like many area bootlegging farmers) drove trucks during the wintertime, transporting "moonshine whiskey" from stills kept in woods and barns during the "very difficult and dangerous Prohibition Era", when extra money was needed simply to survive with adequate food on the kitchen table; enough revenue to pay property taxes, and needed cash to maintain cherished farm equipment. Many proud-but-desperate local farmers (out of economic necessity) capitalized on "the tough times of whiskey deprivation" that were (according to older citizens) caused by the 1920s women's suffrage and temperance movement.

David Henry Anderson's conscientious father profited from the annual "winter bootlegging bonanza", and during the Great Depression, managed to save sufficient funds to buy an additional seven-acre tract of land behind the original homestead from an English immigrant named John Butterton, who (along with *his* descendants) is presently buried in Oak Grove Cemetery on the White Horse Pike in Hammonton. Hence, the small section of forestland is commonly referred to as Butterton Woods, which Dave Anderson presently calls his "personal hunting preserve".

The end of Prohibition and American involvement in World War II gradually brought the USA out of the Great Depression, and Hammonton area farmers enjoyed a time of prosperity with the prices of quality summer peaches and fall apples skyrocketing. Dave's ambitious father was able to expand the family farming operation from one-hundred to four-hundred acres along Walker Road, and then extending his little empire across Union Road to the far end of the property, which was referred to as "Texas", because it was so distant from the original homestead tract. When Anderson's father died in 1974, Dave bought-out his younger brothers Thomas and Frank, and soon became the exclusive owner of the sprawling estate.

David's best friend was an amiable Hammonton High School English teacher named Jack Elder. The two men had been chums ever since ninth-grade, even though ironically, Dave had graduated from Edgewood High in Atco (Winslow Township, Camden County) and Jack from Hammonton High (Atlantic County). On their weekly "Boys Night Out", Dave and Jack would frequent the popular West End Grille on the south side of the railroad tracks in downtown Hammonton, and then habitually enjoy three games of competitive bowling at DiDonato Lanes and Cocktail Lounge on *Route 30* on the east side of town. A week after Thanksgiving, Jack Elder paid a friendly visit to his buddy Dave Anderson's home.

"Hi, Dave! Where's Jill?" Jack asked. "Is she at the grocery store or at the hairdresser?"

"No, she's first taken the kids to school, and then my wife drove to her sister Gloria's place over on Fairview Avenue," Dave informed his inquisitive visitor. "The girls are heading-out to Consumer's Square over in Mays Landing to do some heavy-duty clothes shopping and gossiping. I *swear* that Jill's wardrobe must rival Queen Elizabeth's, Jack. And I think I gotta' build three more closets onto my house!"

"It isn't healthy to swear Dave, especially in a court of law," Jack Elder facetiously joked to his farmer friend. "Aren't ya' gonna' ask where I've been? Or are you so self-indulgent that all you can think and talk about are yourself, your wife, your kids and your huge farm! I mean, start showing a more profound interest in others!"

"Okay, then Mr. Noun, could you educate me about what location you're coming from?" Dave Anderson replied to his public-school instructor pal with a broad grin on his face. "It's not the busy harvest season, so I have the rest of the fall and all winter to listen to your inane prattle."

"Well, I'm just returning from Dr. Joe's chiropractic office over in Atco," Elder said with a straight face. "And Dr. Matt gave me a great adjustment, along with much needed heat and powerful electric stim'. I always get and deserve the four-pad upper and lower back treatment, ya' know! So, ya' see Dave, I'm not playing hooky from school, and I have a legitimate medical excuse for being absent," the gregarious guest continued with his rambling drivel. "But the real reason I go to that clinic in Atco is because the place has a great Hydro-bed, featuring warm water vibrations. And also the clinic has a moving roller bed, or I should say a bed with moving rollers where the muscles, vertebrae, and joints in my back are thoroughly massaged for a full fifteen-minutes. Ya' gotta' come with me some time for a trial treatment," Jack insisted. "It's guaranteed to improve your much-to-be-desired posture, and modify your atrocious bowling game, too!"

"I'll consider your stellar invitation after you accompany me out to Butterton Woods on a little walking expedition," Anderson stated and requested. "Rabbit season will soon be over, and deer hunting starts December 1st. I wanna' check my recently constructed deer stand and make sure no greedy poachers are staking-out the woods with deer bait and plannin' to use my stand as an observation post and shooting platform," Dave Anderson convincingly communicated to Jack Elder. "And after we finish our little Butterton Woods' inspection, we'll head on over to Mary's Restaurant on *206* for a late morning breakfast, my treat of course!"

"Sounds pretty copacetic to me!" Jack Elder promptly replied. "Either Mary's or the Red Barn for breakfast. Either of the two *206* eateries will be just dandy! When a man's stomach is growling like mine is right now, pancakes, bacon, and eggs and strong coffee will taste just as great at either restaurant."

"I remember when *Route 30* used to be the major east-west thoroughfare around here," Dave told his best friend as the friends entered Anderson's red Ford 150 pickup. "But then, the State expanded *Route 322,* and soon the Black Horse Pike was taking traffic away from the White Horse, and giving this parallel highway serious competition with the Philadelphia and Pennsylvania people heading down to the Atlantic City Boardwalk and to the Jersey Shore. And then in 1964…."

"The Atlantic City Expressway had opened right between the White Horse Pike and the Black Horse Pike, and *that* high-speed toll road seriously hurt your family's retail farm market business," Jack finished Dave's all-too-predictable speech. "Dave, I've heard *that* monotonous, redundant sob story a thousand and one times, and quite frankly, it sounds worse than a broken record. Now, let's scoot over to Mary's before it's already suppertime, and we'll have to eat filet mignon instead of hotcakes and eggs! We'll swallow-down some buttermilk pancakes and then tour Butterton Woods to alleviate your paranoia! Ha, ha, ha!" Elder indulgently laughed. "You're a very successful multimillionaire Dave, and all of a sudden you're needlessly worried that your farm market isn't doing as well as it had done forty-years ago! Ha, ha, ha! You should've been an ancient barbarian, because sometimes' you really slay me! Ha, ha, ha!"

An hour later, after sharing and exchanging a few choice anecdotes with several patrons at Mary's Restaurant, and after enjoying delectable breakfasts, Dave Anderson drove his shiny new red Ford 150 (with Jack Elder riding shotgun) back to Walker Road, taking Union Road west from two-lane *Route 206*. The prominent, full-bellied farmer pulled-off the recently paved country road into a dirt lane that separated his main irrigation pond from "the landmark Butterton Woods". A thousand-feet down the dirt trail, the truck's operator gently applied the brakes.

"Okay, Jack. Let's hike five-hundred-feet into the woods and locate my new sacred tree stand," Dave Anderson directed. "If nothing's been tampered with, and if no deer bait is detectable on the ground, then I predict we'll take a quick cruise over to Atlantic City in my new Lexus. And thanks to my good nature, both lunch and your first hundred bucks of gambling money will be on me!"

"If it's *your* sacred tree stand, perhaps we should build a makeshift altar underneath and make it into a shrine! But I gotta' confess that your' buying me lunch is mighty generous of you, Dave!" Jack quipped with a wide smile accentuating his pearly white teeth. "You'll have to sell eight more crates of blueberries next summer than you did last season to make-up for the additional expenditure. But then again," Elder amiably vociferated, "I don't believe I have any other friends that would simply hand me a hundred bucks to casually blow away at the blackjack tables."

Two-hundred-paces into Butterton Woods, on-a-mission Dave Anderson was relieved to discover that his revered deer hunting platform was still securely nestled high up in the sturdy tall barren oak tree, without any sign of senseless vandalism. And the serious hunter was happy to notice that no deer-baiting apple or sweet potato pile had been surreptitiously dumped-off by a greedy, trespassing poacher. Being satisfied that nothing irregular had occurred since *his* last cursory inspection of the area three days before, Anderson was about to remark to Elder how delighted the property owner was about his favorable observations when his keen ears distinctly discerned juvenile-aged voices originating from his far left.

"Duck down!" Anderson softly ordered and then motioned to his less wary companion. "Jack, I think I hear intruders talking behind that clump of pine trees. Let's slink-over there and investigate who's trespassin'!"

One hundred additional feet into Butterton Woods' dense interior the men came across three boys dressed in 1970s winter apparel, lighting left-over caterpillar meshes that had been woven upon and still remained on a short, naked deciduous tree's lower limbs. The new arrivals skulked-down on their knees and intently eavesdropped on the teenagers' odd conversation.

"I told you guys I had a great idea playing hooky and comin' out here in these woods for a couple of smokes and a little mischief!" the first kid said. "Edgewood High's a real bummer, so I thought we'd come out here to the edge of these isolated woods and have a little amusement, ha, ha, ha."

"Great idea, Robbie!" the second kid commended. "It does beat goin' to chemistry class! But make sure you don't carelessly set these woods on fire! I don't wanna' have to spend time in juvenile court explainin' why we're avowed junior pyromaniacs with dreams of becomin' full-fledged arsonists. It might interfere with me watchin' my nighttime TV cartoon shows, ha, ha, ha!"

"Don't flip-out and hit the panic button, Charlie!" the third encroacher laughed. "The only thing ya' gotta' tell the judge is that we ran out of matches, and so did Yogi Bear and his close pal Smoky! This woods' ain't exactly Jellystone Park, ya' know! Ha, ha, ha! Hand me a cancer, stick, will ya'!"

"Shut-up, Steve, before I give ya' a deluxe knuckle sandwich! Your stupid bull runnin' from your filthy mouth is makin' me nervous!" Robbie reprimanded his punk associate/junior comedian. "Now, just look what ya' two clowns made me do! This whole damned tree's caught on fire!"

"It's spreadin' too fast to put-out with all of the leaves and dry brush layin' around!" Charlie panicked and yelled. "Let's bug-out of here quick before the cops and the fire engines arrive. I'm not too good at honestly answerin' tough questions."

"Quick! Let's hustle back to my jalopy on Walker Road!" Robbie shouted at Charlie and Steve. "We'll drive up to the Pic-A-Lilli on *206,* have lunch, and pretend like nothing unusual ever happened! All we did was play hooky and drive through the Pine Barrens to have a bite to eat. And if the cops ever ask us anything, we just took a little nature walk over in Wharton State Forest near Atsion Lake."

The three delinquent youths bolted left, and then wildly dashed out of the burning woods. As the fire rapidly raged, its hunger soon consumed additional trees and bushes. Quickly, Anderson and Elder rose to their feet, hustled over to the roaring inferno, and began tossing dirt and sand onto the flames. But their heroic efforts were to no avail. Soon, firehouse sirens were heard originating from the west in Elm and from the east in Hammonton, so the frustrated men reluctantly abandoned the proliferating blaze and swiftly fled in the direction of the newly constructed tree stand and the nearby red Ford 150. Being reputable adult citizens, neither Anderson nor Elder wanted to be associated with the blaze-in-progress.

Stopping at the tree stand, an out-of-breath Dave Anderson had several extraordinary sentences to express to an equally exhausted Jack Elder. "Jack, I know this sounds like *Twilight Zone* science fiction stuff, but I know those three boys that started the woods on fire," the fatigued farmer revealed. "In fact, I vaguely remember one of them telling me the same story we had just witnessed back at the old Gem teen hangout on Central Avenue."

"I suppose that even the impossible is possible in this day and age," Elder gasped and panted. "Don't keep me in suspense, Dave! Who were the young culprits?"

"You won't believe the *time discrepancy,* but the kid that accidentally set the fire was Robbie Williams, who's now serving time in Camden Prison for wife-beating and for armed robbery," Anderson explained before inhaling three consecutive deep breaths. "And the second derelict thug was a constant troublemaker named Charlie Gallagher, who was always either suspended from school, or serving time in office detention. And the third obnoxious punk was a nasty, temperamental kid named Steve Preston who…"

"Who died in a motorcycle accident in 1990!" Jack remembered and indicated with his mouth agape and his eyebrows raised, forming two brown arches. "Hey, wait a cotton-pickin' minute! Holy cowhide, Dave! I also knew those three incorrigible juvenile delinquents! They were always in trouble, and the vice-principals didn't know what to do with them! But please tell me; how could we have observed the three juvenile delinquent punks setting the woods on fire back in 1978 when we're standing right here in 2007! And with Steve Preston being dead that means…"

"We've just experienced something like a mass hallucination!" Anderson suggested in an amazed tone of voice. "Next time you buy me a drink over at DiDonato Lanes, just make sure it's a ginger ale light. Now Jack, forget all about *our* paranormal experience! Let's exit the woods before the fire trucks arrive. I don't want to have to disclose to either Chief Donio or to Chief Sirolli how that crazy conflagration ever got started!"

"You're right about one thing, Dave!" Jack confirmed in a non-too-confident tone of voice. "For verification purposes, I distinctly remember reading in the *Hammonton News* back in 1978 that Butterton Woods had caught on fire, and that both the Hammonton and Elm fire departments had been dispatched to extinguish the flames. And we just saw a 1978 event transpire from our unique vantage point right here in 2007," Elder emphasized and ranted. "Now, I gotta' confess that I definitely believe in ghosts, in the Loch Ness Monster, and in UFOs!"

* * * * * * * * * * * * * *

The bewildered owner of Butterton Woods was quite certain about a particular cognizance, which Dave Anderson was hesitant of disclosing to his closest friend. "Jack, please don't laugh at me! I don't exactly know how to tell you this truth, but I'm now lost in my own damned woods. This is only a seven-acre stretch of woodlands that I'm quite familiar with and know as well as the back of my hand, yet it seems so vast like, well, like Robin Hood's Sherwood Forest," Dave guiltily divulged to Jack Elder. "I've without a doubt lost my bearings, and my normally dependable senses think we're walking in circles. But what's haunting my mind the most is the idea that Butterton seems to be fifty-times its regular small dimensions. It's like a weird…"

"Time and spatial distortion, a peculiar time and space warp," the English teacher helped Anderson define *their* mutual dilemma. "Say Dave, be quiet and look over there!" Elder whispered while firmly grabbing his fellow trekker's arm and nodding his head to the right. "I don't know whatever happened to the firemen and their trucks, but I just caught a glimpse of a couple of men from a bygone era carrying primitive-looking shotguns. I don't want to get blasted being mistaken for a deer or a rabbit, so let's not confront these newly arrived trespassers in your woods."

The perplexed friends simultaneously crouched-down to further scrutinize the new-found interlopers. David Anderson was shocked to see *his* father Peter, being accompanied by *his* Uncle Joe, ambling through the woods with shotguns in their right hands and with three rabbits each strung together with thin hemp, the dead creatures dangling from *their* left shoulders. Immediately, Dave believed that the sight his eyes were beholding was a cruel mental aberration, because his father had died in 1974 at the age of seventy-one, and equally as astonishing, his Uncle Joe had passed away in 1968. But presently, the rabbit-stalking, deceased brothers appeared to be young hunters not a day over forty, both gentlemen appearing strong, ambitious, and vibrant. After the avid rabbit hunters had meandered out of sight on a narrow woods' path, Anderson, who was nearly traumatized from his most recent "psychic experience", summoned the courage to express his troubled mind to his companion.

"Jack, those men were my father and my uncle, but as you well know, both have been gone for many years," the shocked farmer sadly related. "Dad served in the Army from 1942-'45 and felt compelled doing so, after the terrible Pearl Harbor sneak attack. Uncle Joe ran the farm for those three-years until Pop proudly returned to the States. My father honorably served his country and fought at the Bulge, I believe, and also at Ardennes Forest," Anderson reviewed and described some family history. "He never liked discussing his heroism, but I know he was shot at numerous times by Nazi soldiers, and I know for a fact that many of his buddies were wounded or killed in action."

"This is some sort of convoluted anachronism," Jack Elder said, "and the amazing conundrum is..."

"Speak plain English!" almost-neurotic Dave Anderson sternly objected. "Stop being so disturbingly academic!"

"What I meant to say is that *we* don't belong in the last two times and places our eyes have witnessed," the English instructor clarified, using more conventional nomenclature. "And what our mortal pupils just perceived doesn't belong in *our* 2007 reality. I think there's some sort of crazy anomaly at play here, er, excuse me Dave," Jack promptly corrected himself. "I meant to say some sort of confusion, or distortion of historical time and of physical space. Everything appears to be bent or skewed, or both bent and skewed."

"Have you considered the wild prospect that if Steve Preston, my dad, and my uncle are all dead and buried, then quite possibly we could be dead, too?" Anderson suggested, feeling an element of hysteria settling into his mind. "I mean there's a distinct possibility that..."

"Nonsense, Dave!" Jack sharply interrupted his now thoroughly distraught friend. "We're still breathing, our hearts are still beating, and the other two kids besides Steve Preston we had seen starting the woods on fire are probably still alive in the year 2007. But maybe," Elder pondered and then slowly uttered, "and this bizarre theory may sound as an implausible stretch of the imagination, but maybe the world has ended since our entrance into Butterton Woods, and perhaps Heaven and Hell forgot to inform us of what had happened to our former reality."

* * * * * * * * * * * * *

While still trying to decipher the time-space differentials associated with Butterton Woods, Dave Anderson and Jack Elder persisted in their mania, and after assiduously exploring the vicinity, the duo arrived at an unbeknownst clearing where their keen eyes spotted a pair of early American Indians, apparently holding an impromptu powwow. "Hide behind these two trees," Jack whispered and advised, momentarily taking awkward command. "I can't believe my pupils, Dave! This is absolutely mind-boggling! They're Lenni-Lenapes!"

"Lenny who?" the distraught Anderson stammered. "Sometimes you're speaking to me in an alien form of the English language, where I can't make heads or tails out of your odd jargon! Why would an Indian be called Lenny?"

"Lenni-Lenapes, an old Indian tribe that inhabited this area before the clans were driven west by white British settlers, or put on reservations," the erudite teacher explained in a low voice. "Remember Dave, Indians once populated the entire East Coast, long before there ever was a colony called New Jersey!"

"I get it now," Anderson finally comprehended. "Lenape High School over in Medford has an Indian for its mascot, and my farm market used to get corn from Indian Mills, which is north of Atsion Lake on *206*."

"That's right!" Elder verified in a low voice. "Indian Mills was at one time a reservation for the leftover Lenni-Lenapes. My whole point is that *that* Indian tribe hasn't been around these parts for over a century, and hasn't been wandering-around, hunting for food since the days of George Washington. But don't worry about being attacked, Dave!" Jack softly stated. "The Lenapes were reputed to be peaceful natives that often traded with early South Jersey pioneers. At least, that's what I've read in textbooks! I think your scalp is safe from being non-surgically removed."

"I only hope that some of our demented friends are playing an ugly joke on us, and masquerading around here in Butterton Woods trying to drive us insane," the property owner wished and shared with his all-too-knowledgeable pedagogue pal. "But those two feather-headed Indians patrolling the area with their bows and arrows, who are now walking away into that bracken, look too damned authentic to be wearing costumes and disguises."

"Look, over there!" Jack Elder whispered. "There's a break in the woods, and an open field on the other side with plenty of sunshine beaming-down from the sky. We're almost out of this rustic and very complicated maze; we're gonna' exit this queer contradiction that you had erroneously thought was a small seven-acre parcel of woods exclusively belonging to you."

When the fatigued-but-relieved itinerants eventually departed the weird, verdant flat labyrinth, commonly known as Butterton Woods, the trekkers found no evidence of any red Ford 150 truck, but much to their satisfaction, the woods again appeared (judging from its perimeter) to be its standard dimensions. But Walker Road was no longer paved, and the path was now a very narrow one-lane dirt trail, devoid of telephone poles, electric wires, blueberry fields, peach orchards, farm labor houses, and human activity.

"You know, Jack," Dave Anderson commented before taking two much-needed inhales of oxygen. "It looks like we aren't staggering around in the year 2007 anymore, that's for sure! We're a disoriented pair of time travelers, yes, two pathetic, lost aliens trapped in a different age and time. Look up ahead to what used to be the White Horse Pike!" Anderson implored Elder. "There's an old bearded man behind a horse drawn carriage, heading west toward Berlin, which in colonial times was called…"

"Long-a-Coming!" the scholarly but still-stunned high school teacher answered. "It looks like several passengers seated in the coach are being transported, if not to Berlin, I mean to Long-a-Coming, then to some other western destination, perhaps Camden or Philadelphia. I mean to say, Dave," Jack considered and stated. "Hammonton wasn't incorporated until the 1860s after the Civil War, which quite apparently hasn't even happened yet."

"Now, I get it Jack!" Dave Anderson hollered, exhibiting a degree of enthusiasm. "I see a definite pattern! We've been going backwards in time, ever since we entered Butterton Woods."

"Yes, a reverse chronological order!" Elder astutely recognized and verbalized. "It's all so logically illogical! Consider the three teenagers setting the woods on fire; your' father and uncle hunting rabbits, and then the Lenni-Lenape Indians looking for wild animals to shoot and kill with their bows and arrows," Jack recollected and shared. “This whole incredible scenario is too uncanny to fathom. But somehow, crazily, it all does make a strange sense when you actually think about it!”

The two bewildered amblers trudged ahead, their minds focused on the past, the present, and the future. The compamions theorized that if they had somehow migrated from the twenty-first back into the eighteenth-century, then the duo would have to adapt accordingly to their new time/place environment. ‘Was George Washington the President of the United States? Had the Revolutionary War occurred yet? If so, how many states are now in the Union? Was the War of 1812 going on?’ Jack Elder mused. ‘Have Edgar Allan Poe and Mark Twain been born yet?’

Certain intricate thoughts were also rattling around inside Dave Anderson’s mind. ‘I wonder what my wife and kids look like if I have a wife and kids? I might even have a new wife without having any children? Or I might be a colonial-era bachelor energetically trying to tame my immediate environment!’ Anderson speculated. ‘I wonder if I’m even married at all?’ Both the man’s curiosity and his random reverie were snapped upon again hearing Jack Elder’s shaky baritone voice.

“Dave, there’s a dilapidated house up ahead, and I gotta’ believe it’s yours,” Elder articulated while having difficulty retaining his very active excitement. “There’re several pig and chicken pens in the rear, and a few goats and cows inside a fenced-in pasture. And that old barn is probably used to house the family horse, if indeed you’re wealthy enough to own one,” Jack lectured without any lectern. “But it’s certainly not a Dutch colonial house I see, even though we’re apparently trapped in colonial times! I'm really baffled! This entire bizarre phenomenon is all still very incomprehensible to me!”

“My God!” the still-astounded David Henry Anderson bellowed. “My home-sweet-home isn’t exactly made out of chocolate and strawberry shortcake! But Jack, we’ll have to forget all about the year 2007, and learn how to live and survive in the distant past!”

“You know, Dave. Now I wish that you’d never brought me out to Butterton Woods to check on your highly coveted tree stand,” Jack Elder regretted and complained. “But I’ll tell you one thing worthy of hearing!”

“What’s that?” Dave fearfully replied as the farmer stared at the ramshackle wooden dwelling and accompanying stone chimney, three-hundred-feet ahead.

“It’s a lot better being alive in the year 1750 or 1800 than being dead in technologically advanced 2007,” Jack Elder sermonized to

Dave Anderson. “At least that’s my personal opinion. Take it for what it’s worth! We might as well get on with our uncertain lives, Dave, no matter what century we’re lining in!”

"That'll Be the Day"

It had been a glorious spring break vacation for college seniors Jeff Moore and Fred Durham. The *Rutgers University* seniors had flown from *Philadelphia International Airport* west to Denver, and then boarded a second *United Air* flight out to Palm Springs to enjoy the luxurious Southern California desert sunshine. After renting a sporty car from *Avis,* Jeff drove down Tahquitz Canyon Way from the airport to Palm Canyon Drive, and then headed south on *Highway 111* from Palm Springs to Palm Desert.

"New Jersey sure doesn't look anything like this!" Fred Durham exclaimed from the passenger side of the rented white *Pontiac Grand AM.* "Check-out the red mountains surrounding this desert valley! Pretty magnificent, if I must say!"

"And there's gorgeous girls all over the place," Jeff Moore replied as the driver proceeded south on one-way Palm Canyon Drive. "And what a terrific coincidence, Fred! My sister and her husband are vacationing on a *Mediterranean* cruise, and we get to stay at their cozy Palm Desert pad. The directions are to take *111* south and then take Deep Canyon Road several blocks past Fred Waring Drive, and soon we'll find 105 Cachanilla Court, Palm Desert, 92260 inside a secluded gated community. I sure hope that the pass code entry numbers that my sister gave me to raise the gate are still working."

"You make it all sound too easy!" Fred typically criticized. "First, we have to pass through Cathedral City and Rancho Mirage, which happen to be towns geographically situated between Palm Springs and Palm Desert. Then, I'll read you the specific directions to your sister's place. But I gotta' admit, Jeff. This entire area is spectacular. I've never seen a cloudless dark-blue sky like that before! It's almost like we're traveling on another planet! And the air is fresh and clean too, virtually pollution-free!"

"It sure beats New Brunswick, New Jersey, that's for sure!" the preoccupied driver observed and opined. "The daytime temperatures here in the winter are in the seventies and the eighties. The only downside is that with the desert down here in the valley all around us, there's always more-brown showing than green."

"Who cares?" Fred Durham instinctively challenged his close pal, Jeff Moore. "I'll take dolls in two-piece bikinis over naked deciduous trees any day of the week! And it doesn't matter whether those gorgeous babes are doing spring break in South Padre Island, Texas, or in Palm Springs, California!"

The pair safely reached their ultimate destination and spent four wonderful days in the excellent Palm Desert and Palm Springs resort areas. On Monday, the college roommates strolled along El Paseo, the "Rodeo Drive" of Palm Desert; ate a sumptuous dinner at the Kaiser House, and that evening met several vivacious *UCLA* girls that were staying at the *Palm Mountain Resort,* located at the foot of the scenic *Santa Rosa Mountains* in Palm Springs. Jenn and Sharon were looking for some exciting male companionship, so the four hung-around together on Tuesday and Wednesday, and besides some intense partying, the couples managed to incorporate a few normal tourist activities into their schedules by taking the *29 Palms Highway* into the mountains, and visiting *Joshua Tree National Park,* the only place in the world that has the right combination of climate and elevation for Joshua trees to grow. And then, the following day, the foursome stayed in Palm Springs and that afternoon rode "The Tram" (which slowly rotated a full three-hundred-and-sixty-degrees) up through five separate ecological zones, as the famous "lift" ascended from the hot arid valley up into the chilly snow-clad mountains.

Wednesday afternoon was spent relaxing at the *Palm Mountain Resort* outdoor pool, and then after having supper at the Chop House, over on Palm Canyon Drive. The four carefree college souls trekked over to the Indian owned *Spa Casino* (between Indian Canyon Drive and Amado Road), where everyone tried their luck on the slot machines. On Thursday, Jeff and Fred had to unfortunately adhere to their schedule and drive through the deserts and mountains to Las Vegas, where they had booked two nights at the fabulous *New York, New York Hotel and Casino,* before having to fly back east from Las Vegas to resume their grueling *Rutgers* academic doldrums.

En route to Las Vegas, the young vacationers had been remarking how all houses and motels in the Palm Springs/Palm Desert area were "gated" to extend the idea of "privacy and security" to residents and visitors alike. Then, the conversation naturally switched to Jeff and Fred's most recent *UCLA* female companions. "Jenn and Sharon promised to write us when we get back to *Rutgers!"* Jeff reminded Fred as the Don Juan drove on *I-15* on the way to Vegas.

"That'll be the day!" Fred replied. "And I'm not referring to Buddy Holly's oldies hit record, either!"

"Here's some trivia for you Mr. Know-It-All!" Jeff chuckled. "Did you know that Buddy Holly came-up with the title of that song from words that John Wayne had said in the classic 1956 movie 'The Searchers'?"

"You don't say!" Fred acknowledged. "I'm a big Buddy Holly fan too, you know! It does make sense in that 'That'll Be the Day!' and 'Peggy Sue' both came out in '57. But right now, Jeff, my mind is still focused on Room 301 of the *Palm Mountain Resort,* 155 South Belardo, Palm Springs, California. That was some last night we had spent with those fabulous chicks!"

"The Beach Boys had it absolutely right when the group sang 'Wish They All Could Be California Girls'!" the driver declared with a broad smile expressed upon his face. "East Coast girls are hip, but golden sunny California dolls are definitely where it's at! I mean Fred, who really cares if we lost a hundred-bucks each at the totally magnificent *Spa Casino?"*

"You're absolutely right, Jeff!" Fred Durham amiably concurred while again faithfully riding "shotgun". "You know how I love to eat delicious food, and the Chop House, the Oasis Buffet at the *Spa Casino,* and that LGS Steakhouse on Palm Canyon Drive were really great restaurants."

"And what about the pretty neat mist vapors that were sprayed-out from restaurant canopies on sidewalk pedestrians walking along Palm Canyon Drive," Jeff Moore recollected and shared as the speedster accelerated past a tractor-trailer. "But in spite of the awe-inspiring Tram adventure, the incomparable *Joshua Tree National Park,* the loose atmosphere of El Paseo, and the sophisticated *Spa Casino*, Jenn and Sharon were without a doubt the highlights of our spring break vacation thus far! Let's see what Las Vegas has to offer! I hear it sure beats Atlantic City!"

"Only three more hours and we'll be meandering around on the Strip!" Fred confidently predicted. "And as they say and exaggerate on television commercials, anything can happen in Vegas! Say Jeff. How much did your sister and brother-in-law's Palm Desert house cost?" the *Grand Am* passenger curiously asked the driver.

Jeff Moore sanctimoniously explained that his sister and brother-in-law had gone west seven years earlier; had both gotten licensed in real estate, and that the couple was presently making an attractive living flipping houses. The 105 Cachanilla Court Palm Desert ranch home had cost them five-hundred-thousand-dollars, but it was now on the market for eight-hundred-grand. The New Jersey college travelers mutually decided that real estate was a most favorable and lucrative future career pursuit.

* * * * * * * * * * * * *

Thirty-miles outside Las Vega,s the young men's dialogue again had Buddy Holly as its central theme, with both Jeff Moore and Fred Durham attempting to impress each other with their mastery of picayune details pertaining to the '50s rock star sensation's musical biography.

"You know, Fred," Jeff bragged as the driver navigated the white *Grand AM* through some heavy *I-15* traffic. "Buddy Holly's real name was Charles Hardin Holly and he was from…"

"From Lubbock, Texas," the impatient passenger automatically answered. "And his last name on his birth certificate was spelled H-o-l-l-e-y and not H-o-l-l-y. And H-o-l-l-e-y is how it's spelled on his tombstone. Buddy's buried in…"

"In the City of Lubbock Cemetery," Jeff Moore academically finished his friend's trivial question. "My photographic mind recalls that Holly was born on September 7, 1936, and Buddy unfortunately died on…"

"On February 3, 1959 in a small plane crash just outside Clear Lake, Iowa, not far from Mason City," Fred Durham interrupted. "That winter evening, Buddy Holly had given a performance at the…."

"At the Surf Ballroom in Clear Lake," the driver insisted with egotistical certainty. "But the bus the singer was touring with had broken-down, and so he and the Big Bopper, also known as J.P. Richardson, along with Ritchie Valens. rented a four passenger…"

"A four passenger Beechcraft Bonanza while a terrible blizzard was in progress, in order to get to their next singing destination in Minnesota," the passenger knowledgeably contributed. "But then, the rest of the tragedy is all recorded rock and roll history. Say Jeff," Fred Durham elaborated, "did you know that the Big Bopper, who incidentally had only one major hit record 'Chantilly Lace' was really a former…"

"A former chubby disc jockey from Beaumont, Texas," "Jeff the Navigator" haughtily responded. "And regrettably, the catastrophic airplane crash happened at precisely 1:05 a.m. in a remote Iowa cornfield!"

The *I-15* travelers had reached a stalemate after each knew that Buddy Holly had competed in Hutchinson Junior High School talent shows; had broken the color barrier by being the first white act to perform before a jam-packed audience at Harlem's *Apollo Theater;* that the renowned performer had broken a '50s cultural taboo by marrying a pretty Puerto Rican girl named Maria Elena Santiago, and that the British rock group the Hollies had been named in tribute to the '50s singing legend.

"Let's change the subject back to Jenn and Sharon," Fred Durham suggested. "Although they never sang for Coral Records, which as you probably know was a subsidiary of Decca Records, and despite the fact that neither of the girls wears black-framed, horn-rimmed glasses, or ever professionally sang 'Maybe Baby' or 'Oh Boy!'," the passenger almost arrogantly commented, "That'll Be the Day if we ever see them again! Such is life, I suppose."

* * * * * * * * * * * * *

Soon, the avid travelers finally reached Las Vegas late Thursday afternoon. And after unpacking their bags in Room 528, the duo wandered all over the public sectors of *New York, New York,* familiarizing themselves with all aspects and features of the spectacular casino/hotel. After eating a light supper at an "O. Henry-style Central Park Restaurant" having 1890s' décor and appearance, the twosome left the creatively-designed building to stroll the Vegas Strip, sauntering in and out of the five-thousand plus room *MGM;* the elegant *Mandalay Bay,* and the fascinating architectural wonder known as *Caesar's Palace*, where the pair then sat near a talking statue of the Roman god Bacchus. And after the god-of-wine's verbal presentation had terminated, the itinerant travelers discussed the glittery adult paradise that were visiting for the first time. Jeff had to spoil the wonderful "escape and escapade from reality" by reminding his now-apathetic excursion partner about some other relevant and practical elements of *their* young American lives.

"In a few days, we'll be back in lackluster New Jersey hitting the books and getting ready to graduate," Moore reminded Durham. "And then, it's functioning in the grueling dog-eat-dog real world, after finally obtaining our sheepskins and getting out of *Rutgers*."

"What an enormous bummer!" Fred evaluated and honestly stated. "Why don't you enroll in graduate school and prolong your adolescence as long as possible, just like I intend doing? Jeff, we can successfully delay unnecessary things like marriage, kids, and other annoying adult responsibilities by at least a few years! Then, you and I could become enthusiastic real estate agents, and eventually evolve into reputable property brokers."

"Every once in a blue moon, Fred, when you aren't being disingenuous, you show occasional symptoms of brilliance!" Jeff optimistically joked. "Stop imitating me and find your own sense of identity! And Fred, don't forget that we have to call the *United Airlines'* desk at *McCarron International Airport* tomorrow evening to confirm our Saturday morning flight back to 'Philly."

"Okay, but let's push the exhaustion envelope tonight and tomorrow," Fred Durham facetiously recommended. "We can always sleep on the five-hour flight back to Philly'. And who knows? Maybe one of us will hit a giant jackpot this evening, and we could then forget all about our dreaded admission into adulthood! Let's tour the *Mirage* and the *Venetian* and have a few drinks while we try our luck at the poker and roulette tables. Being twenty-one does have some distinct advantages, you know!"

At midnight, the fatigued and half-inebriated friends returned to *New York, New York* three-hundred-dollars richer, more than retrieving their losses from what the pair had "willfully donated to the *Spa Casino* back in Palm Springs, California". Finally, at three in the morning, the friends managed to return to Room 528 and get some much-needed sleep.

After waking-up at noon on Friday, Jeff and Fred purchased tour-bus tickets (with their "windfall gambling profits") and accompanied some other Vegas vacationers out to the incredible *Hoover Dam* on Lake Meade, where the tourists marveled at the landmark phenomenon built to govern and harness the power of the mighty *Colorado River*. Upon leaving the "colossal engineering wonder", the two adventurers climbed-back onto the tour bus for their pleasant trip back to the glitzy Vegas Strip. Soon, Jeff and Fred were again dining in their authentic-looking "O. Henry Central Park restaurant" and reviewing the sensational highlights of what amounted to their very educational day trip.

"Everybody should come out here and visit this area at least once in their lives," Jeff Moore remarked to Fred Durham before biting into a very delectable charcoal-broiled hamburger. "Atlantic City may have its famous boardwalk, but *New York, New York* even has a small Coney Island-type wooden promenade upstairs. And it's too bad we didn't even have time to try-out that rollicking roller coaster that goes around the first few floors of this magnificent building."

"Well, anyway, Good Buddy. We did get to stroll across the miniature *Brooklyn Bridge* in front of the hotel and take some digital pictures of the replica *Statue of Liberty* and the New York Harbor fire-boat outside," Fred replied.

"I want to hang around the casino floor until midnight," Jeff indicated.

"How come? Do you feel *that* lucky?" Fred asked.

"No, but while you were up in Room 528 using the facilities, I had bought several raffle tickets on that fabulous red and black '56 *Ford Crown Victoria* that's slowly revolving on that platform over there!" Jeff informed his now-amused chum. "Let's go over and inspect that beauty! It's definitely a blast from the past!"

The duo stepped-over to the "nostalgic piece of history" to thoroughly admire its' mint-condition excellence. The interior was in superb splendor, appearing as if the impeccable vintage automobile was brand-new.

"My father has photographs from the '50s when dad had lived in Levittown, Pennsylvania," Jeff Moore casually related to Fred Durham. "And my grandfather once owned a similar '56 *Ford.* Next to Buddy Holly's *Cadillac* convertible and the classic '57 *Chevy*, the '56 Crown Victoria has to be my favorite '50s car. If I win this baby at midnight," Jeff Moore wished and expressed, "and I know it's quite a long shot, Fred, we're gonna' call the *United* desk at *McCarron International Airport;* cancel our scheduled flight, and drive this honey cross country back to New Brunswick. As Aerosmith often sings, 'Dream On'!" the quixotic romantic laughed. "You might snicker, Fred, but I have a hunch that I'm in the running to win this splendid vintage automobile!" Jeff Moore confided.

At midnight, the winning raffle ticket was drawn and announced, and for several dramatic seconds, the flabbergasted New Jersey visitors had trouble catching their breaths and eventually shouting- out their gleeful triumphant yells. "It looks like we're driving this boss chariot back to New Jersey!" Jeff Moore jubilantly shouted to his still-astonished college roommate. "I told you we were going to cancel our flight reservations and drive this honey back East! Say Fred, remind me to buy that Aerosmith *CD* when we finally get back to good old *Rutgers!"*

* * * * * * * * * * * * *

Euphoria reigned supreme as the ecstatic pair traveled east in the newly acquired red and black 1956 *Ford Crown Victoria.* Jeff Moore and Fred Durham spent a full day sightseeing in Denver, and then stayed overnight in attractive *Ramada Inn* accommodations. After a comprehensive breakfast of bacon, eggs, and pancakes, the two were again heading east on *I-70,* and the driver was about to disclose to his relentlessly gabby passenger his personal desire to take *I-80* to Omaha, Nebraska.

"I think you should take *I-70* all the way east, instead," Fred firmly articulated. "*I-80* is too far north, and we still might be subject to an early spring snowstorm. I strongly suggest we take the safer southern route."

"Fred, I just have to honor my inspiration to drive through Clear Lake, Iowa in my handsome '56 *Crown Victoria,"* Jeff honestly revealed. "I gotta' see if the Surf Ballroom is still in existence in memory of the late-great Buddy Holly! Did you know, Fred, that Buddy went on the winter bus tour without the Crickets?"

"Yeah, and the group was supposed to get together again in Minnesota," Durham disgustedly answered. "But as rock and roll history has accurately documented, *that* reunion never happened as a result of the horrible airplane disaster of February 3, 1959, the day the music died, which is profoundly chronicled in Don McLean's unforgettable 'Bye, Bye Miss American Pie'. That's why you really want to take *I-80!"*

"You don't have to be a perceptive clairvoyant to read between the lines! Sometimes, you know me better than I know myself!" Jeff readily admitted.

"Okay, you're the boss!" Fred conceded. "I don't want to stand between you and your dream! If I had done that back in Vegas, then we could never be riding in your fantastic '56 dream machine!"

"Yes, and this baby's been modified with deluxe power steering and brakes, along with a twelve-speaker stereo system," Jeff Moore proudly elaborated. "We just got to be the envy of every car and truck driver that sees us. We'll spend the night in Sioux City, and then journey on to Clear Lake, Iowa first thing tomorrow morning. And if we get distracted, who the heck cares? So what, if we miss a day or two of boring academic classes before we eventually get back on campus!"

"Well, I just gotta' commend you on your originality!" Fred facetiously volleyed back. "You do have a flair for the bizarre! Only another two hours or so, and we'll be on *I-80* on our way to Sioux City, Iowa. I hope we don't get into any serious litigation with any remaining Sioux (sue) Indians! And thank goodness this remarkable car came with temporary license plates!" Durham frivolously punned and jested.

After a good night's rest at a *Holiday Inn Express* on South Lakeport Street in Sioux City, the following afternoon, the red and black '56 Crown Victoria was exiting *Interstate-80* and soon onto *I-35* and heading north toward Mason City, Iowa. Both occupants felt a surge of energy rush through their veins when they were finally on

Route 18 and motoring west in the direction of Clear Lake. Much to their consternation, an early spring snowstorm had descended on the area, and the fellows were caught in what Jeff Moore aptly described as "the beginning of a savage blizzard".

"You'd better turn around," Fred Durham cautiously advised his traveling companion. "Put Clear Lake on hold! Go back to *I-35,* and we'll find some comfortable lodging to see this nasty storm pass through!"

"I'll get gas at that old-fashioned service station up ahead!" Jeff said with an element of disappointment evident in his tone of voice. "Then, we'll turn around and locate a convenient motel just off the Interstate. I should've listened to you in the first place when you were futilely trying to convince me to take *I-70* instead of *I-80.*"

"It's too late now!" the wary passenger gloomily answered as his hardheaded partner pulled-up to the ancient-looking gas pump. "Say, Jeff! This station's closed!"

And then both young men incredulously stared-up at the overhead hanging sign. "*Esso!*" Fred exclaimed. "*Esso* changed its name to *Exxon* many moons ago!" And then, Durham read a sign hanging inside the closed station's dusty office: "Monday, February 2, 1959."

"That's impossible!" Jeff shouted in absolute amazement. "It's Wednesday, March 28, 2006! Are we trapped in some kind of dangerous time warp?"

"I've never been so baffled in all my life!" Fred Durham gasped.

"Let's drive into Clear Lake, find the Surf Ballroom, and discover the honest-to-God truth for ourselves!" the anxious driver replied. "If it's really fantastically Monday, February 2, 1959, then we have a chance of saving Buddy Holly from imminent disaster!"

* * * * * * * * * * *

Snowflakes kept coming-down heavily as Jeff Moore slowly drove the *Crown Victoria* into downtown Clear Lake, Iowa. All of the vehicles he and Fred Durham passed or encountered were vintage 1959 models or earlier. The driver managed to find an available space, and then carefully parked his prized automobile on a side street two blocks behind the famous Surf Ballroom.

"We aren't exactly equipped for this special mission weather-wise," the apprehensive driver cited. "But Fred, I suppose our fall lightweight jackets will have to serve our purpose in being here. It's a good thing '50s kids were very polite, and that security for the big concert will be minimal for us geniuses to figure-out and violate."

"It's almost eight-thirty right now, and with the windows opened a crack, we can hear the great music originating from several blocks away," Fred keenly perceived and declared. "But we'll only have a small window of opportunity to pull this caper off!"

"Let's hope that we can inconspicuously get into the auditorium from a backstage entrance!" Jeff anxiously said to his co-conspirator. "We'll sneak in, and then Fred, leave the rest to me. Remember; our goal is to prevent a major rock star from perishing."

Fred Durham was predictably quick to challenge his friend's very valid talking points. "But what about the Big Bopper and Ritchie Valens? If I recall the story, Dion was also supposed to be on that plane, but Buddy went in *his* place. Maybe if we only rescue Buddy, then Dion will die as his substitute."

"That's the lousy chance we'll have to take!" Jeff Moore replied, showing a degree of conviction mixed with apparent uncertainty. "Let's stop jabbering and start our strategic plan into action. Any police officers or security guards assigned to the show are probably stationed in the audience, or at the front doors, thinking that anyone trying to crash the concert would not be so bold as to enter from the backdoor. Remember, Fred," Jeff Moore strongly emphasized. "It's now 1959 and not 2006. And by all means, let me do all the talking until we get Buddy out of the building and safely into our custody."

As luck would have it, the two young men managed to sneak inside the Surf Ballroom from the unattended rear backstage door, when everyone in the auditorium was paying attention to the talented Buddy Holly singing his medley of stellar hit songs. Fifteen-minutes later, the accomplished performer had completed his grand finale curtain call, and upon exiting the stage, briefly spoke with several other back-stage entertainers involved in the program. Then, the famous singer stepped to the rear wall payphone to make a call, presumably to his pregnant wife.

"Buddy Holly, you'd better come with us!" Jeff sternly insisted. "I have a gun concealed in my jacket. If you dare try to get anybody's attention, you'll regret the consequences and never see Maria Elena again. But we promise you that you won't be harmed! Come quietly with us! It's extremely important! Here's my *Rolex* watch you can hold as collateral!"

After swiftly and surreptitiously exiting the building via the backdoor, and then walking two snow-laden sidewalk blocks to the red and black '56 *Crown Victoria,* the three men entered the car, with

Buddy Holly obediently following directions and sitting in the front passenger side seat. Jeff Moore sat behind the wheel with Fred Durham (also claiming to have a pistol) sitting in the rear.

"Are you two guys professional kidnappers, or gangsters, or what?" the concerned hostage demanded knowing as the famous singer incredulously stared at the expensive *Rolex* watch. "Are you trying to extort ransom money out of me?"

"We're trying to save you from getting killed, Buddy!" Jeff Moore asserted as the driver fired-up the engine while almost simultaneously blasting the heater. "Just relax and listen to our phenomenal story, and then decide for yourself."

As Fred Durham exited the *Crown Victoria* to remove excess snow with his bare hands from the front, back, and side windows, Jeff Moore began his unbelievable dissertation to the now-intrigued '50s rock star. Five-minutes later, the almost frozen human snow scraper re-entered the '56 Ford to engage in divulging additional background information to the now-spellbound singer/hostage.

"You say that there's going to be a small plane crash later tonight, and that I'm going to die in it!" Buddy exclaimed. "How do you know that our bus broke-down; that Dion is sick, and that there's talk about me and two other entertainers flying to Minnesota?"

"It's all history!" Jeff maintained as the chauffeur activated the windshield wipers and then gingerly drove the automobile out of its side-street parking space. "Just listen to us babble for a few hours as we deliberately keep you out of harm's way! I guarantee you, Buddy, that you're not going to believe a single word that your ears are about to hear!"

The very curious listener heard a full-hour of discussion about the past, the present, and the future. Finally, when Jeff and Fred completed their confounding explanations, the still-bewildered front-seat passenger had several pertinent questions to ask.

"Well, what's the damned future like? Will I still be famous? What'll happen to my wife and son?" the awed captive wondered and inquired.

"Well, in the future there's going to be computers and cell phones, and *VCRs* and Apollo moon landings," Jeff inadequately explained as the garrulous speaker drove down Clear Lake's main street in the direction of what he believed was *I-35*. "And your faithful wife Maria Elena will grieve your death for many years. That's what we're trying right now to prevent from happening."

"But if you guys are from the year 2006 as you claim, then why are you driving around in a boss 1956 *Ford?"* Buddy interrogated in a skeptical tone of voice.

"One question at a time!" Fred sternly instructed from the back seat. "First, we'll drive around Clear Lake and tell you all about computers, *CDs,* and cell phones! Then, we'll tell you how we've miraculously obtained this *Crown Victoria!"*

The very interesting conversation continued for another full-hour, as the 2006' time travelers endeavored to convey and encapsulate nearly a half-century of human history and rock and roll music into sixty additional minutes of important dialogue. Soon, the slow-moving red and black vehicle was approaching the entrance ramp that Jeff Moore theorized was the way to *I-35.*

"Jeff, you can't go onto *I-35!"* Fred objected in the midst of myriad swirling and eddying outside snowflakes. "It's still 1959! The highway ramp hasn't been constructed yet!"

"The exit on the opposite side of the highway got us from 2006 into the year 1959, didn't it?" Moore persuasively argued.

"Are you trying to take me into *your* future?" Buddy Holly worried. "Are you guys for real? I think I'd rather stay and live in good old 1959 without this fancy watch! I don't want to live in 2006 before I really have to!"

"You're both right!" the driver promptly acknowledged. "I'll turn around at the first exit and take our distinguished guest back to Clear Lake, now that he's missed his airplane departure flight!"

And after uttering those particular amazing words, Jeffrey Moore stared to his right with his mouth agape, and then in the rear-view mirror observed a similar expression featured on Fred Durham's face. Buddy Holly had remarkably vanished from the front passenger side into thin air. A red *Nissan Maxima* and a tan *Acura* soon slowly passed the red and black *Crown Victoria* after it gradually made its March 28, 2006 entrance onto snow-covered *Interstate 35*. Jeff Moore promptly glanced-down, and much to his utter confusion, his treasured *Rolex* watch was functioning back upon his left wrist.

"Government Problem Solving"

Minerva Graham was a dynamic and animated television personality/comedienne who often "pushed the envelope", exploring the boundaries of civilized propriety and decent sensibility. The stocky lady hosted a popular afternoon women's talk show titled "Ladies Sound Off" that had captured a widespread audience, along with huge national ratings, while generating outstanding commercial revenue. But Minerva Graham had alienated much of her following when the opinionated hostess vociferously came-out of the closet and proudly announced her gay sexual orientation.

Ms. Graham's TV audience problems were only just beginning. Several months later, the controversial female deliberately infuriated millions of loyal Americans, as well as the Administration in Washington, by professing that the Iraq War was both immoral and illegal. A particular statement by the sometimes gruff and offensive hostess (that she had spieled on "Ladies Sound Off") maintained that the Twin Towers in Manhattan had been brought-down by controlled explosives, detonated inside the structures, and not by two crashing airplanes loaded with jet fuel, piloted by mendacious, radical jihadists on September 11th, 2001.

Eddie Rivers was a Hollywood movie star who also had been especially outspoken on the Iraq War issue, claiming that there was no distinct connection between the Taliban in Afghanistan and Saddam Hussein's Sunni Baathist regime centralized in Baghdad. Rivers often delivered fiery speeches at many anti-war rallies in big cities across the United States, and the actor's radical comments and criticisms did not go unnoticed by the media and by image-wary, prominent politicians. But even the left-wing Capitol Building Congressmen and Senators stayed clear of being associated or identified with Eddie Rivers, out of fear of public backlash and subsequent political fallout. "Terrorism is spreading because the President has commanded his military to invade a foreign land, and *that* blatant act of aggression has inspired many Muslims to be recruited into Al Qaeda and into other freedom-fighting Arab religious organizations across the Middle East," Rivers told a boisterous crowd of protesters in Chicago. "Our inept government is directly contributing to the spread of terrorism around the world, and must be accountable for its foolish actions!"

Vincent Crenshaw was an eccentric movie producer who, like Eddie Rivers, publicly came-out against the Iraq War. The retired heavyset film mogul was comfortably living off of his accumulated wealth, and because Vincent had little to lose financially from publicly sharing his political remarks, Crenshaw began shooting left-wing productions that embarrassed the mostly-conservative bureaucracy in the nation's capital. International and domestic issues were harshly analyzed in Crenshaw's "agenda films," and then the cited information had been deliberately skewed to the liberal left point of view in terms of achieving solutions. The reigning central government was both cited and accused of mismanaging the Iraq War; of botching FEMA hurricane relief management; of bollixing-up the American health care system; of incompetently misusing social security funds, and finally, "of "proliferating pork barrel blundering". Vincent Crenshaw (although admired by certain political liberals) was not an honored American in the minds of straightlaced, White House strategic planning personnel.

Eleanor Siegel was a famous recording artist who possessed an extraordinary singing voice. However, after the star vocalist obtained a divorce from her husband, Ms. Siegel became outspoken against the policies of the federal administration, particularly the Iraq War, calling the conflict "another Vietnam". And the adamant entertainer also maintained that the government's preposterous lies and cover-ups about the war had become "another Watergate". Ms. Siegel also appeared with the outspoken Eddie Rivers at many anti-war demonstrations, and was thought of in many Washington power circles as being "a muckraker subversive just like Eddie Rivers". But Eleanor Siegel's bold moral-based stances on contemporary issues did not affect her CD sales, and the outspoken recording artist still retained her flourishing public singing career, despite the controversial artist's harsh castigation about the President and his stay-the-course war philosophy and policy. Plus, the White House staff didn't exactly appreciate her "provocative conspiracy theories"

Sean Price was a popular syndicated newspaper journalist who wrote op/ed pieces for a large news distribution corporation. Price often appeared as a guest on cable network talk shows, and the vociferous cynic frequently rendered his left-wing-slanted remarks. The columnist's militant comments often appalled right-wing audience viewers, along with Price's controversial, reckless barbs and commentaries. Sean Price (just like Minerva Graham, Eddie Rivers, Vincent Crenshaw, and Eleanor Siegel) had contributed to the Washington-based administration's growing unpopularity, which was a general dissatisfaction that was quite evident in national polls, thus automatically creating a plethora of enemies among right-wing Republicans and Bible-Belt Democrats alike.

Reverend Fred Tomms and Reverend Esau Clark were modern-day societal shakers and movers. The black ministers would impetuously play the race card and specifically boycott any major corporation, or actively demonstrate against any vociferous individual that allegedly discriminated against a member of "Black America". The often-protesting verbal TV ministers dually opposed American involvement in the Iraq War, insisting that the great moneys appropriated by the U.S. "trying to transform the Arab World" could be better used for improving the quality of life in American ghettos. And also, the two religious hardliners claimed that tremendous government expenditures could be more favorably utilized for the purpose of promoting a better form of education in inner city public schools.

Even though dissent and freedom of speech are vital aspects of American democracy that are guaranteed and protected by the United States Constitution, for some obscure reason, the seven aforementioned political skeptics (and pundits) either had recently retired from the public scene, or had suddenly and mysteriously vanished from the mass-market television, newspaper, and tabloid gossip columns.

Gregory Sinclair, a multi-billionaire stocks and bonds investor, and potent left-wing American capitalist, thought that something rather suspicious had been happening with the rash of "voluntary departures from public scrutiny". So, the influential entrepreneur had obtained the skilled services of private investigator Matt Dennis to uncover information explaining why Minerva Graham, Eddie Rivers, Vincent Crenshaw, Eleanor Siegel, Sean Price, and the Reverend Fred Tomms and the Reverend Esau Clark had all inexplicably dropped-out of the public spotlight, along with *their* opposition political views and their verbal derisions suddenly becoming obviously silent.

* * * * * * * * * * * * * *

Private Investigator Matt Dennis was professionally interrogating Eileen Gorman, a former '40s film supporting actress about the strange disappearance of her radical nephew, actor Eddie Rivers. Ms. Gorman was very cooperative and demonstrative during what the P.I. described as "my impromptu interview".

"Well, Ms. Gorman. Do you know anything at all about your nephew Eddie Rivers' whereabouts?" P.I. Dennis courteously inquired. "It had been rumored in one of the Hollywood rags that

Eddie had secretly moved to Alaska to practice conservationism. Another report filtering around Los Angeles is that Eddie has journeyed to Tibet, seeking isolation from the rigors of American society. According to the tabloid's claim, your nephew is living a reclusive existence in the Himalayas, because Eddie's become disillusioned with the alleged lies being perpetuated by what he calls 'our untrustworthy government'. Would you care to comment on these speculations?"

"As you know. Mr. Dennis, I'm an old widow without too much sand left in my hourglass, so to speak," Eileen Gorman prefaced her reply. "My nephew is the closest blood relative I have left, and I cherish him dearly. Now with *that* being said, I don't believe one iota any of this journalistic fiction that's been circulating around town. But just like Eddie, I don't trust the government, either, and let me tell you something, Mr. Dennis," the wrinkled woman continued with a stern expression apparent on her elderly face. "Eddie would certainly contact me if he were able to do so! That's the kind of boy he is; very responsible; very respectful of caring adults; very reliable, and very idealistic, too! Confidentially, Mr. Dennis," the aged actress intimated. "I dread the worse, and pray for his safety."

"Well then," Matt Dennis orally proceeded, holding his cheap ballpoint pen applied to his notepad. "You're suggesting, off the record, of course, that something inappropriate or abnormal has happened to Eddie. Perhaps your nephew is possibly being kidnapped, abducted, or being held hostage against his' will? Do I read you correctly?"

"I can't prove any of those suspicions or theories you've just mentioned," Eileen Gorman clarified. "But you're right on target about how I feel. True, Eddie absolutely despises and loathes the paparazzi. True, Eddie's always been introspective, and up to the time of this reprehensible Iraq War, my nephew had generally kept his opinions to himself. And true again," Ms. Gorman editorialized, "Eddie loves the environment, and has done many charity concerts to promote that special cause. But Eddie would never abandon his aunt to become some kind of loner-ecological-pioneer up in Alaska, or a silly Buddhist hermit over in Tibet! That would be too uncharacteristic of him! I believe that my dearest Eddie's been tampered with in some heinous way, Mr. Dennis. I'm quite sure of it! That's my, pardon the awkward expression, that's my true gut feeling, anyway!"

"But what about certain pictures that have recently surfaced in various gossip magazines showing Eddie taking photos' of grizzly bears and caribou up in the 49th State?" P.I. Matt Dennis questioned. "Those pictures appear to be legitimate and authentic!"

"Look, Mr. Dennis. Ever since Eddie got divorced from his cheating wife and lost custody of his two children, he's become a little too introverted in his own personal life, while in the meantime, contrary to his nature, Eddie's become too vocal about certain national and international political matters. In the final analysis, Kind Sir," Eileen Gorman formally asserted, "my nephew's not acting like himself, and as far as those deplorable photographs that have surfaced in certain questionable publications, I don't place any credence in those ridiculous shams, whatsoever!"

"Then, you believe that the photos' shown in the papers are fakes?" the reputable private investigator asked.

"Those doctored photos' are of someone that looks like my nephew, but they aren't of him," Dame Eileen Gorman stubbornly insisted. "I know what Eddie looks like, and those pictures you're alluding to were definitely of someone else. Maybe the general public's been fooled by this ugly, contemptible hoax, but I certainly haven't! My eyesight's still twenty-twenty, after all these years!"

"Well then, thank you for your time," Matt Dennis said. "I'm now off to obtain some additional information from the families of TV entertainer Minerva Graham and singer Eleanor Siegel, who as you know, have also coincidentally disappeared from the Hollywood scene. If I come-up with anything substantial, about your nephew Eddie," the independent detective promised, "I'll certainly let you know what I've discovered first chance I get."

"Thanks, Mr. Dennis!" the worried woman replied. "I appreciate your involvement, since the police think that Eddie is old enough to lead his own life, without his devoted, overly-concerned aunt interfering with the prime functioning of local law enforcement. The cops are mostly concerned with the apprehension of dangerous criminals, and can care less about missing persons. At least, that's the all-too-familiar story I always get whenever I futilely contact the local authorities."

No sooner had Matt Dennis completed his fruitless dialogue with Dame Eileen Gorman and had exited her luxurious apartment, the former police inspector wearing the felt fedora was promptly intercepted by two on-duty military men, a Colonel and a Captain.

"Pardon me, Mr. Dennis," the first officer declared. "I'm Colonel Tom Philips, and this is Captain Roy Ellis. We're from the Army

Intelligence Unit, and we've been dispatched to find you and bring you to headquarters immediately."

"Say, what's this lousy ruse all about? I demand to see your credentials?" Matt Dennis yelled to the military men, for a lack of anything better to say in his defense.

"I assure you, Mr. Dennis, that we're bona fide government representatives," Captain Ellis declared.

"That's exactly what I'm afraid of!" the accosted private detective argued. "I trust the government just about as much as I trust Lucifer in a blue dress!"

"Come along now, Sir!" Colonel Philips encouraged. "You'll be released as soon as our superiors settle a few urgent questions that need immediate answering."

"Whatever happened to the Bill of Rights?" Matt Dennis defiantly asked and challenged. "Are the First Ten Amendments still in effect? Don't I have an opportunity to get in touch with an attorney? Can't I contact my next of kin?"

"Sir, this encounter is just a routine matter, and we expect your full cooperation," Captain Roy Ellis persisted. "Now then, Mr. Dennis. The more aggravation you cause us, the more difficult your plight will become. Just cooperate by accompanying Colonel Philips and me, and I'm sure everything else will fall into place, including your unalienable rights and freedoms as a United States citizen."

* * * * * * * * * * * * * * *

The President of the United States and the Vice-President were meeting in the White House's Oval Office and diligently conferring about current strategy pertaining to the Iraq War, and also analyzing the military initiatives being implemented against Muslim jihadists, along with reputed international terrorist organizations.

"You know," the U.S. President' declared to his trusted V.P., "our society's becoming more cowardly and weak-willed with each successive generation. The feckless newspapers and the anti-war demonstrators are all upset about 3,900 soldiers' lives being *sacrificed* in the Afghan and Iraq Wars. But in *World War II,* over 405,000 American military personnel sacrificed their lives for God and country. That horror was over a hundred-times the *sacrifice* as has happened in our present ongoing Middle East War campaign. And I gotta' emphasize that in 1942, the population of the country was only half of what it is today. The statistics don't lie!"

"And please don't forget, Mr. President, that over 671,000 American soldiers and sailors had been wounded in *World War II,* and that the World Trade Center twin-towers' catastrophe was very comparable to the number of deaths that had happened at Pearl Harbor on December 7, 1941. In fact," the grim-faced Vice-President indicated and then paused, "more people actually died in New York on September 11th 2001 than did in Hawaii on *that* terrible day that 'shall live in infamy'. as Franklin Delano Roosevelt so aptly described the sneak attack."

"The press and the public just don't get it!" the nation's Chief Executive insisted to his right-hand comrade. "It's far better to tackle a problem, or a potential threat, when it's small rather than to have the crisis proliferate into something uncontrollable and massive like *World War II.* When Hitler's minions invaded Czechoslovakia in 1939, I believe, well, nobody in Europe did anything about it," the President pontificated. "But then…"

"But then, soon after *that* experiment with Czechoslovakia, Hitler's army invaded Poland, Denmark, Holland, Belgium, and France, which all fell like vulnerable dominoes neatly stacked in a row," the avid student of history finished the President's thought. "And that world-class villain Saddam Hussein had already invaded Kuwait, and his nefarious intention was to then conquer Jordan, Saudi Arabia, Lebanon, and Syria, just like Hitler had done to the weak European countries a half-century before. We successfully stifled the greedy Arab dictator, and now the press is treating us like *we're* the bad guys."

The intercom situated upon the President's desk buzzed, and his conscientious personal secretary was on the line. "Tell the Secretary of State and the Secretary of Defense I'll be with them in around five-minutes," the nation's highest-ranking official instructed. "I'm in an important conference with the Vice-President, and we'll have a joint meeting as soon as our current business has concluded."

The President's mind then gathered its recollections of *World War II,* and the Chief Executive proceeded with his intense dialogue with his Second-in-Command. "Yes, over fifty-million people lost their lives in *World War II,* and only a small fraction of *that* colossal statistic has been lost in Iraq. History has taught us that it's more plausible to stand-up to a ruthless dictator in the very beginning of his lust for conquest," the President austerely elucidated. "But it was the absence of those weapons of mass destruction in Iraq that turned the press, and eventually the public, against us. Those WMDs, or the lack of atomic bombs, has been *our* embarrassing Achilles heel!"

"Everyone with half a brain realizes that the WMDs had been clandestinely transported from Baghdad to Damascus, just prior to the start of the war," the Vice-President asserted. "It stands to reason that Syria is a Sunni Baathist country, and that Saddam Hussein was a Sunni Baathist. And reliable confidential reports verify that the WMDs had been flown into Syria on Iraqi commercial jetliners, with the passenger seats removed to accommodate the heavy secret cargo. Our intelligence has revealed that the WMDs had been flown in over fifty flights between the two Arab capitals," the Vice-President informatively elaborated. "Syria had just had a dam burst, and the WMD flights were especially ordered by Hussein under the guise of 'disaster aid' to devastated flood victims."

"The main justification for our present Iraq War is that it's really an extension of the original Gulf War," the President blustered. "Saddam Hussein didn't honor the terms of truce. And the arrogant tyrant persistently thumbed his nose at over a dozen UN Security Council resolutions, fifteen I believe."

"Yes, Mr. President," the Vice-President supportively added. "The press and the gullible public should've understood Hussein's evil mindset. Saddam modeled his bellicose Iraqi regime after those of his boyhood heroes, historical predators and maniacs Adolph Hitler and Joseph Stalin. At least, that's what had been documented in our psychological profile of Hussein, prior to the commencement of hostilities over Baghdad."

"Yes, the ignorant liberal news reporters don't comprehend that millions of lives would be lost if *World War III* ever broke-out, and that the high-standard American way of life would be in dire jeopardy," the President stated and commiserated. "A fierce global conflict of such great proportions would be unimaginably catastrophic! That's why we did what we had to do, but the hostile left-wing press will never give us credit for achieving anything significant! We've successfully avoided *World War III* by taking-out dictator Saddam Hussein when we did."

"Right you are, Mr. President," the V.P. praised and commended. "The Twin Towers' tragedy was only the opening punch of Round 1. But the naïve American public doesn't fathom the true purpose of determined Middle East tyrants. Two nations in particular now want to establish a Muslim caliphate by conquering neighboring countries. Those two threats are Syria and Iran, which incidentally, are actually jealous of each other," the Vice-President opined. "Those dual rogue nations sponsor international terrorism, the ultimate purpose of which is to destroy the economy of the United States, bringing this great country to its knees and...."

"And then, to very shrewdly create a devastating Second Great Depression, which will cause subsequent depressions throughout Europe, just like what had happened before the start of *World War II,*" the President concluded and stated. "Then, while the economic vacuum exists, a series of Arab fascist dictators could come to power just like Hitler, Mussolini, and Stalin had done in Europe, but this second time around, the despots would be militant Muslims. And because of the new Great Depression, the United States and Great Britain would then be too crippled to effectively challenge the New World Arab Order."

"Now that we've gotten *that* preliminary topic out of the way," the Vice-President expressed while adeptly changing the subject of discussion, "I need to know how Operation Cloning is coming along. I figured I'd confidentially ask that detail before the Secretary of State and the Secretary of Defense enter the Oval Office."

"Well, only you, me, the CIA, and the FBI directors know about the scheme," the President informed his political colleague. "As you know, Operation Cloning has been secretly created to eliminate certain influential dissidents, particularly those in the entertainment field. The project's primary purpose is..."

"To cleverly replace actors, singers, and outspoken talk show hosts and hostesses, that the naïve public idolizes, and to substitute *them* with physical duplicates, who will all then lead low-profile existences without any dangerous political points of view being expressed at anti-war rallies and on network T.V. It's the ultimate in misinformation campaigns! Okay, Mr. President. Since we've had our exclusive frank conversation," the Vice-President politely suggested, "we can now confer with the Secretary of State and with the Secretary of Defense in order to review our Middle East policy, and we'll also discuss how to improve our current bogged-down, Middle East war strategy."

* * * * * * * * * * * * *

Nine army prisoners with their hands tied behind their backs were being herded together inside a windowless briefing room at Andrews Air Force Base, just outside Washington DC. Nine Special Forces soldiers stood behind the "civilian captives", when Colonel Tom Philips and Captain Roy Ellis, accompanied by a stern-faced, dark-suited government official, entered the large well-lit room.

"Okay, listen up!" Colonel Philips' voice boomed. "Since *we* feel it really doesn't matter one way or the other, Captain Ellis will thoroughly explain to you so-called celebrities what this particular scenario is all about."

"Thank you, Colonel!" Captain Roy Ellis suavely and formally prefaced. "Now then," Captain Ellis continued while addressing Minerva Graham, Eddie Rivers, Vincent Crenshaw, Eleanor Siegel, Sean Price, Gregory Sinclair, Reverend Fred Tomms, Reverend Esau Clark, and Private Investigator Matthew Dennis. "Each of you will be allowed one question after I'm finished explaining why you're here, and where you're going to be personally taken. You've all been accused of treason and sedition while engaging in subversive activity against the United States of America. Your deleterious public comments have been extremely harmful to the national security of our great nation."

"This detention is preposterous!" the corpulent talk show host and war dissident Minerva Graham protested. "I demand access to a telephone, so that I can contact my…."

An alert Special Forces soldier instantly raised the butt of his rifle and smashed it against the back of Minerva Graham's skull. The opinionated talk show hostess's body went limp, and instantly fell onto, and then slumped upon the hard, tan, tile floor.

"Now then," Colonel Philips commanded the remaining shocked war protesters. "I urge the rest of you to show more self-discipline than Ms. Graham had foolishly exhibited. I remind you that you're in military custody, and a similar fate will happen to you if any of *you* loudmouthed civilians violate the terms of information dissemination, just like Ms. Graham had inanely done. Now that you all understand the basic rules, please continue with your briefing, Captain Ellis."

"As I was saying before I had been so rudely interrupted by Ms. Graham," Captain Ellis lectured to his anxious, tethered hostages, "I'm politely telling you this information because *we* believe that you might never return to the United States of America. The government has been developing a secret genetic duplication and replication method, that's presently being practiced in what has been designated 'Operation Cloning'. It's my distinct pleasure to inform you pathetic dissidents that each of you has already been genetically duplicated. We had obtained the necessary cell material from simple blood tests that each of you had routinely undergone, at your own volition, at various doctor's offices and hospitals around the country."

"That's un-American!" Reverend Fred Tomms piped-up. "It's not only an intrusion into our privacy! It's a grotesque form of discrimination against..."

A second loyal Special Forces guard, standing directly behind the garrulous civil rights' leader, administered a savage blow with the butt of *his* rifle against the back of Reverend Tomms head. The obese minister's knees quickly buckled, and the cynical TV minister immediately collapsed upon the tan tile floor.

"You civilian clowns must all have attention deficit syndrome!" Colonel Philips chuckled but stopped short of a giggle. "Now that you've seen what has happened to Ms. Graham and to Reverend Tomms," the amused officer pointed-out, "you'd think that you'd learn to keep your mouths shut when specifically advised to do so. Now, Captain Ellis has already told each of you disgusting war protesters that you'll have one question to ask after he's done speaking. Are you obnoxious imbeciles dense, or what? Please continue with your explanation to these totally uncouth, assembled degenerates, Captain."

"Now, that the government has cloned duplicates of you outspoken anti-war vermin," Captain Ellis proceeded with his critical exposition, "you'll be conducted via Air Force transport from Andrews to Dover Air Force Base in Delaware, and then clandestinely flown overseas. Now, pardon my sense of humor, but Colonel Philips and I will now entertain specific pertinent questions from you' radical traitors."

"I demand that I talk with my lawyer," Reverend Esau Clark barked and objected. "I demand that...."

A third Special Forces guard stepped forward and impacted his rifle butt against Reverend Clark's thick cranium, immediately sending the provocative anti-war activist onto the tile floor.

"You' moronic idiots don't listen when simple instructions are given!" Colonel Philips rebuked the remaining six military prisoners. "You repulsive civilians obviously lack standard Army discipline! You were all directed to ask one question each, and not get onto your soapboxes and utter absurd inflammatory declarative statements. Now then, who's next?"

"Can I make an urgent phone call to one of my attorneys?" the multibillionaire Gregory Sinclair requested.

"Here's an attorney," Colonel Philips indicated as he pointed to the man standing next to him, wearing the dark blue suit and matching tie. "Here's the U.S, Attorney General!"

"The President has decided by special executive mandate that you captives have been deemed detrimental to the security interests of the United States of America, and therefore, you have been enlisted into the military to await further orders," the Attorney General articulated. "The President has the ultimate final supreme say on the matter. Our Chief Executive thinks that your unwarranted threats endanger the stability of *our* country!"

"But why haven't we been given any basic training before being flown overseas?" Eddie Rivers impulsively asked.

"Because you'll be experiencing on-the-job training," Captain Ellis answered with a smile. "You won't need any boot camp, Mr. Rivers, because soon your boots will be on the ground!"

"What's *that* snide comment supposed to mean?" insisted retired movie producer Vincent Crenshaw.

"It means that you've all been determined to be enemies of the government, and must now dutifully serve your country whether you like it or not," Captain Roy Ellis loudly announced. "If you're enemies of the government, you're also enemies of our country! Stop acting like a clan of doltish Neanderthals! Use your God-given scruples for a change! It's all so fundamentally plain and simple."

"But aren't our Constitutional rights being violated?" the famous singer Eleanor Siegel balked. "You don't have dictatorial powers!"

"You'll be promptly flown to either the Afghan-Pakistan border to fight militant Taliban jihadists, or to Al Anbar province, to wage battle against radical Al Qaeda elements," Colonel Tom Philips orally conveyed to his reluctant and befuddled hostage audience. "You pathetic, unpatriotic Ignoramuses will have your own little scouting platoon! You'll receive your weapons and your vital rations, just prior to jumping out of your assigned Air Force plane, and going on survival patrol."

"But I've never parachuted out of an airplane, civilian, military, or otherwise!" newspaper columnist Sean Price squawked and protested. "My civil rights are being trampled upon and…."

True to form, the obedient guard standing behind Sean Price cracked the back of the journalist's head with *his* very effective rifle butt. And a second later, the objecting war opponent's body lay motionless upon the tan tile floor.

"Why are you doing this to us?" P.I. Matt Dennis futilely asked his fully amused military kidnappers. "Doesn't this egregious act you're committing go against everything that the United States, along with *our* guaranteed Bill of Rights' freedom of speech, represents?"

"You'll enjoy plenty of freedom of choice after you parachute either into Afghanistan or into Al Anbar Province," Colonel Tom Philips quite matter-of-factly, sternly replied. "Here's the perfect opportunity for you to prove your patriotism! You'll either fight the jihadist fascist enemy for the United States of America, or join the Taliban or Al Qaeda, and then be hunted-down and killed by *your* country's marvelously brave soldiers. That wonderful privilege, or should I say *right,* Mr. Dennis, constitutes *your* precious freedom of choice!"

“Global Warming Thwarted”

What real mental abnormalities constitute a madman’s mind? Paranoid? Neurotic? Chronic Angst? Psychotic? Delusional? Schizophrenic? Insanity? Fanaticism? How about a combination of any of the aforementioned conditions? One thing is for certain; a poor person is labeled “crazy” when exhibiting any of the states of mind already indicated, but a wealthy person having the same identical emotional dysfunction (as a pauper demonstrates) is automatically identified as an “eccentric” and not as a “lunatic”.

An obsessive/compulsive, multi-billionaire, crazed human being named Jefferson Mason existed. The eccentric tycoon had become one of the wealthiest men in the world, hitting it big in computers and office networking equipment. Mason had later intelligently parlayed his vast amassed fortune into lucrative real estate investments in America, Europe and Australia.

Jefferson Mason had been a shy young man back at Glassboro State Teachers College in the mid-‘50s. The bashful, aspiring history teacher seldom dated co-eds at the mostly female-attended institution, and rarely socialized with the more masculine male classmates, staying isolated in his dorm’ room with his eyes focused in textbooks the full four years of his career preparation. Upon graduating with stellar honors, self-conscious Jefferson decided that American education (along with tolerating its brazen, defiant, insolent *students)* was not his forte, so the shy dreamer boldly risked failure and opened a retail electronics store in a Vineland, New Jersey strip mall.

The frugal fellow saved every penny Jefferson could accumulate. Mason invested his money wisely, and soon thereafter, had a chain of profitable stores in seven South Jersey towns. Never marrying or showing any interest in female companionship, in the early 1970s, Jefferson Mason sold his thriving retail operations, and the ambitious entrepreneur immediately became active in the computer software distribution business, his efforts eventually branching-out into computer networking. By 1980, success upon success had the enterprising risk-taker listed by *Forbes Magazine* as one of the ten wealthiest capitalists in the entire United States.

While in his sixties, Jefferson Mason had been quite actively altruistic, and often engaged in donating to myriad charity and philanthropic causes around the globe. But as the introverted, balding, gaunt-faced recluse turned seventy-five, Mason avariciously hoarded money like a fanatical miser, and abruptly ceased making his generous contributions in assisting his fellow needy human beings.

But the laconic Mr. Jefferson Mason had no heirs to leave his immense fortune to, and the self-pitying hermit often contemplated *his* particular station in life, while perpetually brooding about the advent of his death. Jefferson remained a virtual recluse, residing in his deep subterranean compound, which was situated a thousand feet below his walled-in Princeton, New Jersey mansion.

'All of my blood relatives are dead, and I have no children, grandchildren, nieces, or nephews to be beneficiaries in my will,' the lonely, distraught American aristocrat pondered and lamented. 'But the press doesn't know it, but I have contracted incurable cancer, and the malignancy's already spread to my lymph nodes. According to the medical experts, I only have around six months to live, and I absolutely refuse to have detrimental chemotherapy or radiation done. I've now dismissed my butler, my chauffeur, my maid, and my gardener, all for one obvious reason. None of them will be able to discover my marvelous stealthy plan that I've surreptitiously and ingeniously arranged. It's time to make another stealthy entry into my personal diary.'

> Dear Diary,
>
> Allow me to describe Phase I of my foolproof, perfect, secret plan. My physical double (whom I've promised to pay the sum of five million dollars) has arrived at Cape Canaveral to be launched with a crew of international astronauts into orbit around the Earth. My look-alike facsimile has passed all of the physical tests, and even has my blood type of O Positive. NASA wants to see how a specimen my advanced age can endure the rigors associated with living in outer space.
>
> On the crew's third day circling the Earth, I'll have my Russian military contacts stationed outside Moscow launch a guided missile (I say missile because a GPS missile is much more accurate than an ordinary rocket), and the projectile will obliterate the orbiting space laboratory (with my victimized double inside) right out of the outer atmosphere. The press and the TV media will erroneously report that I've been killed in outer space.
>
> I predict that the U.S. government will accuse Russia of committing the diabolical act, which incidentally, Dear Diary, only cost me an additional ten-million-dollar bargain bribe to complete. General Zinkoff will soon go incognito, and escape to a remote unknown destination; have plastic surgery

performed, and then my old, loyal Cossack acquaintance will settle-down comfortably in either Mexico or in Canada with his small fortune, which of course I'll have deposited in that secret Swiss bank account that I've coyly established in my Russian friend's name. But World War III will be temporarily averted, mostly because the Russians will argue that one of their own astronauts had been killed in the spectacular space laboratory explosion.

Jefferson Mason smiled and then sipped some blackberry brandy from an ice-cube filled glass, while mentally rehashing "Phase II" of his dangerous, unscrupulous strategy. 'I'm seventy-five years old, yet I still strongly desire to live. I find the idea of imminent death quite repulsive! The finest medical attention available can't extend my life beyond what my widespread cancer is currently dictating.'

Then, the scheming, doomed man seriously thought about his futile health predicament some more. 'My liver and lungs have already been invaded by cancer, and will soon start showing symptoms of the dreaded disease. And here I am with seventy-five years under my belt, a mere grain of sand in the Universe's infinite hourglass; its incredible age spanning thirteen billion-years; not to ignore the Earth's very impressive four-five-billion year-existence! I could very well be the richest man on Earth, yet who really cares way out there beyond the solar system in the far extremities of the Milky Way, or anywhere else in any other distant galaxies?

Sighing about his imminent demise, the hermit multi-billionaire resumed his sulking rumination. 'Indeed,' saddened Jefferson Mason imagined, 'my death only really matters if Earth is the only damned planet in the galaxy, or in the Universe, that has developed intelligent life! Then, me being the wealthiest human on Earth would have some relevance and significance, after all! But that's why Phase II of my brilliant plan must be carefully implemented. I refuse to have the world, and all its inferior minions, continue on living, while I'm assuredly going to perish within the next several months!'

Jefferson Mason consumed another mouthful of delicious brandy and then meditated some more. 'Yes; Phase II will be a fabulous prelude to the end of the world according to Jefferson Mason. Why should others with less ability, less motivation, and less savvy outlive me? I'll be safe and secure down here in my underground bunker, much safer than Adolph Hitler ever was in his! Yes;' the emotionally-warped maniac considered and then grinned. 'General Zinkoff has arranged by virtue of another meager five-million-dollar bribe to have his close comrades at several Russian military bases fire-off six ICBMs with nuclear warheads pointed directly at New York City, Washington DC, Chicago, Los Angeles, San Francisco and Philadelphia. And then certainly, the vigilant U.S. military will retaliate with overwhelming vengeance, and soon, the debacle known as World War III will be initiated, thanks to my brilliant cunning. I'll survive the global devastation down here in my air-conditioned, generator-operated compound, while all sorts of havoc, catastrophe and destruction will be occurring up on the surface.

Then, the wealthy, sick, madman continued his bizarre meditation. 'No more Princeton University; or Dartmouth; or Cornell; or Harvard; or Yale, for that matter, ha, ha, ha! Completely annihilated! Ha, ha, ha!' the crazed psycho snickered. 'All of that ongoing colossal calamity occurring on all continents, magnificently initiated and orchestrated by me, the most powerful, indispensable man in the whole wide world; who, by virtue of my clever acumen, will stubbornly endure the terrible global holocaust; and then, I'll live six months or so longer than any other human being on the planet, including the President of the United States, and his soon-to-be asphyxiated secret service storm-troopers! Ha, ha, ha! I'll outlive everyone, even though I have only a hundred and eighty or so precious days remaining.'

The following morning, after partaking of a cereal, toast and orange juice breakfast, Jefferson Mason again took pen-in-hand and opened his personal autobiographical black leather diary that might never be read by another human being. 'I don't know why I'm keeping detailed records for posterity, when quite probably, there'll be no damned posterity,' the elderly, maniacal, disease-infected fiend thought and chuckled. 'Oh well, I'm writing these splendid words for my own personal satisfaction, and not for anyone else's individual reading pleasure. I remember when I was a kid, my parents had an atom bomb shelter built in the basement of their home with adequate food and provisions to last a full month. But I have to admit that my sturdy, well-constructed, self-sufficient subterranean compound, along with its adequate food, liquor, and water supply, will last as long as I will, basically, six-to-ten lonesome months! Ha, ha, ha!' Of course, while the rest of humanity will be dead!"

* * * * * * * * * * * * * *

Oh, My Dear Diary,

Only two more anxious days before my sagacious scheme will be launched into most-wonderful action. Much to my meticulous organizational skills, the unwary world's apathetic population has no knowledge or suspicion of their prospective extermination. After my duplicate likeness is blown out of the atmosphere from inside the orbiting International Space Laboratory tomorrow morning, like clockwork, Phase II will go into operation with World War III rapidly ramping-up to warp speed. And while the Americans and the Russians are having their savage Armageddon with their awesome ICBM exchanges and bombardments, I'll then systematically commence with Phase III of my in-genius machination.

Yes indeed, in the past year, I've also satisfactorily bribed criminal and espionage elements along with certain Muslim terrorists all over the globe, who out-of-spite, have great animosity for Americans, and for American freedoms. The result of my well-planned methods will cause a gigantic dust veil to envelope the entire Earth; a tremendous cloud so incredible in size that it'll make the meteor concussion that had eliminated the dinosaurs seventy-to-ninety million years ago seem like mere child's play. Yes, Dear Diary; a sequence of hydrogen bombs will crash into various targeted volcanoes around the planet with such fantastic ferocity that Global Warming will become much more than a contemporary buzzword, or popular catch phrase.

Phase III will mean that tremendous nuclear explosions will occur to Mt. Etna in Sicily; to Mt. Vesuvius outside Naples; to Stromboli, also in Italy; to Krakatoa in Indonesia; to Mauna Loa in Hawaii; to Mount Fuji in Japan; to Popocatepetl in Mexico; to Mont Pelee in Martinique; and finally, to U.S. Mt. St. Helens, Mt. Shasta, Mt. Hood, and to Mt. Rainier, all situated in America's northwestern region. Such a gargantuan dust cloud shrouding the sun's rays would immediately envelop the whole globe. Soon, the polar regions and their massive glaciers will melt, but hopefully, that occurrence with happen well-after the human population will have been totally exterminated, or should I say 'eradicated,' to politely use a much more benign term. Only I, Jefferson Mason, shall miraculously escape the total horrific devastation and cleverly outlive the remainder of the human race! This I promise, my dear diary.'

'Yes, thanks to my need to survive, an incredible 'greenhouse effect' of such enormous and monumental proportions will make the disappearance of the prehistoric dinosaurs seem like a trivial, geological event,' the psycho-minded egomaniac concluded. 'And a secret is only a secret if it is kept by only one person, and not ridiculously shared. That's precisely why I prefer to act as a lone wolf! Of course,' Jefferson Mason greedily reasoned, 'my knowledgeable and wholly competent Arab and Russian co-conspirators are in on separate parts of the clever ruse, but they hate Americans with a passion, and will gladly participate in my grand design, just to slaughter as many millions as they can by firing-off the already acquired projectiles at selected volcanoes. I had illicitly obtained the missiles on the black market from Pakistan, from Iran and from North Korea, and soon thereafter, my well-connected contacts clandestinely smuggled the lethal devices into my state-of-the-art launching facilities, conveniently hidden in strategic places all over the world. Those selfsame, formidable weapons of mass destruction that I've furtively obtained had been originally purchased by my former agents and international employees,' the mentally ill psychopath recalled with a smile.

The lunatic billionaire took a deep breath, and then analyzed his particular physical, sick plight some more. 'Yes; only the self-centered doctors over at the University of Pennsylvania Hospital know of my grave medical problem, but they're bound by the physician/patient privilege to not reveal any pertinent information about my deteriorating physical health to anyone. Even though my thoughts are sometimes erratic and disconnected,' the deranged fanatic speculated and rationalized, 'I'm still a veritable genius, and therefore, rightfully deserve to outlive the more inferior members of my mostly mediocre species.'

And then Jefferson Mason thought about the lack of love and romance in his life, and justified his fabulous prosperity and his current aversion towards his fellow man by wickedly reckoning, 'I had to stay focused on my great dream of ascending above the competition and totally winning in the end,' the delusional, egocentric, rogue-scoundrel assessed. 'A nagging wife and bratty children would've taxed my creativity, and would have put a strain on my financial resources. If I had to be dedicated to *them*, I could've never accomplished what I had done. I had very intelligently devoted my entire existence and energy to pursuing the Queen of Diamonds, and I obstinately refused to be subordinate to, or be henpecked by the very demanding Queen of Hearts.'

And indeed, for a fleeting minute (during a rare moment of sentimentality), Jefferson Mason recalled his Oakcrest High School heartthrob Charlene Wilson, and his Glassboro State College dream girl Gina Thomas; each of whom later had led lackluster lives, had married, and divorced rather ordinary husbands; and both females soon became typical mothers trapped in totally mundane, miserable, middle-class existences; the women living and drowning within a Darwinian world teeming with boundless opportunity and abounding in intense individual and corporate competition.

'But ten years ago, I did send Charlene and Gina checks for a million dollars each, but then I deliberately ignored both their efforts to contact and personally thank me for my fine generosity. I deliberately shunned having close associations with others, especially women; *that* very necessary practice being employed so that I could concentrate my enviable talents on achievement and on being exclusively objective in my proclivities; and consequently, my sacrifices and endeavors were blessed by me not having bothersome emotions influencing the outcomes of my keen decision-making. And just look what I've attained and what Charlene and Gina have done with their very lackluster pathetic lives!' Jefferson Mason concluded. 'They've both been content being minor cogs inside of small wheels, not ever realizing that they could be big wheels themselves! I'm glad I didn't waste my life endeavoring to be just like everyone else in this dull and drab convoluted world! On the contrary, I've always derived satisfaction from being productive, self-reliant, resourceful, and successful!'

The progressively disconsolate man then thought about Princeton, New Jersey, and about the excellent university, and how he had often declined giving guest lectures at the institution out of his fear of public speaking, and also, out of disdain for close human contact. And then attempting to switch his ever-deteriorating mindset from the negative to the positive, Jefferson Mason recollected living in San Diego, of visiting the outstanding Balboa Park Zoo there; of appreciating the architectural splendor of the Hotel del Coronado, and of viewing the beautiful rugged cliffs and placid coves along the La Jolla coastline without anyone (close to him) to share those most pleasurable sites. 'Yes, I do miss Southern California after living there for twenty-two marvelous years,' the melancholy maniac sobbed. 'The trips and vacations to Palm Springs and Palm Desert, the great restaurants on Palm Canyon Drive and on El Paseo, all fond recollections, but definitely, irrelevant and minuscule to the enormous task at hand. Why should other less deserving people enjoy the amenities of those terrific places when I must die a mere half-year from now! If there's a God in heaven, I must curse Him for my rapidly spreading cancer!'

* * * * * * * * * * * * *

The emotionally unstable, mercurial-tempered, multi-billionaire suddenly became temporarily elated, sitting inside his isolated deep bunker compound, a full thousand feet underground. The crazed spectator curiously viewed on his giant flat-screen television evolving news reports of the mammoth International Space Laboratory's recent explosion. Mason poured a glass of blackberry brandy and contemplated the successful implementation of Phase I of his twisted plot to survive the remainder of his doomed species.

'Yes; my unwary physical double has just been erased from existence!' the obsessed villain summarized. 'Everyone will think that I've been blown to smithereens with all my atoms, cells and molecules instantaneously scattered into outer space in a unique sort of contemporary, astronomical cremation, ha, ha, ha! But obviously, I've not been blown into oblivion as everyone now believes! To the mini-minded populations of the world, my passing will be just a momentary bit of gossip and tabloid dissemination, and nothing more. But I intend to have the last laugh on so-called 'civilization'; yes, I most certainly will! Ha, ha, ha! The pea-brained inhabitants of Planet Earth will soon become hysterical rats desperately scampering all over creation, desperately seeking shelter from inevitable extermination! Much to their frustration, the pathetic masses will soon-be learning histrionics instead of history inside my experimental well-contrived Earth laboratory! Ha, ha, ha!'

The mentally superior yet emotionally underdeveloped iconoclast had very methodically taken the time to deactivate the elevator leading-down from his palatial mansion to the well-equipped and handsomely furnished subterranean "survival compound". That strategic precaution would ensure that Jefferson Mason would indeed out-live his fellow man. 'Yes, tomorrow morning, World War III will commence, and it'll soon be followed with missiles impacting into Mt. Vesuvius, Krakatoa, Mt. St. Helens, Mt. Rainier, Mt. Etna and the rest of geography's most important and destructive volcanoes. I'll mastermind the end of humanity and not leave it up to definite incompetents like Satan or Jesus Christ!'

And then Jefferson Mason's defective mind reflected on the present state of mortal affairs some more. 'Perhaps I'm Vulcan reincarnated, the defunct and obsolete Roman god of fire and metallurgy; yes, the Roman resurrection of the Greek god Hephaestus,' the mentally sick fiend hypothesized. 'Yes, now I distinctly remember learning in my college Greco-Roman Mythology class that the word 'volcano' had originated from the god Vulcan's name, ha, ha, ha! Yes indeed; I am the very capable author, producer and director of this morbid, tragic play now spawned into progress! Let Mt. Stromboli and Mt. Hood violently erupt and completely pollute the atmosphere, all occurring at my omnipotent command! My supreme powers are limitless! My invincible will is final! I shall ultimately prevail! Ha, ha, ha!'

* * * * * * * * * * * * *

A series of extremely loud explosions suddenly rocked the underground bunker, and soon tons of debris descended into its well-fortified interior. A team of thirteen Delta Force commandos stormed into the compound with weapons and searchlights, just after the emergency generator had failed, and the overhead and wall lights had gone out. Soon, the lifeless body of Jefferson Mason was discovered beneath a fallen beam and underneath large fragments of crumbled concrete. The evil architect of the world's end had swallowed a cyanide capsule just before the elite squad of soldiers had forcefully entered the area, so the wily multi-billionaire had died of his own volition and not from the series of powerful military blasts that had been detonated.

"The nutcase fanatic's dead!" Major James Nelson determined upon feeling Jefferson Mason's neck. "No pulse evident on his frail wrists, either! Forensic tests will determine exactly how this perverted humanitarian had died, but the important fact is that he's dead, and that the world's no longer in jeopardy from his demented insanity! What a diabolical plan his vile mind had hatched! Better him being dead and not us, Captain!"

"Yes, indeed Major," Captain Gene Donohue agreed and verified. "It's a good thing we managed to bypass the deactivated elevator and climb-down that elevator shaft with our high-powered stun grenades intact! And it's also a good thing that the Russian authorities and our Arab intelligence agents found-out about this nefarious monster and his devious blueprint for international calamity," Captain Donohue knowledgeably added. "This demonic predator absolutely loathed his fellow man, and fortunately, the vindictive knave wound-up destroying himself in the process! And Mr. Mason had everything going for himself too, but then the fiend became too selfish, too excessively covetous, and...."

"And despicably wanted to start World War III and next eradicate his fellow man as if we all were disgusting insects and fleas," Major Nelson confirmed with a serious-looking frown showing on his grim, gritty face. "And there're hundreds of other crazy loons with all kinds of grievances out there, having similar weird notions and delusions of grandeur; but luckily, those random culprits have less money and less resources than this psycho Mr. Jefferson Mason possessed. Most of the country's most bitter enemies are without a doubt anarchistic socio-paths having demented concepts of what's right and what's wrong, finding fault with everything *outside* of themselves! If this loon's nightmare had reached fruition, and had not been expertly foiled by our superb intelligence network," Major Nelson emphasized to Captain Donohue, "then *we* would've been sent back to Neanderthal times, with us and our accursed descendants again living in caves and going back to being slaves to a primitive, subsistence existence. Culture and civilization would've had to begin all over again!"

The well-trained Delta Force commando soldiers all stood there, totally amazed at what had just happened, and contemplated what had almost transpired had *they* not so decisively acted and violently intervened. Then, the attack squad's fearless second-in-command had something salient to say.

"Major Nelson; you're assuming that some people would've survived the unparalleled worldwide destruction!" Army Captain Donohue conjectured and then stated to his immediate superior. "And Major, everyone out there in the media all along had been deceived and felt that this twisted-minded maniac had been a benign benefactor to humanity, and also a kind contributor to society's greater good! Philanthropist my eye! Now we fully understand this loose cannon Jefferson Mason for what he actually was, and for what he really represented. Needless to say, a harmless benefactor and philanthropist he was not!"

"This delusional old codger's malicious strategy wasn't just a fascinating whim or an idle idiosyncrasy," Major Nelson evaluated and verbally communicated. Thank God that this mentally ill crackpot never got the chance to employ Phase II and Phase III of his perverted, heinous plot, or else, Captain Donohue," the commanding officer of the undercover mission maintained, "we wouldn't be standing here having this casual conversation right this minute!" Major Nelson convincingly and solemnly replied. "We'd both hopefully be in Heaven and asking St. Peter at the fabled Pearly Gates exactly how the *hell* we ever got there!"

"Twelve Modern Labors"

Stephen Fischer, a resident of rural Pine Road, was quite upset when he had learned that his last remaining aunt had died. Aunt Marie Mayor of Taylor Avenue, Baltimore, Maryland had always favored Stephen, and had often doted on him whenever she had the opportunity. In the sixties and the seventies, Uncle Henry Mayor and Aunt Marie would frequently visit Steve's hardworking parents at their place of business, Pete's Farm Market on the White Horse Pike in Hammonton, New Jersey.

"I remember when I was a kid, whenever my family visited Baltimore, Aunt Marie and Uncle Henry used to take me to Gwynn Oak Amusement Park, and a few times to Trimpers Rides on the boardwalk in Ocean City, Maryland, too," Steve told his cousins Jerry and Richard Berkheimer at *their* aunt's viewing inside the huge funeral home on Bel Air Road in the Overlea section of the city. "I'm sure going to miss her and her kindness towards me. But ever since Uncle Henry passed away, Aunt Marie had become a quiet recluse. Certainly, not the person I remember her being in her earlier days."

"She never had a driver's license, and after Uncle Henry passed on, Aunt Marie had to rely on the rest of the family for transportation around Baltimore, and for simple things like groceries, and taking care of her property," Jerry Berkheimer respectfully explained. "And she had a very large lawn to maintain, too. My brother Rich and I cut the grass at least once a week every weekend, during the spring, summer, and fall for ten consecutive years."

"And Aunt Marie was so meticulous and fastidious," cousin Richard Berkheimer added. "Her house was almost like a museum, and everything in the small mansion had to be exactly right, all the time. The story goes that *our* grandparents had lived in Alpena, Michigan, and grand-pop was an industrious timber man who had leased forestland from the government. At one time, he had over fifty lumberjacks working under his employ. Anyway," Richard continued with his glorified narrative, "a wicked fire burned-down the whole logging camp, and also the nearby dwelling, or should I say 'homestead,' and the family lost everything because people didn't carry any insurance back in those days in the early 1900s. And so..."

"And so, later, the family came east by train from Michigan to stay with relatives here in Baltimore," Jerry Berkheimer informed his New Jersey cousin Stephen Fischer. "That is, after grand-pop had died of tuberculosis in Alpena, so Aunt Marie was the eldest of seven children, and she by necessity became her brother and sisters' substitute parent, raising *your* dad, Uncle John, *our* mom, your Aunt Vera, and also Aunt Tina, Aunt Elsie, Aunt Lillian and Aunt Catherine. Times were exceptionally tough back then," Jerry stressed and then paused. "We just gotta' believe that Aunt Marie's teenage life had been somewhat ruined, because she had assumed adult responsibility at too young an age."

"Yes, things were certainly pretty hard in the so-called 'good old days'," Stephen Fischer evaluated and shared with his cousins. "But if I recall from family gossip, after Aunt Marie had married Uncle Henry, the college graduate soon became a construction engineer, and the couple traveled and lived all over the world, including Egypt, Italy, France, Spain and Greece. So, there was some enjoyment in Aunt Marie's life, despite all of the early adversity she, had suffered and endured, and I suppose she always made a big fuss over *us* when we were kids, because Uncle Henry and her never had any children of their own."

"I understand that the three of us are going to be pall bearers," Jerry informed his brother and his New Jersey cousin in a low voice so as not to disturb the other mourners. "It's only right that we can carry Aunt Marie to her final resting place, considering that she had carried us around when we were infants."

Two months after the Baltimore funeral of Aunt Marie Mayor, Stephen Fischer received a certified letter in the mail from the office of Byron Tucker, Esquire, of Baltimore, Maryland. In the legal missive, the attorney stated that his firm had been assigned to administer and execute the will of Marie Helen Mayor, and that Stephen's inheritance from the woman's estate was a large Grecian urn featuring the image of a classical Greek hero, along with the mythological champion's various adventures painted on all sides from top to bottom. "You'll be receiving your extraordinary item via UPS delivery, and the package will be shipped next Tuesday," the estate's lawyer indicated in his letter. "This unusual-but-exquisite rare gift represents your entire inheritance."

Stephen Fischer felt dejected upon reading the surprising news. 'I always understood that Aunt Marie believed that I was her favorite nephew,' the disappointed recipient of the Grecian urn thought. 'I suppose that *that* all changed when Uncle Henry had died, and then Jerry and Rich began taking care of her property, and doing errands for her. After all, I was here up in New Jersey, and my cousins were only a mile away from Overlea. And besides,' Steve continued his train of concentration, 'Aunt Marie probably exhausted most of her savings with medical, hospital expenses, and expensive nursing home care. I recall that she had spent one full year in a convalescence home. Jerry and Rich probably inherited her brick ranch home and the remaining cash was more than likely divided among *my* other seven cousins living in the Baltimore vicinity. I suppose there's much merit in the old adage, 'Don't count your chickens before they're hatched!'

The following Friday afternoon (right on schedule), the familiar local brown UPS truck pulled into Steve Fischer's U-shaped, asphalt driveway and delivered a rather heavy package labeled "Fragile: Handle With Care". After thanking the cheerful driver, the new owner of the Grecian urn carried the carton into his house and decided that he would open it after supper. At eight p.m. Fischer used a sharp knife, and carefully sliced the intricately wrapped cardboard shipping box, and next folding the four flaps back to the sides. Inside a well-insulated inner container was a "hideous-looking" urn with the Twelve Labors of Hercules painted in vertical circles from top to bottom. Stephen casually examined the strange, gaudy item and shook his head to express his personal dissatisfaction.

'This object was probably obtained when Aunt Marie and Uncle Henry had spent two years living in Greece, both years residing just outside Athens I believe,' Fischer conjectured as his melancholy eyes studied the odd-looking object. 'This baby's definitely going into either the attic or the cellar. I wouldn't wish this grotesque-looking artifact, if indeed it is an ancient artifact, on my worst enemy, or on my all-too-fortunate cousins Jerry and Richard Berkheimer, as far as that's concerned.'

Stephen poured himself a generous amount of *Southern Comfort* over fresh ice cubes, and began imbibing the delicious caramel-flavored liquor. Out of curiosity, reaching-up to his bookshelf, the homeowner grabbed a seldom-read encyclopedia volume and read on the subject of ancient Greek mythology. The curious peruser randomly thumbed through the pages until his fingers came to a heading that appropriately read: "The Twelve Labors of Hercules". As the slightly depressed man gulped-down several more ounces of delicious *Southern Comfort,* his eyes and attention alternated between what words he was reading and what images and scenes were represented upon the "rather ugly" recently acquired Grecian urn.

'Let's see now,' Steve pondered after pouring his second potent glass of *Southern Comfort.* 'It states here that the hot-tempered hero Hercules had killed his wife, and out of sheer anger, had burned his house down with his dead spouse still inside. As a punishment for his wicked deeds, King Eurystheus of Mycenae assigned Hercules the task of performing twelve super-difficult labors to atone for his egregious misdeeds,' Fischer comprehended and mentally visualized.

In his initial labor, Hercules first choked to death the vicious Lion of Nemea, the carcass of which the muscular fellow immediately returned to King Eurystheus to keep as a coveted souvenir. The second superhuman task was to travel to a place called Lerna to kill the nine-headed Hydra, which terrorized anyone who accidentally came close to its native swamp. 'Whenever a head of the Hydra was chopped-off,' Stephen laughed while reading his dusty book and drinking more of his tasty whiskey, 'another one would instantly grow back in its place. But then, Hercules seared each of the nine necks off with a burning brand, so that the heads eventually could not sprout-out again. Pretty ingenious solution for a brawny guy like Hercules to creatively solve such a challenging dilemma, ha, ha, ha! Hercules had invented cauterizing! Ha, ha, ha!'

After swallowing-down another mouthful of his favorite liquor, Stephen continued his spontaneous analysis of Hercules' twelve arduous labors. 'The third obligation was capturing a wild stag that was sacred to the hunting goddess Artemis; the fourth detail was to kill a great ferocious boar, and the fifth command was to clean the filthy stables of Augeas that contained thousands of ill-tempered horses and cattle possessing loose bowels. 'What a smelly mess *that* terrible environment must've been!' Fischer giggled as the half-intoxicated imbiber read and drank some more. 'Hercules used his great strength to change the course of two rivers, making the separate diversions flow and flood right through the stables as if they were teabags. And the sixth demanding labor was to chase away a flock of huge, predatory, carnivorous birds using *his* trusty bow and arrow. Say, these labors are not only funny, they're quite interesting, too!'

After refilling his glass of *Southern Comfort* and replenishing his ice cube supply, Stephen Fischer resumed his academic-but-whimsical investigation into the Twelve Labors of Hercules. 'The seventh labor, which appears both in the book and on this oddball urn, has Hercules journeying to Crete and capturing King Minos's legendary monster, the Minotaur, and then putting the wild beast on a boat and transporting the beast to King Eurystheus' palace in Mycenae. The next grueling project of Hercules was to kill Eurystheus' enemy, King Diomedes, and to disperse *his* hostile man-eating stallions out of their sturdy stables. The ninth tough labor was to steal and bring back the girdle of the Amazon Queen Hippolyta, which the Greek hero had cunningly accomplished using both charm and guile.'

Then, the new urn owner assessed the remaining three scenarios. 'These fantasy stories, or should I say 'extraordinary myths,' are wonderfully intriguing,' Stephen admitted. 'Ancient people probably were totally bored with the difficulties of everyday life, so the inhabitants invented this crazy outrageous fiction, making-up what we today call mythology, to simply entertain and inspire one another.'

Next, the nearlyinebriated Fischer imbibed the balance of his mellow *Southern Comfort* and groggily struggled through the three remaining labors: the tenth job was to bring back the cattle of Geryon, and in the process, the hero creatively formed the Pillars of Hercules, now Gibraltar (then Calpe) in Southern Spain, and Abyla in Northern Africa, with the wine-dark Mediterranean Sea flowing between the two landmark rock masses, directly into the Atlantic Ocean. In Hercules' eleventh labor, the punished icon had to retrieve and bring back the Three Golden Apples of the Hesperides, and also, briefly hold-up the sky for the very demanding Titan known as Atlas. 'And finally,' Fischer conscientiously read and paraphrased from the informative encyclopedia text, 'there was an assigned private expedition which the strong fellow had make down to the Underworld.' The belching reader and urn scrutinizer proceeded to learn about Hercules courageously trekking-down to Hades for the purpose of releasing the dead champion Theseus from the Chair of Forgetfulness, and next single-handedly capturing and bringing the formidable three-headed dog Cerberus up from Hades, and finally, proudly carrying the savage cur directly to King Eurystheus in Mycenae.

The overly indulgent drinker closed the Greek Mythology section and slid it onto the coffee table in front of the cranberry leather couch upon which Stephen Fischer was sitting. 'I'm a trifle dizzy and fuzzy-headed, but I'll be all right! I actually enjoy being in this happy state of mind!' Then, the lonely businessman thought about his downtown Hammonton pharmacy; about his marital separation from his wife Michelle, and about her gaining custody of their children, Maryann and Justin. Fischer then recollected how Michelle (instead of receiving alimony) was drawing a thousand-dollar a week settlement salary from the drugstore business. 'I know of a guy living down Stone Harbor named Ernie who owns seven drugstores all over South Jersey, and three of his thriving establishments have already been bought out by *Rite Aid*,' Stephen reasoned. 'Ernie's my idol, and I'll gladly model my future life after his! I'll be the next drugstore tycoon in New Jersey, just wait and see. All I have to do is start accumulating available going-bankrupt pharmacies! Ha, ha, ha!'

And then, Stephen Fischer focused his attention on the Herculean Grecian urn that he had just strangely obtained by virtue of inheritance. Staring at what his now-dull mind perceived as a 'bad-conversation piece', the totally soused contemporary "apothecary" spoke sarcastically to the inanimate urn. "Oh, mighty and intrepid Hercules! If you're dwelling inside this horrendous-looking Grecian vase, please have the courtesy of showing yourself! Ha, ha, ha! I dare you to come-out of that ceramic pottery jug, or whatever the heck it is!"

A puff of light green smoke wafted-up and eddied-out of the ancient urn, and then a gaseous, two-legged form leaped-out onto the den's Oriental rug, and next, the vaporized, archaic-looking muscleman gradually grew from a mere foot-high to a remarkable height of nearly seven-foot-tall. The impressive, bearded fellow (actually a splendid itinerant/anachronism) sported a wide frown on his weather-worn, tan countenance that immediately intimidated the shocked and startled possessor of the Grecian urn. Hercules was indeed a tremendous sight to behold.

"What's going on here?" startled Stephen Fischer stammered. "Who are you? You look a lot like the illustrations of ancient Hercules I had seen in a book I've just recently viewed, and you also bear a peculiar resemblance to the famed fellow repeatedly painted on that Grecian urn! Are you the legendary Hercules?"

"Indeed, I am!" the incomparable giant bellowed in a booming voice that made the hanging light suspended from the wooden cathedral ceiling shake. "And I'm here in *your* reality because you had just summoned my name. Actually, I haven't had decent employment in over a hundred-years, so I'm really bored and eagerly chomping at the bit to attempt some brave act that truly requires plenty of strength and dexterity. What is your name, Master? Are you a wealthy king or rich potentate? Perhaps a powerful wizard, or maybe an experimenting alchemist?"

"My name's Stephen Fischer, and I *am* some sort of an alchemist," the staggered homeowner answered, sobering-up from his *Southern Comfort* fantasy adventure in a hurry. "Tell me, now Hercules, why did you kill your wife and burn-down your house according to the descriptive myth I had just read?"

"That's personal business between King Eurystheus and me," the hero loudly responded as the hanging lamp again began vibrating. "As you can plainly see and discern, I can speak many languages, including yours. That particular natural ability came over the centuries with the terrible curse that has kept me captive inside that miserable urn since ancient times. Now then, do you wish to learn more about our relationship, or should I say, about *our* unique partnership?"

"Sure Hercules, anything you say," Stephen reflexively acceded and complied. "After all, I am your Master, and basically, my secret wish is probably your command."

"Not exactly!" the huge hero disagreed. "Well anyway, I still have to endure two additional Masters after you, Stephen Fischer, before I'm finally liberated from my horrendous three-millennia incarceration," the mighty Hercules informed his almost-mesmerized new Master. "And just like I had obediently performed exceptional deeds to satisfy my moral debt to the very vindictive King Eurysthesus," the illustrious champion elaborated, "I'm presently committed by the tyrannical king to enact twelve new labors for *you*. All you have to do, Master, is utter the code word 'Heracles' and I'll appear and assist you out of a major crisis or problem. Is that information perfectly clear?"

"Please, Hercules. Give me some guidance. What does 'Heracles' mean?" the intrigued owner of the urn asked.

"Heracles is actually the Roman name for the Greek appellation Hercules!" the immense strongman explained. "Are you especially dense? Perhaps a slow-learner, or what?"

"Have you ever met Aladdin's genie?" Stephen frivolously inquired, lacking something more rational and more appropriate to communicate.

"Who the Hades is Aladdin, and what's a genie, if I may ask?" Hercules wanted to know.

"Never mind! It's all totally irrelevant to our essential relationship!" Fischer smartly replied.

"Okay about that!" the massive figure vociferated, almost loud enough for distant Pine Road neighbors to hear. "Now remember this essential instruction, Stephen Fischer. If you urgently require my vital services, just say the name 'Heracles' and I'll show-up and merrily help you out of your predicament, just out of sheer obedience. Now, I suggest that you not drink any more alcoholic beverage and that you sip-down a cup of hot black coffee, and then take two aspirins before retiring to bed. And don't take a hot or cold shower, either. You might slip and fall-down in the tub, or cubicle, and if you're unconscious, you can't possibly summon me to your rescue in order to help you out of your dilemma. And besides that," the inflexible Hercules emphasized with a stern expression featured on his visage, "I'm a little deficient in administering quality medical aid! I should've taken a few fundamental lessons from Hippocrates! And finally, Master, I'll dutifully perform twelve special labors for you as I had done for the despotic King of Mycenae!"

And after announcing those marvelous words, recommendations, and explicit directions, the famous hero instantaneously shrunk-down to one-foot in height, and then quickly jumped high into the Grecian urn, with his inimitable laugh echoing-out of the top of the wondrous object.

* * * * * * * * * * * * * *

The following Monday afternoon, Stephen Fischer left his Bellevue Avenue Towne Pharmacy in his manager's charge and drove ten-miles north on two-lane State *Highway 206* to the popular local eatery, the Pic-A-Lilli Inn, which was frequented by South Jersey pineys, black leather jacketed motorcycle enthusiasts, and in-need-of-a-bath deer hunters. 'The Pic-A-Lilli has great hot wings and terrific baby-back ribs!' the hungry apothecary thought as his vehicle passed the popular Red Barn breakfast and lunch spot on his left. 'And not too many people from Hammonton go there, so I'll just enjoy a great dinner, sitting at the bar before the noisy supper crowd arrives. It's too early for *Southern Comfort,* so I'll just settle for a couple of *Coor's Lights*.'

All during his ride up *206,* the 'chemist' contemplated his 'almost surreal' encounter with the authentic Hercules. 'That weird visitation had to be some sort of aberration, a phantasm of sorts,' the prospective tavern patron assessed. 'I don't place too much credence in the experience whatsoever, simply because I had been partially drunk during the entire inexplicable encounter. Greek mythology went-out of vogue over two-thousand-years-ago. Perhaps I'll need psychiatric care if the perplexing illusion ever happens again,' the driver of the brand-new white Nissan Maxima mused. 'I don't want my delicate psyche haunted by disturbing redundant hallucinations.'

The hot wings and the pork ribs were delectable, and on his way back from 'Indian Mills', upon passing Atsion Lake to his right, Fischer remembered something that he felt needed to be addressed. 'I want to get an estimate for new tile in my hall bathroom. I'll take *County Route 536* through the pine barrens and meet-up with my former brother-in-law at his place over in Waterford to discuss the price and installation,' the full-bellied driver decided. 'It's six p.m. and Ollie's probably just getting home for dinner. I'll pull-over and give him a call on my cell phone. I don't want to get a traffic ticket from an overly ambitious backwoods cop on patrol. Pretty soon, even game wardens and forest rangers will be giving motor vehicle citations in this money-hungry state!'

After steering his white Nissan Maxima onto the deserted road's grassy shoulder, Stephen opened his cell phone, but much to his frustration, the battery was too weak to transmit an adequate signal. And then, the driver's acute hearing detected a hissing sound. 'Oh no! Of all the bad luck! When I pulled over to make the phone call, I got a flat tire. Pretty soon, it'll be dark, and now I can't call Triple A for road service. Sometimes, it doesn't pay to be too law-abiding!' the demoralized driver regretted and concluded. 'I knew I should've driven down to *Route 30* and taken the Pike west to Waterford. This lousy shortcut through the dense forest has proven to be a veritable nightmare. Twilight's setting-in, and it's quickly getting dark out. Damn it! I used to know how to change a tire back in the sixties, but these new-fangled crank jacks are completely alien to me.'

Stephen disgustedly exited the comfortable automobile and evaluated the damage to his right front tire. The disgruntled driver angrily opened his trunk and removed his lug wrench. 'Tire's only get flat on the bottom!' the incensed motorist mused, trying to think in a more positive and constructive frame of mind.

A junkyard hound-dog was wildly barking several-hundred-feet away, and *that* fearsome sound was the only sign of any possible human habitation along the desolate country road. Remembering his 'mental manifestation' in his home's den regarding the inherited Grecian urn, Fischer instinctively mumbled the name 'Heracles', and much to *his* surprise, the notorious hero from antiquity appeared upon solicitation.

"Do you require my immediate assistance, Master?" the brute of a man asked. "This metallic mode of transportation you've been utilizing seems to be debilitated. How may I help you?"

"If you can," the amazed owner of the Grecian urn uttered, "lift up the right front side of my vehicle, er, I mean, of my modern chariot while I change the tire and put a donut, er, I meant to say, a new tire onto the front wheel. Can you do that?"

"Easier done than said!" the exceptional seven-foot-tall physical specimen answered with a broad smile. "But only as long as I don't get my cherished lion-skin dirty. This furry, itchy outfit is the only haberdashery I have, you know!"

Within five-minutes, the flat tire had been successfully replaced with the donut, thanks to Hercules' incredible strength and inexhaustible energy. The fantastic show-off even held the front of the car two-feet off the ground with only one hand during the whole tire change. And after the first labor had been comprehensively completed, the fabulous marvel instantly disappeared into thin air, presumably journeying-back to his Grecian urn enclosure. The changed tire, along with its flat counterpart, represented the only evidence of the hero's former presence in that desolate, back-road setting.

'One down and eleven to go!' Stephen recalled and counted. 'After visiting my friend Ollie in Waterford, I'll take my Nissan to AT Auto Clinic first thing tomorrow morning. I dare not tell Anthony or Lou about how I managed to change the tire in the dark on a deserted country pine barrens' road. There're entirely too many skeptics and cynics in this modern age! Who says that magic and mythology are obsolete?'

Three nights later a terrible spring storm descended on Hammonton, and at three a.m. a bolt of lightning (accompanied by a loud thunderclap) scorched a tall oak tree situated next to the jinxed pharmacist's Pine Road abode. The trunk of the enormous tree uprooted, and the bulk of its weight crashed-down onto Fischer's house, and violently penetrated the roof with jagged limbs entering Stephen's bedroom. Immediately, the aroused and frightened bed occupant summoned his new-found servant 'Heracles'.

"Yes. Master. What can I do for you?" the fearless hulk requested. "You're quite lucky that my indispensable services are available twenty-four hours a day, seven days a week."

"Are you mentally retarded or what, Hercules? Can't you see that I'm trapped in my bed and have nearly gotten killed by this humungus tree crashing-down through the ceiling!" the flustered act-of-God victim yelled. "And besides that, I'm getting all wet! Act quickly and get me out of this room right away, and then remove the encumbering tree limbs before the entire roof collapses and crushes me right into the floor!"

"Do you have an ax?" Hercules calmly asked. "The job can be done in a jiffy if I have the proper implement!"

"Yes, but a chain saw can do the task a lot quicker!" the still startled resident insisted and exclaimed.

"Forget this modern technology stuff that I don't know how to operate!" Hercules petulantly replied. "You can't teach an old mutt new tricks, you know! A simple ordinary ax will do just fine. I'll easily perform the perfunctory task you've mandated before you can ever recite the Greek alphabet from alpha to omega! But Master, make sure your ax isn't a mere toy hatchet!"

"Okay, go quickly into the garage. That's the room where I park my car, er, I mean my white chariot," Stephen anxiously instructed and clarified. "You'll find an ax in the corner of the garage near the laundry room door, er, I mean right near the particular door leading into the house!"

Astonishingly, Hercules was able to chop the invasive tree into small parts and then mechanically chuck the heavy chunks through the huge hole in the ceiling and roof, directly into the back yard in a matter of ten minutes. Stephen was freed from his entrapment, and when the urn owner turned-around to gratefully thank his rescuer, Hercules had already disappeared without a trace of ever being in the bedroom to render *his* inimitable assistance.

'I don't know if having Hercules around is a curse or a blessing!' Stephen pensively thought. 'I'd have him repair the roof, but I don't want to expire another wish. I don't know if it's a coincidence or not, but ever since I've gotten the Grecian urn, I've experienced a horrible bad luck skein. Perhaps the urn *is* cursed. I've never had a tree plummet through my bedroom ceiling before! It'll cost me a small fortune to get a carpenter here and fix the devastation. Oh well, I guess I should consider myself fortunate to still be alive! Thank God the heavy rain has stopped!' But then the still jittery homeowner had a change of heart and mind. Out of necessity, he again summoned Hercules to start repairing the damaged roof at daybreak.

"No problem, Master!" Hercules agreed to undertake the simple project. "I'll easily do this side job. I promise that I won't charge you for overtime! And I'll even give you a small bonus in the meantime. Is there anything else of a minor nature that requires my attention before I get started on this elementary-type roof repair project?"

"Yes, Hercules. You can carry the heavy desk that the furniture store had delivered yesterday from the side screen porch into the computer room, er, I mean into the spare room at the other end of the hall," Stephen ordered. "I'm sure that *that* additional minor job I've just mentioned will be minuscule and picayune when compared to slaying a nine-headed dragon, er, I mean Hydra; or venturing down to Hades, or holding-up the sky for Atlas while the Titan performed a special favor for you by skillfully retrieving the three golden apples!"

And as had remarkably been demonstrated before, Hercules (with facility) completed his assigned roof labor and attendant desk transport favor, and then magically vanished in a puff of green smoke, without ever waiting-around to be either thanked or acknowledged.

* * * * * * * * * * * * * *

Three days later, the Pine Road resident was preoccupied inspecting certain materials left off by a tractor-trailer to be used to erect a white picket fence around his well-manicured backyard lawn. 'Why should I pay three workmen four-hundred-dollars each when I could economize and have Hercules do the required work for gratis?' the parsimonious pharmacist determined. 'After all, I still have nine labors remaining, and my temporary Greek genie will efficiently and competently get the job done.' So, without any additional thought, the owner of the inherited urn spoke the magic name "Heracles."

"Hercules, I want you to construct this white picket fence around the perimeter of my back yard," Stephen commanded his Grecian urn servant. "It would take three workmen an entire day to finish the job. How long would you estimate that it'll take you? Six-hours, I would guess."

"A half hour at the most," the musclebound fellow replied and promised. "The building of the fence isn't even a Promethean task, let alone an arduous Herculean task. This third labor will be like stealing milk and honey from a baby gorilla."

"Make sure you don't allow any of my nosy neighbors to see you in action," the wary homeowner imperatively insisted. "I don't want them to report any suspicious activities to the police. I've had enough personal trouble lately without having any unnecessary added aggravation!"

"Allay your silly fears, Master!" Hercules assertively exclaimed. "Confidentially, whenever I initiate a labor, you'll be the only one who'll be able to witness my stellar performance. All that any other people in the vicinity will see is a puff of green smoke appear, and then later, again form and finally vanish. Yes, smoke without mirrors is my personal motto!"

A week after the white picket fence had been "professionally erected and completed", Stephen Fischer stepped-out of his Bellevue Avenue pharmacy and ambled two blocks to the Hammonton Post Office on the corner of Central Avenue and Third Street. Three hooded Ku Klux Klan members were distributing literature in front of the federal edifice, the phony subject matter describing the hate organization's opposition to asbestos that had been recently discovered in the demolition of a local municipal building. The six-foot-seven hooded Klan leader attempted handing the harried local businessman a pamphlet.

"Get that freakin' brochure and shove it where the sun doesn't shine!" the town apothecary strenuously objected. "You're just trying to give some legitimacy to your offensive hate propaganda, and coyly using asbestos as a vehicle to accomplish your sinister goal."

"Watch your tongue, Buddy!" the burly surly Grand Dragon shouted directly into Stephen's face. "You could've just declined my solicitation courteously, rather than become so damned belligerent."

"I don't have to stand here and argue with you three losers!" the livid pharmacist countered his new-found adversaries. "Go advocate your discrimination and your violence tactics somewhere else! Your vile primitive, hate philosophy belongs in an earlier century!"

The three insulted Ku Klux Klan members grabbed their vocal critic and began jostling the local businessman around. Fischer immediately uttered the name "Heracles", the superhero obediently appeared, and soon very expertly tossed the first Klan member onto the post office's slanted roof; the second antagonist was wildly flung into a nearby maple tree, and the third instigator was swiftly hurled onto the flagpole of the Hammonton Police Station, situated next door to the Post Office. A crowd of twenty spectators watched the melee develop and progress, but all the stunned bystanders could see were three bodies shooting-out in different directions from the central point of conflict in front of the town Post Office. Thus, the fourth sensational labor had been successfully consummated.

That afternoon, Stephen drove his shiny white automobile to the Bank of America office located on the corner of Broadway and *Route 30,* (the White Horse Pike) to make a business deposit. Two heavily armed, masked bandits entered the establishment and ordered all customers to get-down on the floor. Fischer confidently whispered the magic name "Heracles", and the dependable ancient Greek showed-up in a second; grabbed the first confused crook, and quickly tossed the thug into the bank's opened vault. And then, in the blink of an eye, the invisible, invincible muscleman latched onto the second culprit, and flung the surprised criminal through a thick pane glass window, knocking the dangerous crook unconscious. Then, Hercules gave Stephen Fischer a wink that only *he* could perceive before the servant of the urn crystallized into the oxygen, hydrogen, and nitrogen gas around him. Challenging Labor Number #5 had been satisfactorily performed.

The following week was uneventful with the charmed pharmacist going about his daily routines without any significant complications or difficulties. On Monday, Fischer did his standard laundry and dry-cleaning visitation. On Tuesday, Stephen enacted his evening grocery shopping at SuperFresh and ShopRite. His biweekly haircut was done on Wednesday at Salon FX, and the Hammonton resident's Thursday evening Bruni's "extra-thick" tomato and cheese pizza was greedily consumed. And then predictably, the lucky owner of the Grecian urn played cards and drank beer with "the boys" on Friday night at the Sons of Italy Garibaldi Lodge on North Third Street.

On Sunday afternoon, Fischer drove his impeccable Nissan Maxima to the town's gravel carnival grounds on North Third Street and boarded a chartered bus headed for the Showboat Casino on the boardwalk in Atlantic City. The Hammonton Lions Club was sponsoring the trip (and a fundraiser) that was earmarked for its sight and hearing projects, and being a past president of that noble organization, the pharmacist wholeheartedly supported the event.

Midway between Hammonton and Egg Harbor, the bus veered off the White Horse Pike and skidded into a ditch, just barely missing a telephone pole. Several passengers were shaken-up, but no one had been seriously injured from the jolt of suddenly stopping. Before anyone could exit the tilted vehicle, Stephen softly uttered the name "Heracles", and the genie-like giant showed-up and with dispatch, pulled the bus (much to the passengers' utter astonishment) back onto the shoulder of the highway, thus allowing the driver to again pilot the large vehicle eastward towards Atlantic City. Labor #6 had been officially accomplished.

The next week Steve and his best buddy and pinochle partner Mark Benedetto drove to South Philadelphia to attend a Philadelphia Phillies and New York Mets baseball game at Citizens Bank Park. In the seventh inning, the Pine Road fan excused himself to a Men's Room on the stadium's second level, and while inside the crowded quarters, Fischer was accosted by several irate Mets' fans, who took umbrage with the Hammonton man's red Phillies cap. Soon, a loud verbal altercation ensued.

"Give me that hat so I can spit into it and hurl the crummy thing into that trash can!" the first obnoxious and drunk Mets' fan demanded. "That red hat's an abomination!"

"Yeah, Creep! Do as my pal is sayin', or else you'll wind-up in the trash can, too!" the second nasty itinerant Queens punk directed. "I always said you Phillies' rooters were garbage! Ha, ha, ha!"

Before the New Jersey rooter ever complied with the rude jerks' orders, the accosters targeted victim casually articulated the name "Heracles" and in the next thirty-seconds, both two-hundred-and-fifty-pound bullies had been simultaneously elevated off the tile floor (seemingly against the laws of gravity), and then hastily thrown over two lavatory stalls, landing directly upon the seated and defenseless bodies of two other taken-by-surprise Mets' fans. Stephen Fischer shrugged his shoulders while staring at other Mets and Phillies fans (standing with their mouths agape) inside the crowded men's room, and then after conducting his bathroom business, the triumphant fellow nonchalantly returned to his box seat rejoining Mark Benedetto, who never learned of the incredible 'Men's Lavatory incident". Deed #7 had been effectively executed.

On the following Saturday morning in June, Stephen decided to drive to Atlantic City and use his fifty-dollar cash coupon at Bally's Casino before the valuable comp' would expire. While walking along Pacific Avenue, the stroller was solicited by a rather obese blonde prostitute. The anxious gambler refused her brazen offer, and then the hooker's pimp leaped-out from behind a parking attendant's small building and wielded a knife that was pointed directly at the pedestrian's chest. The prospective Bally's patron muttered the name "Heracles", and two-seconds later, a ball of green smoke formed, suddenly distracting the astonished pimp brandishing the sharp blade. The invisible servant next lifted the struggling scoundrel off the sidewalk; stepped-over to a black hearse that had stopped at a traffic signal; opened the back compartment's latch, and next energetically deposited the puzzled bully inside, before hastily slamming the door shut. Consequently, Labor #8 had become history.

Tuesday evening, June 26th arrived on the kitchen calendar, and Stephen Fischer motored east on *Route 30* to engage in his weekly ritual of grocery shopping at SuperFresh and at ShopRite. June traditionally meant blueberry season to Hammonton area farmers, the community advertising itself as "The Blueberry Capital of the World". At nighttime, many Mexican farm laborers would hang-around outside the Wal-Mart and also next to the SuperFresh store, having nothing better to do with spending their idle time.

While casually pushing his loaded shopping cart out of the busy SuperFresh chain store, Stephen noticed five Mexicans desperately attempting to break into his prized white Nissan Maxima. "Hey you! Stop or I'll call the police!"

"Look here, Gringo. Shut your mouth, or you'll be pushin' up daisies in the nearest cemetery!" the chief instigator threatened in broken English as his on-a-mission companions continued to manipulate the automobile's door handles. Without wasting another precious second, Stephen pronounced the noun "Heracles!" and before anyone could say "enchilada" or "hacienda", five over-matched and totally vanquished dizzy Mexican aggressors wound-up in the nearby Salvation Army Deposit Bin. Hence, Labor #9 came to fruition.

* * * * * * * * * * * * * *

On Sunday afternoon, July 22, 2007 Stephen Fischer was driving north up *State Highway 206* to again consume some scrumptious hot wings and pork ribs at the notorious Pic-A-Lilli Inn. 'I only have three more Herculean labors to use to my benefit,' the possessor of the splendid Grecian urn comprehended. 'I'll have to employ discretion and choose how I should wisely utilize my last several emergency Greek hero interventions. But honestly,' the worried pharmacist pondered and evaluated. 'I've never had such unexpected arguments and disputes with bellicose people cropping-up *before* I owned the ornate, gaudy-looking urn. Oh well, there's placid Atsion Lake on my left, and I'll be at the Pic-A-Lilli in less than two minutes.'

Inside the popular Pine Barrens establishment, the jukebox was playing loudly, and groups of boisterous pineys and raucous bikers were preoccupied with playing pool and air hockey games on the available tables, and several locals were busy taking turns aiming darts at a wall target board. The new arrival sat-down upon a black bar stool and gave his order to the accommodating waitress on duty. An attractive biker girl and her scruffy-looking escort were seated at the far corner of the crowded bar and sharing drinks and laughs with a gang of tattooed Harley Davidson guys wearing cut-off blue denim jackets with the designation "Renegades" emblazoned on the back.

After consuming his spicy meal and downing three brown bottles of cold *Coor's Lightd,* the bashful, self-disciplined Hammonton businessman paid his bill, left a generous tip, and then exited the lively tavern. Fischer's path was followed by a bevy of drunken bikers, one of whom shouted a derogatory criticism in the departing diner's direction.

"Hey, Jerk! what's the big idea of making goo-goo eyes at my girlfriend!" the mean-looking, scar-faced dude hollered in front of his amused peers, who were egging him on with continuing his bullying taunts. "Me and my Harley friends are gonna' make mince meat outa' ya,' whether ya' answer me or not!"

Eight fierce-looking bikers (that looked like they hadn't taken baths or showers in months) quickly surrounded their suddenly-beleaguered prey, who soon abandoned his generally lackadaisical attitude. "Heracles!" Stephen bellowed loudly enough for his un-illustrious, new-found adversaries to hear.

"What did you call me?" the jealous and acrimonious instigator asked. "You're gonna' be road kill, Buddy!"

A wild brawl instantly ensued with bodies flying all over the place as the then-invisible Hercules assiduously attacked his unwary opponents and swiftly knocked their torsos over parked cars and motorcycles. Several bearded pineys who loved fisticuffs got into the fray, and the pugnacious locals too were appropriately mauled and disposed of by the incomparable Greek strongman. In less than a minute, eleven tough guys and their previously vociferous dates were sprawled all over the popular inn's parking lot, moaning, groaning and gasping for air. Stephen Fischer then casually sauntered-over to his white Nissan Maxima; nonchalantly climbed inside; quite deliberately fired-up the engine, and slowly backed out as if nothing irregular had ever happened. Modern Day Labor #10 had been brutally fulfilled.

* * * * * * * * * * * * * *

The lazy hazy days of summer were coming to a close. In late August, Stephen had taken a few automobile excursions over to the Ocean City and the Wildwood boardwalks with his best pal Mark Benedetto, but no incidents of any consequence had transpired with ill-tempered, self-appointed, destructive enemies. But the roller coaster on Hunts Pier had stalled at the top of the steep first hill, and soon Hercules had been summoned to free the amusement ride (with the two Hammonton natives aboard) from its encumbrance. Thus, much to Stephen Fischer's disgust and Mark Benedetto's relief, Labor #11 had been enacted near the Wildwood Boardwalk.

On Labor Day, the Grecian urn possessor received a call from his sister Anne, who had just purchased an ultra-modern duplex in sunny South Padre Island, Texas. The conversation between the siblings was cordial, but nevertheless, quite surprising to the brother.

"Steve, how would you like to fly-down here from Philly' to South Padre?" Anne affably invited. "It's a really neat place. Phil and I would love to have you as our honored guest. It's only twenty-miles north of the Mexican border; the beaches are phenomenal, and the summer crowds ought to be gone, so we'll practically have the whole island to ourselves. And as you might not know, South Padre Island is called the 'Shrimp Capital of the United States'."

"South Padre Island!" Steve imagined and stated. "Isn't that the new Fort Lauderdale where the college kids go on their spring break?"

"Yes, but that's just in March and April, and you'll be down here in September when the entire resort has been nearly evacuated by tourists. And the Gulf's water temperature should be in the high seventies and low eighties," Anne convincingly framed her invitation. "It'll be like a week in paradise. You'll be going from the Blueberry Capital of the U.S. to the Shrimp Capital!"

"Are there any direct flights from 'Philly?" Fischer wanted to know.

"You'll have to take Continental Airlines, 'Philly to Houston," Anne specifically explained. "That'll be around a three-and-a-half-hour flight. And then you'll have to fly Continental from Houston to Brownsville, another full hour in the air. Phil and I will pick you up at the airport once you land. And then, South Padre is only twenty or so miles north of Brownsville. You won't even have to rent a car."

"Great info' ! I'll book plane reservations for the week of September 25th to October 2nd," Fischer related as he circled the important dates on his kitchen wall calendar.

"Terrific!" Anne exclaimed. "Phil and I can't wait to see you. He's driving down from our California home in Palm Springs and should be here tomorrow afternoon. I'll call my husband on his cell and tell him the good tidings. So long, Steve. And as the classic song goes, 'I'll see you in September'." Click.

The next few weeks elapsed rather smoothly for Stephen Fischer, who then boarded Continental Flight 177 at precisely 2:05 p.m. from the D Concourse of Philadelphia International Airport. In another ten-minutes, the southbound jet was taxiing-down the runway, and seconds later, gracefully ascending into the air. The first hour and a half of the flight was not inordinate, but then suddenly, somewhere over Tennessee, three Muslims dressed in conventional western-style business suits and ties stood-up and began screaming commands while holding and waving switchblade knives and Korans.

"Okay you American pigs; be prepared to die and sacrifice yourselves to Allah!" the leader of the ruthless hijackers arrogantly yelled. "In case you're wondering, one of your pilots in the cockpit is a Muslim associate of ours, and the entire plane is now under our control!"

"And if you're curious about how we had smuggled our weapons aboard with all the tight airport security," a Muslim accomplice bellowed, “the knives had been strategically placed under our seats by Arab security workers at the ‘Philly Airport.”

“Heracles!” Stephen Fischer softly said amidst gasps and delirious cries coming from the mouths of hysterical passengers and flight attendants. In another ten-seconds, the invisible, indestructible Greek hero began flinging the terrorists’ bodies all over the anterior part of the airplane, smashing and breaking their skulls open with his pummeling blows. And then, the relentless ancient Greek champion easily cracked-open the cabin door with his powerful right fist, and savagely molested the shouting Arab co-pilot, who was then violently strangled, dying instantly from a broken neck and a fractured cranium. Thus, the twelfth and final Herculean labor had been achieved.

* * * * * * * * * * * * *

The national newspapers and the major TV and cable networks intensively covered the incredible “jet plane massacre”, and no passenger interviewed could logically account for the “very extraordinary salvation from impending disaster”. Stephen Fischer eventually recuperated from his most recent ordeal, and after returning home from glorious South Padre Island on October 2nd, the somewhat-disappointed vacationer was pleased to receive a phone call from his Baltimore cousin Eleanor Damysen.

“Hi, Steve,” Eleanor began. “I have a favor to ask of you. I hope you can oblige.”

“If I can render assistance, I’ll be more-than-happy to help,” Fischer suavely answered. “What’s your pleasure?”

“Well, Steve, Aunt Marie Mayor had left me a funny-looking Grecian urn that I understand is quite similar to the one that you had inherited,” Eleanor elegantly prefaced. “So, since I’m not the least bit interested in keeping my artifact, or whatever it is, and since you have a matching one in your care, would you be interested in obtaining the second urn. If so, I’ll wrap it up carefully, and send the hideous-looking artifact to you via UPS. You could have it by early next week.”

“Is the character represented on the external paintings Heracles, er, I mean, Hercules?” the befuddled but suddenly intrigued Hammonton apothecary inquired. “That’s the one that I have. The grotesque-looking item features Hercules!”

“No, I asked around and checked the illustrations, or paintings, or whatever the depictions are in a reliable encyclopedia, and the designs all seem to be renditions of an ancient Greek hero named Achilles," Eleanor informed her now-inspired New Jersey cousin. "You know, the guy with the vulnerable heel!"

"Well Eleanor, to tell you the honest-to-goodness truth, I'm not exactly enamored with *my* Grecian urn, either," Stephen bluntly replied, feigning disappointment. "But for you, I'll suffer through having another atrocious-looking jug, if it'll make you satisfied that a dependable person such as myself will safely keep and loyally guard Aunt Marie Mayor's set of hideous-looking, ancient urns."

“Parallel Developments”

Twin brothers Frank and Fred Davies were 1981 graduates of Hammonton High School, North Liberty Street, Hammonton, New Jersey 08037. From their early youth the twins were complete opposites both in demeanor and in physical prowess. Fred Davies was always an extrovert and a competitive athlete while his twin facsimile Frank had a shy personality genuinely punctuated with humility and modesty.

In June of 1987 Fred graduated from Philadelphia’s *Temple University* with a law degree and Frank evolved out of New Brunswick’s *Rutgers University* with a master’s degree in biology research. In the fall of 1991 during a dual ceremony Frank and Fred ironically married twin sisters Lois and Eleanor Cataldi of Bridgeton, a large town situated twenty-four miles southwest of Hammonton.

In order to celebrate their fifteenth wedding anniversary Frank and Lois booked a Mediterranean vacation featuring two nights in Barcelona and a seven-day-cruise aboard the resplendent Regal Adventurer. Coincidentally, Fred and Eleanor (through the same travel agency) also made arrangements on a similar vacation aboard the Regal Adventurer, but the former couple’s scheduled dates were Wednesday September 13th to Saturday the 20th while the latter pair’s sailing dates were several weeks later from Wednesday, October 4th to Saturday October 11th.

“How come Fred and Eleanor aren’t going to accompany us to Europe?” Lois asked her husband as they waited for the van to pick them up for the thirty-mile drive to *Philadelphia International Airport*. “Do we have leprosy or something?”

“Certainly not!” Frank politely answered. “My brother and I mutually agreed that we should take separate vacations touring Spain, the French Riviera and Italy. We thought it would be too confusing for everyone we met or communicated with by having two sets of identical twins. And besides Lois,” Frank persuasively communicated, “you honestly don’t get along too keenly with Fred and quite candidly I don’t hit it off too well with my loudmouth sister-in-law, er, excuse me, with your twin sister. And I do believe Lois that the eight people we’re traveling with will be more compatible with us than Fred and Eleanor will ever be. In the final analysis that’s the bottom line!”

“I suppose I have to subscribe to the basic wisdom you’ve just expressed!” Lois confessed. “Here comes the van now zipping down the Pike approaching our driveway! Let’s carry our four pieces of luggage from the front porch.”

"And as you know, Lois, Fred and I have different sets of friends," the husband emphasized and clarified. "And as a matter of fact so do you and Eleanor. Warren and Melissa Mottola are much more mellow and gracious than Fred and Eleanor will ever be. And I want this trip to be as relaxing and comfortable as possible without those two garrulous nitwits ruining every meal and every sidebar excursion on our hectic itinerary!"

"Yes, my dear Husband!" Lois verified. "We seem to harmonize better with retired science teachers and their accountant wives than we do with relative lawyers and their flamboyant spouses. Warren is studious and academic just like you are," the wife maintained, "and Melissa is generally quiet and likeable. I guess it's because she's always concentrating with numbers and figures at work. That's why she and her soft-spoken husband aren't wild and crazy lunatics like Fred and Eleanor are!"

The cranberry-colored van pulled into the two-story gray colonial home's U-shaped driveway and halted right where the cement walk bordered the asphalt driveway. Immediately the driver hopped out of the vehicle and introduced himself.

"Hi, I'm Tom Dixon!" the man cheerfully greeted. "Why don't you two hop into the van and join your friends! I'll take care of loading your bags into the back storage compartment."

"Thanks!" Frank politely acknowledged. "You look trustworthy enough Tom! It's great to see that courtesy hasn't gone completely out of fashion! My wife and I appreciate your fine gesture!"

Frank and Lois were immediately welcomed by Warren and Melissa Mottola, who were seated near their pretty office manager daughter Lisa and her handsome fiancé David Winters, a young and serious corporate jet pilot. Other passengers in the enormous cranberry van were Jimmy and Joanne Valerio, a construction contractor and an accountant respectively with Joanne being employed in the same CPA's office as Lois. Rounding out the party of ten Europe-bound-Americans were Dr. Rose Jeffries (an infectious disease specialist at Camden's Cooper Hospital) and her new-found friend Judy Marks, a comptroller for a large automobile agency in Marlton, New Jersey. Soon after Tom Dixon had carefully arranged the new baggage in the van's rear, he re-entered the vehicle, slammed the door shut, fastened his seat-belt and casually started-up the engine.

The thirty-mile drive from Hammonton to Philadelphia was quite pleasant. The late summer scenery still displayed deciduous trees with ample green leaves about to assume their predictable autumnal hues. The men's conversation focused on the latest professional baseball and football scores and the rising stock market while the ladies preferred exchanging dialogue on the best clothes to take along on the trip and the various sights to be explored on the general itinerary. In a short forty-five minutes the van stopped in front of the *U.S. Airways* terminal in the newly renovated section of *Philadelphia International Airport*.

After paying Tom Dixon the appropriate fee and tip for his vital services, the ten passengers hired a skycap to transport their twenty pieces of luggage inside to the *U.S Airways* ticket counter. That particular procedure was conducted rather expeditiously and after the necessary passports and photo' ID's were officially checked, five minutes later the ten anxious travelers passed through the airport's tight security check.

"I hate being treated like a terrorist!" Lois complained. "But Frank, you're so mild-mannered that it's just like water off a duck's back to you."

"Why get upset with taking your shoes off and having them scanned along with your other personal belongings?" the husband passively accepted and stated. "Why become neurotic about what you can't change! And since everyone flying out of 'Philly has to go through the same process, it's perfectly tolerable! After all Lois, we're not being discriminated against!"

"Sometimes, you're so soberly philosophical!" the wife sincerely complimented. "That's one reason why I was so attracted to you when we first met at that wild party in Atlantic City! I really admired your calm disposition!"

"I'll try not to talk too much on the seven-hour flight to Barcelona!" the husband bantered tongue-in-cheek. "And I'll speak even less on the grueling eight-hour trip on the way back!"

"I can't believe we're actually going to Europe!" Lois jubilantly exclaimed. "I mean I've read about it in high school textbooks and in encyclopedias," the spouse marveled and said, "but now it's like a dream come true! Let's make the most of it! It might be a once in a lifetime opportunity!"

"Yeah, Honey!" the normally laconic husband readily concurred. "After going eight times to the Caribbean and twice to both San Diego and Las Vegas, this long jaunt sort of represents a departure from the ordinary. Outside of a cruise boat stop in Caracas, Venezuela, this is really only our second removal from the North American Continent. I hope we have a smooth flight!"

"I checked the forecast on the *Internet,*" Lois assured. "And it's going to be clear skies all the way to Barcelona except for an hour of mild turbulence. I can't wait to leave the New World for the Old! Maybe next time we can do Madrid, Paris, London and Berlin instead of Barcelona, Marseilles, Rome and Naples!"

"Anything you say, Lois! Anything you say!" the husband reiterated. "And just think! Thanks to modern-day airport security we only have to wait two hours before we finally board our wonderful airplane! We're scheduled to take off at 5:45 p.m. and then finally arrive in Spain at…."

"At approximately 7:45 a.m.!" Lois alertly finished Frank's sentence. "Already we're trapped in a time warp and soon destined to suffer significant jet-lag! But don't worry! We have the rest of our lives to recuperate!"

"You should do stand-up comedy, even when you're sitting down!" Frank mused and expressed. "Now let's interact with our eight friends before they receive the impression that we're both anti-social in addition to being extremely introverted!"

The seven-hour flight from Philadelphia to Barcelona was *not* interrupted with an hour of rough air pockets (as Lois had predicted from reading various weather reports) and a two-hour movie, random magazine scrutiny and a decent chicken and rice meal had sufficiently distracted the passengers from their lengthy confinement and overall travail. A weak drizzle awaited U.S. Airways Flight 948 when it finally touched-down and landed on its destination runway on Spain's eastern coast.

The passengers had to be transported by bus from the tarmac to the Immigration and Customs Terminal, an adventure *not* characteristic of most major big-city U.S. airports. *That* specific inconvenience was followed with an hour-long-delay while waiting for the passengers' baggage to arrive on the Barcelona terminal's luggage carousel.

"I hope that this isn't indicative of the remainder of our tour," the usually reticent Frank Davies remarked to Jimmy Valerio. "I suppose it's true that we Americans are quite spoiled and too used to instant gratification."

"Yeah, Frank!" Jimmy nodded and confirmed. "It could be said that Americans are like wristwatches, always thinking 'Get-there, get there,' while many Europeans are like grandfather clocks practicing the mantra 'Take your time, take your time!' Maybe we'd be happier with pacifiers in our mouths!"

"It's only 8:45 a.m.," an eavesdropping Warren Mottola reminded his male companions. "We have all day to squander if we ever escape this suitcase acquisition and retrieval area."

"You're absolutely right there, Warren!" Frank diplomatically commented. "But I insist that it's over three-hours too early for the old Spanish noon-to-three siesta tradition. And as you've so appropriately suggested Warren, let's act like amiable and cooperative tourists rather than as typical dissatisfied and ultra-critical picayune Americans."

At last, the luggage carousel was activated and the tired but now-rejuvenated Flight 948 new arrivals anxiously grabbed their suitcases from the rotating black belt slats. The multilingual Barcelona Customs personnel were friendly and professional in processing the several hundred folks through the initial security screening. After obtaining five luggage carts at the end of the "Immigration responsibility," the party of ten Americans hired a driver and a van to convey them to the Apsis Atrium Palace Hotel at 656 Gran Via de les Corts Catalanes, situated right in the heart of Barcelona's most elegant downtown shopping district. The twenty-five minute drive through the city allowed the ten Americans to view and evaluate the Spanish metropolis and compare it to certain American cities cataloged in their mental repertoires.

"They seem to have massive congestion gridlock, just like New York, L.A. and 'Philly!" Warren Mottola' observed and said. "But I'm especially impressed with their highway system and the use of tunnels. And everything, including the buildings and streets, seems to be well-maintained and really clean."

"I particularly like the architecture and how the four buildings at intersections are at catty-corners and not at right angles to the streets like they are in cities back in the States," Jimmy Valerio contributed to the conversation. "That unique construction pattern automatically makes each intersection more open and visible. Barcelona seems to be an urban paradise with lots of parks, fountains, monuments and museums," the observant building contractor added. "I do believe that the Europeans take more pride in their cities than Americans tend to do with theirs. Driver, what boulevard are we now on?"

"Las Ramblas!" the van chauffeur answered. "And that's the famous *Columbus Monument* we just passed! We're now only ten minutes from your cozy hotel."

"The sights are magnificent!" Joanne Valerio exclaimed. "We'll definitely have to take a double-decker bus tour and sit on top, weather permitting. I like the idea of open-air top-deck buses! I've already seen several dozen of them that were conducting tourists around this beautiful city!"

"And the shrubbery and flowers are really fantastic!" Lisa Mottola noted. "This part of the city is like one giant botanical garden! And they have lots of bougainvillea here just like we saw in..."

"In La Jolla and in residential San Diego!" corporate jet pilot David Winters remembered and finished. "And there's many sycamore trees along the boulevard too! Barcelona is very much like southern California except for the rain. I hope the sky clears up later today!"

"Yes, it will," the driver authoritatively replied. "And I suggest that you take a stroll down the Passeig de Gracia after you become settled in your hotel rooms. It's a terrific shopping area just two blocks away from the Apsis Atrium Palace. I highly recommend it and I guarantee that you won't be disappointed. It's rather exceptional!"

After the ten new arrivals checked into the hotel, a bellboy escorted Lois and Frank Davies to the elevator and then up to their second-floor room, which had a marvelous balcony view of the Gran Via de les Corts Catalanes. Frank was so happy to get to his room and take off his shoes that he gave the helpful attendant a generous five Euro tip.

"Hey, before you leave, how do we put the lights on?" Frank inquired. "These light switches don't seem to work!"

"Sorry, Sir. My mistake for not telling you!" the bellboy instantly apologized. "You have to place the plastic room key in this wall slot here just after you open the door. The key insertion makes the lights go on. It's a measure we use to conserve energy and electricity."

"I see! Pretty nifty and practical!" Lois earnestly admitted. "Maybe we Americans could learn something from other cultures if we cease being so independent and arrogant. Thanks for sharing that important information with us!"

After the hotel porter left the Davies to their own privacy, another minor crisis soon developed. Lois couldn't figure out how to flush the toilet.

"There's no flush handle!" Lois informed her equally puzzled husband. "There just has to be a handle somewhere! I feel so stupid and incompetent right now!"

After searching and experimenting for a full minute, Frank was surprised to discover the solution to the riddle. A flat rectangular silver metal wall plate (that appeared to be part of the bathroom's décor) served and functioned as a useful flush handle.

"Mystery solved!" Frank declared, pretending that he was a contemporary Sherlock Holmes. "I just wish the bellboy or the person at the desk would've explained that simple secret, or should I say *that* simple method to us! They just assume that we've been to Europe before and are familiar with the different habits and customs. Anyway, realistically speaking Lois, good old Yankee ingenuity and perseverance are difficult to stymie."

"Now, you're beginning to sound haughty just like your obnoxious twin brother!" Lois facetiously kidded. "Nothing can defeat or stifle Fred! And now your inflexible attitude is contrary to acceptable!"

"And now you're starting to sound a lot like *our* overbearing sister-in-law!" Frank creatively joked. "If the slightest deviation is not a calamity, then it most certainly is a disaster! What a mental case Eleanor is and always will be!"

"Let a smile be your umbrella is indeed *not* Eleanor's favorite maxim!" Lois diplomatically assessed. "That vicious sister of mine possesses the combined personalities of Lucretia Borgia and Medusa the Gorgon! Need I say more to support my premise and your analysis?"

That afternoon, the light drizzle subsided and the Davies took the airport van driver's recommendation and sauntered down the magnificent Passeig de Gracia, a splendid boulevard replete with spacious sidewalks, fabulous buildings, ritzy department stores and swanky fashion emporiums. The fascinating scenery was both overwhelming and breathtaking.

"This thoroughfare makes New York's Fifth Avenue look like an ordinary dump!" Frank sarcastically interpreted. "It's without a doubt the most excellent street I've ever walked along!"

"Now, you're again sounding exactly like your disgusting brother Fred!" Lois quipped and benignly chastised. "Stop acting like a ruthless uncivilized cynical American barbarian!"

"And you're again sounding just like Eleanor!" Frank asserted. "Stop chiding and reprimanding me as if I'm a five-year-old wet-behind-the-ears kid! Please Lois, kindly show me some more respect and consideration!"

"Well, to change the subject," Lois Davies astutely said, "many of the structures on this fantastic avenue were designed by Antoni Gaudi, a world-renowned Spanish architect."

"Probably, our English word 'gaudy' comes from the guy's name!" Frank deducted and articulated. "Everything on that building over there across the street seems exaggerated and garish!"

"I don't know about *that* uncharitable comment!" Lois replied. "But I had read about Gaudi in a brochure about Barcelona down in the hotel lobby while you were busy checking in. His work is still very popular here in Barcelona and actually the architectural genius has a huge reputation throughout Spain and Europe!"

"Look at that roof on the opposite side of the boulevard!" the mildly perturbed husband pointed out. "It looks like dragon scales accentuated with medieval fantasy towers. And that ostentatious apartment house on the corner looks like it belongs with the Flintstones back in prehistoric Bedrock! This Antoni Gaudi fellow was so out in left field that he's entirely out of the stadium!"

"You could never appreciate another person's artistic or personal expression!" Lois rankled. "Now your true feelings are fully exposed! Deep down inside Frank, you're an ingrate just like your hostile twin brother is!"

"And you're hostile and argumentative just like *my* vitriolic sister-in-law, who happens to look exactly like you!" Frank volleyed back.

"Well, at least my problem is not partially genetic like yours is!" the wife caustically lectured. "Both you and Fred need the services of several priests and a squad of psychiatrists!"

According to Spanish custom, supper was not served in the hotel dining room until 8 p.m. During the delicious dinner Frank (out-of-character) got entangled in a minor wrangle with Dr. Rose Jeffries, a political liberal.

"These Spaniard natives all seem rather cold and indifferent to Americans!" Frank generalized with a frown on his countenance. "They mostly seem apathetic, not to mention pathetic!"

"I've seen equally unconcerned dispassionate people, walking the streets of downtown 'Philly or New York!" Dr. Jeffries abruptly challenged. "I think you're being a little too judgmental!"

"You probably voted for John Kerry in the last Presidential election!" Davies vociferated. "I can tell by your tone and by your attitude that you're a devout left-wing liberal from the word 'go'!"

"How I vote is my own conscience," Dr. Rose Jeffries protested. "And I've learned from experience that nothing tangible can ever be achieved by debating either religion or politics! I suggest that *you* change the topic of discussion!"

"Why are you being so confrontational and belligerent?" Lois Davies disputed with her usually tranquil marital partner. "I'm becoming a trifle embarrassed with your new-found tirades and I don't condone them at all! It's all contrary to your general nature!"

"And I'm becoming pretty tired of *you* being non-supportive of your loyal husband!" Frank snidely affirmed. "Behind every man there's a woman, and that's exactly where she belongs!"

"Now you're proving that you're truly a right-wing male chauvinist!" Dr. Jeffries indicted her formerly mild-mannered philosophical opponent. "A dedicated conservative right-wing male chauvinist at that!"

"And Rose, you're probably a militant left-wing save-the-environment and an avid save-the-whales advocate!" Frank angrily responded. "All you left-wingers have some perverted idealistic agenda to pursue like valuing animals over humans! You're all on the brink of abandoning capitalism and adopting socialism as an honorable way of life! Your history heroes are probably Karl Marx and Vladimir Lenin!"

"I see no reason to prolong this regrettable verbal altercation!" Warren Mottola interrupted the argument. "We're all here in Europe to have fun and recreation and not to verbally assault and attack one another! Now let's all drink to our newly engaged couple, Lisa and David!"

"Yeah, David!" Frank unfortunately yelled while frivolously raising his glass in a mock salute. "The next time the *pilot* light on my basement hot water heater goes bonkers, I'll know exactly who to call!" Davies loudly said, deliberately insulting the young commercial jet operator.

* * * * * * * * * * * * *

Day two of the European vacation was much more harmonious and favorable for the Davies than day one had been. Frank had attributed his recent aberrant behavior to being overly fatigued from the seven-hour-flight. The rain had ceased and a cloudy blue sky had appeared over Barcelona's delightful sixty-eight-degree temperature. After enjoying a hardy breakfast in the hotel's main restaurant, the party of ten purchased tickets for the "city bus tour," which originated on the Placa de Catalunya, only four blocks from the aforementioned Apsis Atrium Hotel. The twenty-five-mile bus excursion entailed twenty-eight stops where tourists could get off at their leisure, sight-see and next board another double-decker open-air bus on the grand circuit and then get off at another place of interest along the scenic itinerary.

"Look, Frank!" Lois indicated as the bus passed from the Passeig de Gracia onto Calle de Cerdena. "There's the La Sagrada Familia (the Sacred Family) Cathedral. The tour pamphlet says it was designed by the great Antoni Gaudi in 1882. It's still under construction although Gaudi died way back in 1926!"

"It's marvelously built!" Jimmy Valerio recognized and attested. "As you know I'm in the construction business but I've never before seen anything quite like this terrific architecture! It's a combination of both primitive and modern! Just look at those unbelievable spires or towers or whatever you want to call them! They're worthy of any person's admiration!"

Evidence of Antoni Gaudi's brilliance was very abundant all over the bustling city as the tour bus passed by the Pare Guell, the Museum of Catalunyan Art, the Pueblo Espanol, the city's main university campus, the Maritime Museum and the Picasso Gallery. Not far from the waterfront the touring party exited the bus on Las Ramblas and stepped in the direction of the Gothic Quarter, an alluring section of Barcelona with buildings and residences dating back to the Thirteenth Century.

"Let's stroll up this narrow alleyway!" Lois suggested to the less rambunctious members of the group. "It looks rather intriguing and adventurous!"

"And the natives probably don't have clothes dryers, because all of the laundry is hanging out of overhead windows!" Frank articulated, again finding fault with his environment. "Maybe they don't own washers either!"

"Regardless," Lois mildly countered, attempting to get the erratic exchange of words back on topic. "Let's see how far this alleyway extends! The walks on both sides are quite narrow and a compact car can barely squeeze by in the center!"

"That's why most of the people in this city have motor scooters and motorbikes!" Warren Mottola concluded and explained. "There's not too many large American SUVs speeding around town, that's for sure! And those new Mercedes Smart cars are now the vogue over here! Don't forget!" the science teacher elaborated. "Gasoline is around eight-dollars-a-gallon and is sold in liters just like Coke and Pepsi are back in the States. That's precisely why most conscientious Europeans must be frugal and economical."

"Why do they call them Smart cars?" David Winters asked. "Do they have artificial intelligence generated by an on-board computer?"

"No!" Warren laughed and corrected. "Smart stands for Small Mercedes Art car! At least that's what I overheard a tour-guide telling a curious tourist on the bus!"

The commercial ancient alleyway (that was dotted with small neighborhood grocery stores and bakeries) stretched for over a mile, and upon leaving the very historic medieval area, Warren perceptively spotted the Roman Arch, a brick copy of the famous Arch de Triumph in Paris.

"The edifice is made out of Roman bricks," Warren academically told his exhausted companions. "The flat brick is about half as wide as those currently used in the United States and it *was* standard building material throughout the ancient Roman World."

"I thought you were a science teacher?" Joanne Valerio asked. "You seem to be an expert on history too!"

"Yes, Warren," Judy Marks chimed-in. "You must study dictionaries and encyclopedias both day and night to have knowledge of a trivial fact like that! No wonder why kids are bored in school!"

"I majored in science, but minored in history at *Rutgers!"* Warren Mottola clarified. "But sometimes it's hard to divorce one subject from the other! For example," the erudite teacher elucidated, "architecture is a science that has a certain history! That's precisely when and where the two distinct disciplines integrate!"

"Barcelona is the most beautiful and most exquisite city I've ever toured and that includes Las Vegas and San Diego!" Lois Davies opined. "Even though the brochure I had read stated that it has a population of nearly two million, I haven't detected one slum or ghetto yet anywhere! It's truly unbelievable and exotic!"

The fatigued trekkers stepped into a small soda fountain and purchased Seven-Ups and Pepsi Colas to be drunk outside. Frank generously treated everyone to their beverages.

"You want to know something," the biology research specialist stated and complained, "they charge you extra if you drink the sodas outside. They sort of rent the table and chairs to you. It's a little different than how food merchants do business in the States!"

"Yes, it is!" Lois agreed. "In the States soda fountains don't have twenty outside tables and sixty outdoor chairs! That's what I consider one of the main differences between Barcelona and 'Philly!"

Day two of the European vacation trip elapsed without any major incidents occurring. The travelers were satisfactorily adjusting to the six-hour time differential and were indeed becoming more social and less irritable. All ten American tourists were highly anticipating the seven-day voyage on the Regal Adventurer, the highlight of the trip being less than twenty-four hours away. The New Jersey visitors readily agreed that certain aspects of life were full of gratifying moments.

* * * * * * * * * * * * *

Saturday, September 16th arrived on the calendar, and at breakfast Judy Marks announced to the group that the ugly three-day weather pattern that had hovered over and near Barcelona was now drifting east towards Italy.

"That makes sense, Judy!" Frank acknowledged and commended. "Weather in the northern hemisphere moves from west to east and generally so does the jet stream."

"That's why our flight back to 'Philly will be eight hours, a full sixty-minutes longer than it took getting here!" Warren objectively added. "We'll be going against the headwind caused by the strong jet stream flow in the upper atmosphere!"

"Before we check-out of the hotel at noon and meet our pickup van driver," Lois mentioned to Frank, "I want to go to the Passeig de Gracia and view its splendor one final time, while I'll really be in quest of purchasing some decent postcards to put into a new photo' album."

The Davies did walk the magnificent Passeig de Gracia and had only two brief hours to inspect marvelous sights that hadn't been observed and explored before. Frank seemed back to his quiet-disposition self but then remembered an unusual scene he had witnessed on the balcony the previous evening (at midnight) while Lois was taking her hot shower.

"While you were getting ready for bed, I stood on our suite's small terrace and was relishing the beauty of the Via de les Gran Corts Catalanes," Frank prefaced his observation. "The wide boulevard is really totally terrific when lit-up at night."

"Yes, and it's so wide that it takes a full minute to cross," Lois recalled and exaggerated. "I especially like the double-lanes on each side and the corresponding wide pedestrian walk paths next to them before the crosser finally gets to the four main lanes. The wonderful boulevards of Barcelona are not safe havens for careless jaywalkers, that's for sure!"

"Well, anyway," Frank continued as the pair finally reached a newspaper and souvenir stand. "While you were in the shower, I witnessed over three hundred midnight roller blade enthusiasts speeding by on the pedestrian walkway. It was pretty phenomenal! I counted each and every one of the three hundred and eleven of them. Instead of wild motorcycle gangs they must have roller-blade clubs here!" Frank humorously conjectured and revealed. "It's certainly less expensive than owning and driving gas-guzzling cars around Barcelona! Say, Honey. Here's a colorful book about the city to take home as a memento of our trip!"

"I don't want that one!" Lois emphatically disagreed. "I prefer this one!" she insisted as she handed the specific item to the souvenir stand proprietor.

"Allemagne!" the stand owner bellowed.

"He means the book's written in German and not English!" the husband recognized and interpreted.

"Entonces yo quiero uno en Engles, mismo eso uno!" Lois directed the salesman in broken stilted Spanish. "Then I want another one like the one I had selected in English!"

"Don't be ridiculous!" Frank strenuously objected. "The one I had wanted you to choose was all about the entire city and not just about the architectural works of Antoni Gaudi! Stop being so damned stubborn Lois!"

"You're again sounding like you're impersonating your rotten twin brother!" the aggravated wife steadfastly protested. "You're rapidly becoming the dispute king of American tourists! You've been far from hilarious lately!"

"And you're now evolving into a carbon-copy of that vicious viper, Eleanor!" Frank accused his spouse in a bellicose tone of voice. "I suspect that somebody evil and jealous is putting a heavy wicked curse on our relationship!"

The volatile couple hardly spoke to each other on the van trip from the Apsis Atrium Palace down the picturesque Via Laietana, which led to the Passeig de Colom and ultimately to the docked Regal Adventurer. All ten tourists seated in the vehicle transport took a final stare at the elaborate lengthy and wide gray paver-stone promenade that accentuated the incomparable Barcelona waterfront.

Obtaining the required Sea Passes was easily facilitated, once the ship's new passengers showed their passports and other relevant identifications to the courteous harbor terminal personnel. Everyone was allowed to board at 1 p.m. and the newcomers had six-full-hours to unpack and investigate all of the massive fourteen decks until the scheduled first seating supper in the Magic Carousel Dining Room at six-thirty (with the vessel's disembarking at 7 p.m. sharp).

In the grandly decorated Magic Carousel Dining Room, the waiter and assistant waiter introduced themselves to the ten American diners at their table. "Good evening, ladies and gentlemen! I'm Cem (pronounced Gem) and this is my very able assistant Tomas. I'm from Turkey and Tomas is from Czechoslovakia. We're here to cater to your every eating need!" Cem said in almost perfect unaccented English. "It will be our pleasure to serve you!"

Frank formally introduced everyone at the table to Cem and to Tomas and then ordered two bottles of Merlot for the assembled gourmets to enjoy. Soon the conversation turned to the other travelers aboard the ship after the well-trained waiters began attending to *their* individual duties.

In short time, Frank Davies' recently acquired Dr. Jekyll and Mr. Hyde alternating personality again unexpectedly surfaced. "You all must know, some of these Europeans aboard this vessel are quite rude!" Frank began his impromptu criticism. "I was standing in Line H inside the harbor terminal acquiring Lois's and my Sea Passes when this nasty grumpy elderly Spanish man tried to wriggle into a spot at the Line G counter and then pushed me out of his way!"

"What did you say or do to the impetuous old fellow?" Warren Mottola curiously asked. "I'd think that his aggressive behavior would've warranted at least a perfunctory 'Excuse me'!"

"Well, I quickly raised my left elbow and deflected the old ill-mannered coot directly out of my standing space!" Davies bluntly reported, much to his wife's utter humiliation. "And besides that scenario Warren, this afternoon at lunch up at the eleventh floor Quarterdeck Buffet, Lois and I were seated at a table for four when a Hispanic lady signaled to me with sign language if she and her mate could sit down. I suavely said 'Si! Hable Engles?' and the snobby witch answered 'Portuguese!' Then neither the woman, I'd say she was in her fifties, nor her self-centered husband ever once again glanced at Lois and me during their entire meal. It was as if we were lepers or convicts or inferior beings or something! The only friendly people on this boat are good old Americans! You can pick them out in a second by their cheerful and happy demeanors!"

"Frank, I think you'd better stop speaking so loudly!" Lois rebuked. "You never know when you're going to offend someone sitting at another table!"

"Well, let them sue me for all I care!" Frank automatically and indiscreetly returned. "Let them sue me, even if they're rude Europeans and not merely Sioux Indians!" the slightly intoxicated man awkwardly joked.

"Now, just wait a cotton-pickin' minute!" Dr. Rose Jeffries boldly challenged her philosophical adversary. "I strongly suggest that you stop making unsubstantiated prejudicial statements and unfounded gross discriminatory stereotypical generalizations!"

"You're sounding too much like a cowardly liberal again!" Frank yelled across the table at the now-flabbergasted infectious disease doctor. "You're always crusading for a dumb cause! Get a grip on reality, will ya'!"

"And you're sounding more and more just like your haughty obnoxious brother Fred again!" Lois aptly injected into the three-way exchange.

"And I think you're deliberately mimicking Mrs. Eleanor Davies!" the indignant husband snarled back. "She's a venomous viper if there ever was one!"

"Folks! This is supposed to be a happy occasion for all in attendance!" Warren Mottola adroitly interrupted, acting like both a referee and peacemaker. "I'd like to now propose a toast to officially honor my daughter Lisa and her fiancé David's engagement! Let's all sincerely drink to their future health, wealth and happiness!"

* * * * * * * * * * * * * *

At 6 a.m. on Sunday morning, Frank Davies opened the curtains to cabin suite 8322 and admired the superb view of the city of Marseilles. 'It's September 17th,' he thought. 'I vow to myself that I have to be more diplomatic and I must also stay away from initiating controversial subjects, especially with Lois and with that nasty despicable leftist Dr. Rose Jeffries.'

The passengers aboard the Regal Adventurer were given three separate tour options at each port-of-call. 'We could've toured Marseilles but instead Lois, Warren, Melissa and I have chosen the small fishing village of Cassis!' Frank reviewed in his now- somewhat remorseful mind. 'I'll try my best to make this day pleasant and enjoyable for all concerned! Wow!' Davies considered. 'There must be at least fifty tour buses lined up down there! You'd certainly need that many to accommodate the three-thousand four-hundred travelers aboard this super-mammoth ship!'

After a quick visit to the eleventh deck buffet for breakfast, Frank, Lois, Warren and Melissa assembled in the fourth floor Metropolitan Theater, were swiftly assigned to Bus #6, and then wearing small stick-on #6 badges, the four guests waited for their tour designation to be called.

"I think it's best if *we* hang around together on all five scheduled tours in France and in Italy," Warren privately suggested to Frank. "Lisa and David are lovebirds and only have romance on their minds and Dr. Rose and her roommate Judy tend to have radical political views that are diametrically opposed to ours. Otherwise, we'll have to be constantly defending our conservative viewpoints! Dr. Rose has already labeled you and me 'Neocons.' I believe that in this specific case Frank, distance from that militant Marxist is the best remedy in order to avoid conflict!"

"I totally agree with your recommendation!" Davies instinctively answered. "Prevention is always better than cure! Even Dr. Rose must realize *that* obvious medical truth!"

The ship had its own sophisticated security-check system and the passengers' Sea Passes served as viable substitutes for the customary passports and photo' IDs. Soon the four friends were on Bus #6 and heading through Marseilles traveling from the "New Port" to the "Old Port," which featured numerous scenic marinas loaded with local fishing boats, Mediterranean schooners and extravagant yachts owned by the rich and famous.

"Notice that the residences' principal rooms all have three sets of shuttered windows facing the street," the French female tour guide explained in English. "Notice too that the city is built in a semi-circle. Marseilles presently has a population of around one million people and it remains the second largest metropolitan area in France. On your left is the classic Byzantine Cathedral, a favorite of tourists from around the world. And up on that hill overlooking our proud city and the gateway to the Mediterranean stands the impressive Cathedral of Notre Dame de la Garde with its magnificent gold-leaf towers," the knowledgeable guide described. "And soon we'll be passing by our Theatre National de Marseille La Criee. This part of the city with its many fancy stores and cafes looks very much like Paris's Champs Elysees, which incidentally in English means the Elysian Fields! Looking out toward the sea," the upbeat woman loquaciously stated, "you'll notice a fort or prison situated on a small island. That's where the Count of Monte Cristo was held captive in the classic novel written by Alexandre Dumas, who as you know also wrote the book *The Three Musketeers*. And as we travel along the coast toward Cassis, please remember that the genius painter Vincent Van Gogh was often inspired by many of the area's olive groves and vineyards situated along that route!"

"This city is definitely beautiful, but in my humble opinion, I still like Barcelona better!" Lois whispered to Frank.

"Me too!" came his rather convivial reply. "Everything looked a bit newer and cleaner on the Passeig de Gracia and on Las Ramblas compared to what we're now seeing in Marseilles."

Tour Bus #6 left the main highway and the skilled driver slowly navigated the vehicle along steep winding roads above rugged jagged cliffs until it stopped at the summit of the white precipices overlooking gorgeous Cape Canaille, a full 1,300 feet above the placid Mediterranean.

"The guide said that this spectacular view is actually from a higher elevation than the one from the top of the White Cliffs of Dover! In fact, it's the highest cliff overlooking the sea anywhere in Europe!" Lois marveled and informed.

"It's truly sensational and breathtaking!" Frank confirmed. "Let's take some pictures of Melissa and Warren and then they can reciprocate! Just look at those fabulous homes with orange tiled roofs situated down there near the Mediterranean. I gotta' admit, it's all very enticing and extraordinary!"

The remainder of "Day 4" in Europe was inconsequential. The bus passengers were then taken with dispatch to the quaint fishing village of Cassis where they were left off on the outskirts of the town to be transported into the center while sitting in compartments of small trains on wheels pulled by cute diminutive locomotives of various colors. "The Mayor of Cassis insists that all tourists enter the village on these trams because of traffic congestion and pollution!" the tour guide explained.

"The City Mayor sounds like another radical left-wing liberal environmentalist, just like Dr. Rose Jeffries!" Frank complained to Lois. "He's probably an officer in Greenpeace and in PETA, too!"

"Now, now, Frank!" the amused wife giggled. "Let's not become cantankerous, and let's simply pretend that we're normal tourists out to sample the exquisite fishing village, peruse its leather shops and then take some pictures of us standing in front of the fine waterfront cafes and restaurants. This is no time to act like a bullheaded contentious American, now, is it?"

"I suppose you're right!" the husband reluctantly conceded. "This is no time to *harbor* any animosity!"

That evening, Cem and Tomas served the party of ten delicious suppers of surf and turf followed by large portions of baked Alaska for dessert. "I wonder how the chef could fit an entire state like Alaska in his oven!" Frank jested with even Dr. Rose getting a brief chuckle out of his somewhat witty comment. At 9 p.m. everyone enjoyed the lively show "Broadway Sights and Sounds" staged in the Metropolitan Theater, which was followed by an hour's social activity at the Anchor Bar's piano lounge and then by some casual gift shopping along the ship's expansive promenade.

"Thanks for not being so verbally combative today!" Lois praised her spouse. "You're again mastering the art of being civil!"

"I'm trying my best!" the husband solemnly pledged. "Believe me Lois. I'm attempting to be calm and tranquil! I'm really working on it! But for some remote reason I'm finding it quite difficult!"

* * * * * * * * * * * * * *

On the morning of "Day 5", Frank, Lois, Warren, and Melissa again stepped down the "gangplank" for the next stop on their wonderful sea odyssey. A "tender" would ferry two busloads of tourists to the mainland since Villefranche had no deep-water dock where the Regal Adventurer could moor and anchor.

"I always wanted to tour Monte Carlo," Lois began. "Because it's where Grace Kelly had married Prince Rainier in a fantasy-type storybook wedding! I can't wait to see the cathedral where the event took place!"

"We have to remember that Monte Carlo is the name of the casino in Monaco," Warren Mottola scholarly remarked and corrected. "People often get the two terms mixed-up and call one the other. Monaco and Monte Carlo are two different things!"

"It's too bad we had to make a choice between Monaco and either Nice or Cannes for our one-day shore excursion," Melissa piped-in and regretted. "Confidentially, I'd like to visit and explore all three places."

"You could do this exact same cruise again and see totally different things at every port!" Lois Davies concluded and shared. "Perhaps we can do it again before we're...."

"Before we're all in wheelchairs having dual oxygen tanks on the rear while gasping for our last breaths!" Frank said, while completing his wife's thought with terminology that showed a distinct insensitivity toward the handicapped. "I want my wheelchair to have chrome dual exhaust pipes!"

"That horrible statement was in poor taste, and I hope you think things out more in detail next time before you again say something off-color!" Lois disciplined her husband. "You're more tolerable and less miserable when you're being introspective with your mouth zipped shut!"

"I swear that both you and Dr. Rose have no sense of humor!" Frank argued in defense of his vulnerable ego. "Neither of you know the definition of the word 'amusement'."

"Let's act a little more aristocratic now that we're mingling with highbrow society here in the French Riviera, even though in reality, we're just middle-class Americans and not Counts or Countesses!"

Warren intelligently intervened. "I really never aspired becoming a wealthy snobbish aristocrat anyway!"

Tour Bus #5 stopped on the Avenue St. Martin near the Monaco Oceanographic Museum, the institute where Jacques Cousteau had conducted much of his essential nautical research. Not far from the very excellent museum was the Prince's Palace situated atop Monaco Rock, where the thoroughly enchanted tourists observed the hourly changing of the guard.

"The tour guide said that if Monaco were ever attacked by an enemy, then France would come to its defense!" Frank related to Warren. "When's the last time France ever won a battle? Was it before or after Julius Caesar?"

Although several eavesdropping American tourists found levity in Davies' assertive remark, Lois certainly did not. "You're again being very sarcastic and offensive!" the wife reproached as she approached her opinionated husband. "Do I have to tell you exactly who you're reminding me of?"

"No *Eleanor!"* the husband intentionally wrangled. "I wasn't making a public speech! I was merely whispering something in private to Warren! Why does every little conversation that I have elicit scorn from your lips?"

"Well, your boisterous whispers sound like they're being shouted into a bullhorn let alone into a megaphone!" the wife passionately countered. "Right now, I believe that you're evilly transforming into your cavalier twin brother right before my very eyes!"

"Guys! Let's take a stroll over to the Cathedral where Princess Grace and Prince Rainier were married and are now buried!" Melissa Mottola wisely advised. "Then we can ramble over to the Monte Carlo Casino. We have two full hours to burn before we have to board the bus."

"The casino isn't open until this afternoon!" Warren recollected and quoted from a guidebook he had read. "And they charge you a ten Euros admission fee just to pass through the fancy doors! That's close to fifteen dollars! You're way behind even before you insert a coin into the first slot machine! I guess they want to keep all of the riffraff out!"

The foursome discovered a park located behind the city square that featured an array of colorful tropical plants, flowers and palm trees. Pictures were taken with digital cameras and then Warren noticed that all traffic in the square had been terminated to allow for the filming of a rap video in progress.

"Look, there's the famous rapper Bee_G being driven in that black Mercedes convertible. He's being chased by an anonymous villain in that gold and black Rolls Royce," Warren uttered in pure amazement. "This MTV video must be costing tens of thousands of dollars to film!"

"That lousy rap music is a scourge to America!" Frank opined. "It's corrupting the minds and hearts of our youth while it's eroding the very morality of society! And it's all done for the love of money! Bee_G doesn't care one iota about the damage he's doing to teenagers from Portland, Maine to Portland, Oregon. The hedonistic narcissist is a complete egomaniac. And the worst part about it is that rap music isn't even music!"

"Frank, please be quiet!" Lois simultaneously admonished and pleaded. "We're surrounded by Bee_G's film crew and several of his intimidating three-hundred-pound Titan bodyguards, and they're standing only twenty-feet away! Be more discreet! They might not savor what you're saying!"

"I'm tired of your perpetual, uncouth character assassinations!" Frank fiercely reacted. "You're not exactly the most supportive wife you know! I'm only trying to explain myself to Warren!"

"I just don't want to see you causing a scene with your ongoing diatribe!" the wife emoted. "And I want you to know that for the first time the word 'divorce' has entered my mind! I find your behavior ever since this trip began most abominable!"

"Look! There's an ice cream parlor over there on the corner!" Warren nervously indicated. "Let's all cool off with some tasty treats! Vanilla cones might just do the trick!"

"I'm lactate intolerant!" Lois answered. "I can only eat yogurt, and that's on a full stomach!"

"That's not all that's wrong with my fickle wife!" Frank condemned and divulged. "In fact, that's just the most minor flaw! Right *Eleanor!"* he alluded.

"You're mentally sick!" Lois yelled back. "You're a detestable disgrace to humanity!"

"At least, I'm human!" Frank hollered back, getting the immediate attention of Bee_G's formerly nonchalant, enormous bodyguards.

"It's going to be a long six-mile bus ride back to Villefranche," Melissa accurately predicted. "Let's all please learn to temper our tempers!"

That evening after supper, the normally compatible foursome attended a terrific one-man performance in the Metropolitan Theater starring Domenick Allen, a former member of the rock group

Foreigner. All during the outstanding show, Lois and Frank sat mum and as still as statues. The Mottolas sensed and suspected that major conflict was about to erupt.

* * * * * * * * * * * * **

"Day 6" of the European trip was Tuesday, September 19. As usual, Frank and Lois and Warren and Melissa met at the entrance of the Metropolitan Theater at 7:30 a.m. to await assignment to their designated tour bus and to obtain their associated bus badges.

"This was a really tough choice," Melissa began to test the waters and see if there was any apparent current riptide existing between Frank and Lois. "We could've gone to Florence but instead we selected Tuscany on the advice of our travel agent."

"Let's see what happens!" Lois blandly answered. "It's too late now to change horses in midstream."

"Tuscany's famous for Chianti wine, alabaster statue products, olive trees and excellent leather goods!" Frank said without any trace of rancor evident in his tone of voice.

"Yes, and I understand that many Renaissance painters found the Italian fertile valleys and the gentle sloping Tuscany hills as interesting backgrounds for their creative works," Lois Davies contributed. "And the weather's going to be eighty-two degrees, something between ideal and perfect!"

Tour Bus #8 traveled north from the port of Livorno along an elevated industrial highway stretching over several kilometers of marshland in the direction of Pisa. "I know many of you had desired to see the Leaning Tower and have elected to fore-go Florence to sight-see Tuscany. Believe me, you've made a wise decision and you won't be disappointed. Pisa and Florence are both located on the Arno River," their guide Maria said into her bus microphone, "which has over the centuries silted up. Thus Pisa, being situated inland, has over the years declined as a trading port and Livorno has risen. You'll all be totally enthralled and thrilled with both the medieval towns of Volterra and San Gimignano," Maria claimed. "Volterra even has some Roman ruins but actually during your short visit, you'll all feel like you're time-traveling back a thousand years into the past as you shop in narrow streets that haven't changed too much in appearance in the last millennium."

Stellar high poplar and cypress trees randomly dotted the many vineyards and olive groves, as Tour Bus #8 was maneuvered around curvy bends while it ascended thirty-miles inland, going-up hill after hill on the gradual ascension to Volterra. Dreamy clouds wafted by in the valley below as the spellbound tourists feasted their eyes on the remarkable landscape. Frank, Lois, Warren, and Melissa all felt as if they had wondrously entered a magical fantasy realm.

Volterra, and later that morning San Gimignano, were true medieval-type anachronisms, highly regarded special places to behold. The couples bought several leather belts, handbags and wallets in each town without any incidents, problems, haggling or dilemmas occurring. Lois was contemplating Frank's severe vacillating Jekyll and Hyde personality swings, but then she dismissed them as 'signs of manic depression' and was indeed glad that her husband's deportment appeared being 'back to normal.'

Since the total tour lasted a full ten-hours, lunch was served at a remote farmhouse that specialized in tourist visitations. A full-scale three-course-meal was prepared and presented with the first dish being pasta, the second meat and vegetables and the third being dessert, all in small but very attractive servings. Chianti wine (grown and processed on the farm) was then poured into tall-stem glasses to complement the fine delicious food.

"The only negative feature of this country farm is that they only have two bathrooms, one in the adjoining room, and the other in the farm's office," Lois perceptively stated to her friends seated at the long country farmhouse table. "It's a little inconvenient for forty-eight touring adults with overactive kidneys. But then again, this is Italy and not New York."

"It sure beats the lavatory facilities back in Volterra," Frank uttered in a non-threatening voice. "A fat woman sat behind a table and charged us a half-Euro each to use the toilets. This is one distinct advantage of public bathroom accommodations in the States as opposed to here in Italy. At least the two patron bathrooms on this farm seem to have some degree of privacy."

"And we had to waste fifteen-minutes of our tour time standing single-file in a long bathroom line; at least the women did," Melissa Mottola remembered and offered. "What am I saying? It was a co-ed bathroom with a series of stalls! There were no gender designations! But over here they call them W.C.'s or Water Closets and not Men's Rooms or Ladies Rooms!"

"At least, we haven't seen any holes in the floor with two feet painted on the cement showing the lavatory patrons where they have to stand," Frank pointed out to his listeners. "Several guys back in Jersey had told me that's what they had experienced at stops in certain parts of Italy. I'm glad we haven't discovered them yet!"

"Frank, I'm going outside to the farm's office to use the facilities," Warren judiciously hinted. "I'll beat the crowd, if ya' know what I mean!"

"Good idea. I'll go along and make sure you aren't molested by a savage poplar tree or by a demented chicken wandering around," Davies amusingly jested. "You might need my inexpensive personal protection."

After returning from the office's bathroom and then partaking of the delectable Tuscan meal, Frank and Warren were surprised to see that the farm's two "multi-functional" office secretaries had moved to the gift shop to wait on customers from behind the counter because the diners all had to exit the building/restaurant into the gift shop area in order to return to the bus.

That evening upon the cruise ship was "Dress-up night" and everyone eating in the Magic Carousel Dining Room had to wear formal apparel. After dinner the party of ten enjoyed the Russian duo of Tara and Alexandre performing their professional ice-skating skills in the ship's spacious Ice Arena and the show's stars had a cast of twelve very talented skaters accompany them in enacting their very complicated maneuvers.

"This colossal ship has almost everything!" Warren bragged to his favorite companion. "Even an ice-skating palace almost big enough for the Philadelphia Flyers to play an ice hockey game!"

"I had read where the Regal Adventurer is so huge that if you stood it vertically from stern to bow," Frank summarized and stressed without exaggeration, "the colossal ship would be as tall as the Empire State Building. Now that's what I call really thinking big! Hey Warren," the biology researcher related, "I can't wait to get out of this encumbering monkey suit!"

"Well, good Buddy. Glad to see that you're back on an even *keel!*" Warren Mottola merrily joked. "You had me a trifle worried there for a while, and that's the honest-to-God truth!"

* * * * * * * * * * * * *

Wednesday, September 20th was "Day 7" for the fully acclimated Mediterranean tourists now cruising aboard the ultra-modern Regal Adventurer. Again, fifty-buses were lined-up at the dock at Civitavecchia, the modern-day gateway to Rome. Rosemarie, the gentle Bus #15 tour guide, was conscientiously explaining to her captive audience the overall layout of Rome. "The Vatican lies on the north side of the Tiber River, but on the south side is where the original Seven Hills of Rome are located along with the major shopping districts and ancient ruins. Our first exciting stop this morning will be the incomparable Vatican Museum."

The thirty-mile drive from Civitavecchia to Rome took an hour and a half, due to heavy traffic congestion first showing itself ten miles outside the city. "Subways and underground parking are nearly non-existent because every time a construction crew begins excavating somewhere," Rosemarie educated her receptive listeners, "important archeological ruins are usually uncovered and work must be halted. Therefore, as you might've presumed, there's little new construction going on in central Rome."

At the Spanish Steps, a second gray-haired tour guide named Luigi was picked up who, like most Italian men, was an incessant chronic cigarette smoker. But the veteran host was quite experienced at shuttling his tourists through the Vatican area and his presence was well-known to the various security guards and Vatican attendants.

"Today, the entrance line for the Vatican Museum is only four blocks long," Luigi mentioned to his assigned disciples, "but in another two hours it'll be eight blocks in length. Be happy that you've luckily arrived here at the most desirable time."

"I can't believe all of the beggars hanging around the outside wall trying to exploit the pilgrims and the visitors' good intentions," Frank suddenly criticized to his wife. "It's astounding how people will sometimes use religion to achieve their selfish devious ends!"

"These are poor homeless people that have probably somehow evaded the welfare safety net and have inadvertently fallen between the cracks," an irritated Lois replied after solidly nudging her husband in the ribs with her right elbow. "Now please stop acting so uncultured and give your undivided attention to Luigi."

"I know that some of you have with difficulty sacrificed seeing the Trevi Fountain, the Pantheon, the Castel Sant' Angelo and the Forum for the sake of touring the Vatican and the Colosseum with me, but believe me when I say," Luigi appropriately pontificated and embellished with an Italian accent outside St. Peter's Basilica, "you haven't made the wrong decision. Perhaps sometime in the future you all can return to the Eternal City and see all that you've missed this first time around."

Luigi patiently distributed certain "Whisper Phones" to his assigned tourists so that they could place a plug into an ear and listen to his extensive narratives by turning up the volume. The lengthy line moved rather quickly and in forty-five minutes Luigi was conducting his "students" through the immense Vatican Museum, which exhibited long narrow galleries ornamented with huge wall tapestries and various invaluable marble statues. The highlight of the tour (beyond a doubt) was the incomparable Sistine Chapel, which possessed a tremendous arched ceiling displaying numerous paintings painstakingly created by the inimitable Renaissance genius Michelangelo.

"The frescoes were recently cleaned-up and they look as good as new," Luigi proudly explained to his tuned-in audience. "For your information Michelangelo also designed the uniforms for the Pope's Swiss Guards and in addition the Master had sculpted the famous Pieta, which you'll all see and admire later this afternoon inside St. Peter's Basilica."

"If they had Baptismal water basins in this church then it could be called the cistern chapel instead of the Sistine Chapel," Frank foolishly joked to his close male companion.

"Stop being so disrespectful and irreverent!" the eavesdropping Lois chastised her sardonic mate. "This is the Pope's favorite and most sacred chapel! Don't you have a conscience?"

"Shhhh!" two very stern-looking Vatican attendants reflexively implored, as they held their index fingers up to their lips, signifying the need for silence. "Shhhh!" they repeated.

"Sanctimonious Fools!" Frank uttered to Warren while effectively drowning out Luigi's voice on his Whisper Phone. "I wouldn't be surprised if God were to boot those snobbish 'Shhhh!' idiots right out of heaven!"

"Shhhh!" the Vatican attendants again reminded the talkative and impious tourists that were either standing or meandering about.

After leaving the awesome Sistine Chapel, a tour guide and his group discourteously cut in front of Luigi and immediately the two all-too-proud leaders became embroiled in a heated disagreement. Luigi began hitting the other guide with his Bus #15 lollipop sign while several security guards deliberately ignored the saber rattling and quickly paced away from the minor imbroglio.

"Hey, Pal. I'll give you a fat lip if you keep hassling my friend Luigi!" Frank yelled to the now-perplexed and flustered maverick tour guide. "Back off!"

"Frank, don't get involved!" Lois desperately pleaded. "You're behaving just like your lawyer brother Fred would in this situation!"

"Maybe I'm inheriting some of Fred's traits and he's getting some of mine!" Frank hypothesized and suggested.

"Don't be preposterous!" the perturbed wife answered. "That's totally absurd! I do believe that ever since this vacation began you're regressing in maturity instead of advancing! If you can't act your age, then please act your shoe size!"

"Shhh!" two Vatican foot patrol personnel very characteristically breathed-out from behind rigid index fingers. "Shhhhh!" they reiterated in animated fashion.

Two hours later, Frank Davies somewhat redeemed himself by performing a good deed on the opposite side of the Tiber outside the Colosseum. A young black girl wearing a "Detroit" sweatshirt was running to catch-up with several of her friends (who wanted to take a picture with three men posing and costumed in ancient Roman soldier uniforms) when she tripped over a slightly raised cobblestone and landed hard on her right elbow. Frank rushed over, asked the girl if she could move her arms and legs and then clasped his fingers around her waist and swiftly hoisted the still-in-shock victim to a standing position.

"At least you still have an ounce of decency in you!" Lois chided after Frank had executed his admirable humanitarian deed. "You might actually be the chivalrous Sir Walter Raleigh reincarnated! Helping others was one of your better qualities before we got married. Thank goodness you're once again a benefactor to society!"

"I'd do the same for you if you lost your balance," Frank retorted, showing a degree of rancor in his tone of voice. "I'm basically a gentleman and a Good Samaritan despite what *you* might think!"

"Thanks a lot!" an insulted Lois adamantly objected. "I would hope that you'd scurry over twice as fast for me! I guess I had just overestimated you!"

That sultry afternoon the passengers assigned aboard tour bus #15 devoured the traditional three course meal at an exclusive Rome hotel and then continued their tedious tour by returning to the Vatican for an inspection of St. Peter's Basilica.

"St. Peter must be a rich guy because he owns this vast structure plus hundreds of churches and schools all over the world!" Frank quipped. "He must be as wealthy as Bill Gates!"

"Frank, stop being so repugnant!" Lois disapproved, shrugging her shoulders. "You're rather repulsive and reprehensible at times!"

"Sometimes, I just got to be candid! That's why they call me Frank!" the husband stupidly joked.

"Your sense of humor leaves much to be desired and is none too amusing," the wife fired back. "You're even more bullheaded than ancient Greek mythology's Minotaur! At least *he* had a lame excuse for his stubbornness!"

"Guys, let's all politely listen to Luigi's lecture, even though it's now getting quite monotonous and boring!" Melissa Mottola proposed. "And just think. Tonight, in the Metropolitan Theater, the Regal Adventurer's multi-talented Singers and Dancers will be doing 'Hollywood in Motion.' Now that's something half-decent to be looking forward to."

At the first sitting dinner, neither Cem's sumptuous fillet mignon nor Tomas's scrumptious "sorbet delight" could adequately cheer-up Frank and Lois Davies from their mutual enmity and from their obvious dual emotional depressions.

* * * * * * * * * * * * *

On "Day 8" of the comprehensive European trip ("Day 6" aboard the Regal Adventurer) Frank, Lois, Warren, Melissa, Dr. Rose Jeffries and Judy Marks were all assigned to Bus #13, which they obediently boarded on the Naples dock.

"Where are Lisa and David?" Dr. Rose innocently asked. "Those two infatuated and hypnotized lovebirds don't mingle too much! They're too focused on each other!"

"They're more ambitious and adventurous than we are!" Melissa Mottola explained. "They're touring downtown Naples, then taking a ferry to the Isle of Capri and next taking another one from Capri to Sorrento where they'll be gallivanting around. They promised to meet up with us in Pompeii."

"That sounds like a pretty rigorous and exhausting day!" Judy Marks remarked with a smile. "I hope Lisa and David can avoid the notorious pickpockets and purse snatchers constantly patrolling downtown Naples! Those crooks especially thrive on ripping-off vulnerable American tourists!"

"They'll both be so tired that they'll probably miss having sex tonight!" Frank uncouthly and distastefully theorized and said as the group stood in a circle waiting to climb aboard Bus #13.

"That last comment was rude and crude and totally unjustified!" Dr. Rose sternly protested and challenged. "You should rinse your mouth out with *Lysol*!"

"Either that, or learn to bite your tongue!" Lois verbally piled on. "I'm embarrassed to say that I'm married to you! You're becoming a pathetic excuse for a human being Frank!"

"I think you're all making mountains out of molehills!" Frank exclaimed like a true bona fide egomaniac. "Learn to lighten-up, will ya'!"

After everyone had clambered aboard Bus #13, Monica, the designated tour guide, diligently distributed the by-now-familiar Whisper Phones. "As the bus leaves the Port of Naples, which incidentally is famous for the invention of pizza, we'll be skirting the city and driving past Herculaneum and Pompeii, both towns that had been destroyed by the volcanic eruption of Mt. Vesuvius on August 24th, 79 A.D. to be exact. Then we'll be heading to Sorrento on the peninsula and taking the nearly forty mile scenic drive along the magnificent Amalfi Coast all the way down to Salerno," Monica expertly orated. "So just sit back and relax and be prepared for at least seven miles of walking before this invigorating ten-hour tour is completed."

The first stop just outside Sorrento was a local establishment called Miss Bellevue, a factory outlet that manufactured exquisite inlaid wood dining room tables with elaborate matching chairs, tea wagons and house furniture. The pieces exhibited in the showroom were quite intricately made and the tourists all marveled at the tremendous degree of craftsmanship that went into achieving the highly sophisticated-looking final products. Frank and Warren were tempted to purchase appealing double-pedestal dining room tables (and matching upholstered chairs) that were listed at 3,500 Euros.

"That's about the equivalent of $4,700.00," Warren smartly acknowledged after doing a quick arithmetical estimate in his head. "That's what I call a bargain! You don't see stuff like this displayed at furniture stores back in the States!"

"But then you have to worry about shipping the set all the way across the Atlantic and who knows what condition it'll be in upon arrival back in Hammonton?" Frank objectively evaluated and maintained. "It's hard to return damaged goods when you're four-thousand or so miles away from the source!"

"Maybe, on our second trip to Italy, I'll have the courage to make the acquisition," Warren keenly answered.

"That's an un*warran*ted comment! You've never demonstrated a moment of courage since the day you were born!" Frank Davies arrogantly and caustically remarked. "You've been about as intrepid as an army deserter as long as I've known you!"

Warren Mottola abruptly left Frank's company to rejoin Melissa, who was preoccupied chatting with Lois, with Dr. Rose Jeffries and with Judy Marks, all concerned about Frank's annoying and insulting statements. A half hour had elapsed before the forty-eight tourists were instructed to again ascend the familiar steps into Bus #13.

"The classic song 'Come to Sorrento' was not a love melody," Monica matter-of-factly began her next memorized dissertation. "In fact, the lyrics are a political message, a past sincere appeal for certain lawmakers and officials to return to the city to organize a new government."

"Doesn't that obnoxious witch ever shut up?" Frank said to Lois. "She's giving me an intense headache that won't quit!"

"Here, swallow down a couple of aspirins!" the wife insisted as she frantically opened her purse to retrieve a small plastic container. "How am I going to enjoy all of the exotic bougainvillea sprinkled in with prickly pear cactus and the totally gorgeous array of other flowers when you're chronically complaining and finding fault with everything and anything? Haven't you noticed the majestic trees flourishing throughout Italy?"

"What about them?" Frank acerbically reacted. "What's so damned special about the trees? Trees are trees, aren't they?"

"In Tuscany, in Rome and all along this entrance to the marvelous Amalfi Drive," Lois explained, "the trees' limbs have been sheared off at the bottom and in the middle to form handsome canopies. I suppose it's been done to provide ample shade because they don't have nearly as many woods and forests here in Italy as we do have back in the States. That's the only suitable logical explanation I can think of!"

"Maybe, here in Italy, they have a surplus of unemployed lumberjacks!" Frank unrealistically and indiscriminately joked. "Unemployment abounds here because they have plenty of lazy non-industrious citizens! That's what the heck happens when you have a mostly socialistic type of government. Dr. Rose must feel right at home here in Italy! Most of the parasitic people in this country despise capitalism and free enterprise! That's why they'll never be as prosperous as we Americans are!"

"You're being absolutely implausible and irrational!" Lois profoundly protested. "I think I'll be sitting with Melissa for the remainder of the tour!"

"Now, you're again sounding like my bitchy sister-in-law!" the husband accused. "When we get back to Room 8322 be sure to check your passport and make certain that the name Eleanor Davies isn't printed on it! Better yet, examine your Sea Pass to determine whether or not your entire identity has been surreptitiously changed!"

"And closely check *your* passport and determine if the despised name Frederick Davies isn't typed on it!" the now emotionally disheveled wife snapped back. “You’ve become ruder than sin and cruder than petroleum!”

“We’re now officially entering the world-famous Amalfi Drive!” Monica exuberantly announced into her trusty microphone. “Many rich Neapolitans maintain resort homes here! Notice that some residents use their concrete roofs as their garages because their homes are built on the sides of the mountains overlooking the sparkling blue sea. Those types of homes are usually the most expensive! There’s nothing like this physical beauty anywhere else in the world!”

“It looks exactly like La Jolla along the California Coast just above San Diego!” Frank shouted and disagreed from his sixth-row seat, much to Lois’s mortification.

“Thank you, Sir!” Monica cleverly and graciously responded. “I’ll make a note of that fact and definitely mention it on future tours!”

The panoramic view of the mountainside town of Positano was quite outstanding, appearing as if it belonged on canvas in a masterpiece painting as it nobly lorded over the serene Mediterranean. Buildings and dwellings appeared terraced, one on top of another, in some instances fifteen structures high all the way up the mountainside. Only one main street passed through the entire town and security patrol personnel with communications’ radios stopped traffic in one direction for a full half hour so that vehicles could smoothly travel in the opposite direction. Then the traffic monitors alternated the procedure for a full half hour to accommodate and alleviate northbound congestion.

“They need some Yankee ingenuity around here to build some decent highways!” Frank thought and then impulsively blurted out. “In the States this over-populated town would be referred to as a ghetto or a barrio!”

“How are they going to possibly build parallel roads on this mountainous coast?” Lois incisively questioned her husband. “It would be a bizarre undertaking, that’s for sure!”

“We American capitalists can accomplish almost anything! That’s why we’re the envy of the entire world!” Frank egotistically boasted. “We’re born entrepreneurs!”

“Please be quiet and listen to Monica!” Dr. Rose Jeffries commanded from her seat directly behind Frank. “Show some courtesy! Your unsavory opinions aren’t exactly being relished or cherished by the other passengers!”

“Your totally silly politically correct nonsense is contrary to the operations of the objective adult mind!” Davies mercilessly ranted to

Dr. Rose, much to her chagrin and humiliation. "It's a revolting social sickness that rivals any infectious disease!"

The somewhat-exhausted trekkers stopped in Amalfi (a large hillside town that resembled Positano in sublime appearance). The group ate the standard three-course lunch served at a posh hotel and then with renewed energy again boarded the tour bus for the anticipated trip to historic Pompeii.

"The traffic on this narrow street is quite horrendous, almost brutal!" Frank curtly mentioned to Monica. "And these people flying around the wicked curves on motor scooters are a definite hazard. This entire street is treacherous! How many turns did you say this winding road has?"

"Around two-thousand-five-hundred!" the effervescent tour guide recollected and confirmed. "Of course, that's an approximation!"

"That's about two-thousand four hundred and ninety-nine too many!" Frank negatively bellowed. "How do they get accident victims and emergency cases to the nearest hospital?" Davies relentlessly persisted. "This lengthy snake-like road is excessively dangerous!"

"By helicopter!" Monica replied.

"That makes sense because anyone in need of medical attention would otherwise die from traffic congestion let alone from lung congestion!" Frank condescendingly exhaled. "Where did you learn to speak English?"

"I spent three-years living in Brooklyn!" Monica patiently replied.

"Shut up!" Lois reprimanded as she gave her husband another healthy dig in the ribs with her sharp left elbow. "Shut up! Stop asking so many irrelevant annoying questions!" she angrily parroted.

"You're hysterically overreacting!" Davies fired back.

The archeological treasures of Pompeii were quite exceptional, ranging from the well-preserved gladiator practice arena to the antiquated amphitheater, where Greco-Roman plays were once performed. Then Monica led the tourists on a walking trip around the "resurrected city" that Mt. Vesuvius had violently buried under thirty-foot of volcanic ash.

"Notice the elevated rocks in the center of the street!" Monica indicated. "Residents would use the raised rocks to cross the road because raw sewage had used natural gravity to flow down the street from the higher ground to your left to the lower end of the city to your right!"

"The ancient Romans didn't know crap about crap!" Frank boisterously nitpicked. "I'll bet that the Italians have learned *that* particular tradition from their primitive ancestors! The E-*truss*-cans all had double hernias, especially the men!"

Monica just stared incredulously at Frank Davies while *his* disbelieving wife dragged him to the back of the crowd to avoid potential friction in public. "The people of Pompeii had a fascination, or should I say a special fixation with sex!" Monica pointed out to her remaining listeners. "Please observe this bit of graffiti drawn on this wall. Look closely! It's an exaggerated male reproductive organ!"

"It's homo erectus, even if the ancient Romans weren't gay!" Frank boomed for all to hear. "That graffiti was probably drawn by a *porn'* again Christian!"

Monica was stunned and at a complete loss for words at the speaker's general audacity and brazenness. Lois then pulled her marital partner into an alley and again lectured him about his "total lack of decorum."

"Lately, there's been nothing sentimental or commendable about you Frank! You've managed to deride many people including your good friend Warren on this supposedly wonderful tour!" Lois screamed out of control. "You're an insult to your country and to humanity!"

Frank intensely scrutinized his Sea Pass to verify his identity. "Truthfully Lois, I'm not myself. Today I actually think and believe I'm my ill-tempered brother Fred!"

* * * * * * * * * * * * *

That evening, Frank and Lois dressed for supper and hesitantly departed Cabin Room 8322. The couple remained non-verbal as they entered the vacant elevator that promptly conducted them down to the fifth deck Magic Carousel Dining Room. The emotionally distraught feuding couple obstinately entered the ship's restaurant not realizing that the whole place was virtually devoid of human activity.

When Frank and his peeved wife arrived at their familiar table, they were appalled to see that Fred and Eleanor Davies were already seated there. Frank was the first to comment on the weird parallel coincidence.

"What are you two misfits doing here?" Davies exclaimed in absolute astonishment. "This is more of an ugly aberration than a blessed miracle!"

"Where are Warren and Melissa, Lisa, and David, Dr. Rose, and Judy Marks?" the virtually mesmerized Lois Davies asked, almost in a trance.

"This ugly encounter totally defies logic and reason!" Fred incredulously replied. "You two are on this ship two weeks later than you're supposed to be! This is supposed to be *our* European vacation!"

"Something's mighty peculiar here!" Eleanor Davies stated from her seat in a disconcerted tone of voice. "And I must admit that Fred and I have been acting rather strange lately. He's been sounding like *you* Frank and I've been sounding exactly like *you* Lois! *Our* confused minds just couldn't account for those crazy anomalies!"

Just then, Cem and Tomas appeared to further complicate matters on the already-bewildering scene. "Welcome folks for your final dinner on the cruise!" Cem mysteriously began his odd-but-powerful discourse. "And today is Thursday, September 28th, 2006, what you four targeted passengers might consider a compromise date."

"You four dupes might think that Cem and I are working for the Regal Adventurer, but actually, we're delighted to report to *you* four honored people that we have another even more successful employer!" Tomas obscurely and cynically stated. "This ship, or should I say this heinous trap, happens to belong to someone *you* commonly allude to as Lucifer!"

"Yes, valued Guests, Tomas and I are shrewdly recruiting new clients and patrons for our awesome Master," Cem evilly informed.

"The terminology 'eternal slaves' would certainly represent and constitute more accurate language!" Tomas enlightened his rather astounded and appalled audience. "The four of you are now specimens, or should I say carefully selected participants in a new innovative *moral,* or should I say a new innovative *immoral* experiment involving the unique confluence of time and space. Congratulations Francis, Frederick, Lois, and Eleanor!" Tomas diabolically declared and snickered. "You're all about to be dishonorably inducted into a most premier organization!"

"Now, be ready to consume some delicious Deviled Clams for an appetizer, some Deviled Crab-meat for your main entrée and some Devil's Food Cake for your very palatable dessert," Cem confidently and confidentially related to his stunned prey. "You unfortunate nominees have no choice in this delicate awe-inspiring matter for indeed, all four of you naïve morons have just involuntarily surrendered your free wills!"

"No *Angel's Food* cake aboard Satan's favorite ship! Welcome to the enigmatic Prince of Darkness Regal Adventurer!" Tomas scrupulously clarified, much to the dismay and horror of his four victimized recruits. "Cem and I are greatly exuberant, way beyond *your* very limited human imaginations! This truly and undeniably is a most thrilling event! We've finally met our work quotas! We're now mercifully emancipated from perpetual drudgery! Freedom is finally ours! Thank you so much for *your* inadvertent cooperation!"

And then, with an absence of ceremony, both Cem and Tomas cryptically transformed into frightening zombies and next into incessantly laughing skeletons. In a matter of seconds, and without any indication of resistance, Frank, Lois, Fred and Eleanor obediently joined *their* un-illustrious and totally accursed damned company on a mysterious journey into infinity.

"The Christian Republican Left"

Powerful members of the Fraternal Order of Constructionists had in 2040 AD founded the exclusive "Society of the Christian Republican Left". The newly-established secret brotherhood believed that the United States of America had sinfully drifted away from its original "divinely inspired purpose and direction". The new-found movement started in Delaware, the nation's "First State," and its three most influential members were Samuel Wilkes, a prominent Dover and Wilmington banker; William Rogers, a devout right wing conservative Anglican minister; and Richard Adams, a very wealthy "old money" importer/exporter.

The "CRL" had its historical roots in certain fundamentalist chapters in Rehoboth Beach, Lewes, and Bethany Beach, all Atlantic seashore resort communities having religious origins; and then "the growing movement" spread-out from those respective Delaware communities, gradually establishing clandestine chapters (exclusively chartered among White Anglo-Saxon European stock Americans) in Dewey Beach, in Fenwick Island, in Milford, and in Smyrna. From those humble origins, the fledgling organization gradually matured to having a membership of over one million serious advocates and adherents in all fifty states. The CRL had little to do with liberal "left wing politics.," which its ultra-conservative membership virtually unanimously abhorred. The unique oxymoron title "Christian Republican Left" received its appellation from the cartel's founders' secret salutation of deliberately greeting one another by shaking their left hands.

Samuel Wilkes, the renowned Delaware financier, William Rogers, the fire-and-brimstone Episcopalian televangelist, and Richard Adams, the affluent and dynamic international products and commodities dealer met on July 4th, 2155 in Wilkes' luxurious penthouse atop the Star of the Sea Condominiums, overlooking the Rehoboth Beach boardwalk and beach, with the tranquil Atlantic Ocean gleaming in the background. The trio of determined men shared parallel philosophical opinions in regard to what they considered the "corrupt denigration of American democracy by immoral socialist left-wing Democrats".

"In five short years, it'll be 2160, the 540th anniversary of the noble Pilgrims' landing in Massachusetts at Plymouth," Minister William Rogers reminded his all-too-adamant colleagues. "This nation was gloriously founded on the idea of religious freedom; yes Gentlemen, on the premise of *Christian* religious freedom long before the Constitution was savagely perverted to allow Arab radicals and terrorists to roam about freely from mosque to mosque with designs of undermining our national security. Yes, my esteemed Colleagues; in the beginning," William Rogers lectured and emphasized, "Massachusetts and Rhode Island belonged to the Pilgrims and the Puritans; Pennsylvania to the Quakers and other devout Protestant denominations; and the Maryland Colony to the Catholics. Just look at what Godless deviations have occurred in the United States of America since our mostly Mason founding fathers had authored and endorsed the Declaration of Independence and had later conducted themselves admirably in the Revolutionary War! The last hundred years have been a dangerous, immoral, precipitous slide down an extremely slippery slope!"

"Your God-inspired comments, William, have hit the bull's-eye right in the center of the target area," Samuel Wilkes commended the fiery Reverend Rogers. "Hopefully, in the new national era, *we*, the rightful leaders of our *ordained* organization, will ensure that Thanksgiving Day will be the new 4th of July. Our country will experience a political and spiritual Renaissance, just like Italy and Europe had a magnificent cultural Renaissance in the 1400s," the banker enthusiastically prognosticated. "We must engineer and initiate our plan so that we can use our political and financial clout to have a rebirth of Christian values in America. We must take back our country from the atheists, the gays, the blacks, the woman's rights advocates, and the anti-war dissidents," Samuel Wilkes implored his co-conspirators. "Our nation must have a much-needed rebirth, and then quickly revert back to its original purpose for existence. America must return to possessing a moral compass firmly based on the Ten Commandments, and our country's philosophy should *not* be predicated on exploiting dangerous liberal interpretations of the First Ten Amendments. Our numerous enemies," Wilkes reminded his associates, "both our internal and international adversaries," the wealthy financier qualified, "have, with the collaboration of soulless, amoral and greedy lawyers, advanced *their* sinful causes and agendas. The abusers are using the Bill of Rights along with the rest of the sacred Constitution to pervert and traduce our fundamental national values. Indeed Gentlemen, our heritage is in serious jeopardy! Wouldn't you agree with my assertions, Richard?"

"Yes; without a doubt," the very rich and on-a-mission Richard Adams concurred with the very prestigious Samuel Wilkes. "The Pilgrims had inadvertently landed on the Cape Cod peninsula at Provincetown before heading onward to the Massachusetts mainland,

and ironically, today, Provincetown along with *our own* Rehoboth Beach are havens for gays and lesbians, avowed practitioners of debauchery who believe that they're free to openly practice their vile Sodom and Gomorrah licentious lewdness in public. These arrogant in-your-face sinners are both unabashed and unashamed of their baneful, disgusting, reprehensible behavior. Now Gentlemen," the prominent banker continued his narrative, "it's up to us as dedicated directors of the CRL to put a stop to this disgraceful demonstration of evil before the wicked travesty ravenously consumes America from sea to shining sea."

"And getting back to history, then the thirteen eastern colonies became the thirteen original states with our Delaware being one of them," Minister William Rogers reviewed and stated. "I say in all good conscience that America is doomed to the fires of Hell unless this blessed land returns back to its Puritan roots and its Christian family values. It's no longer sufficient simply being the minority Right Wing Neocons, Gentlemen. Our Christian Republican Left must gain control of the United States, and return our blessed land to the same sober, ethical state of mind that existed back in Philadelphia in 1776. Now Gentlemen," the rhetorical manipulator of words continued his didactic narrative as if *he* were occupying a church pulpit, "I firmly believe that 13 is a lucky Heavenly-favored number. We should start our Bible-inspired campaign by first purging sin out of Delaware, and then systematically cleansing the remaining twelve original colonies of Satan's evil practices. Yes, I insist that 'ethic cleaning' shall begin with 'ethnic cleansing!' Are our honorable militias in the northeast ready to conduct their separate crusades against God's avowed enemies? Are they ready up in New England?"

"Yes, Sir!" the dedicated-to-the-cause Samuel Wilkes confirmed to William Rogers. "All of our eager-for-action commando units are prepared to assassinate the thirteen targeted governors; the twenty-six Senators, and the other listed dangerous Congressmen, diplomats, lawyers and judges. The CRL will soon have control of the entire eastern seaboard, in a year flat, I predict," Samuel Wilkes flagrantly boasted to his impressed comrades. "Especially with the support of our most elite members being in charge of all thirteen National Guards from Georgia right up to New Hampshire and Maine. And my capitalistic Wall Street associates are chomping at the bit to lead and finance the inevitable insurrection, just like patriotic Stephen Girard had used his personal fortune to help the Patriots' defeat the British during the War of 1812."

The three CRL leaders then discussed the methodology that would accomplish their immediate, sinister objective; that is, to gain dominion of the original thirteen eastern seaboard states. First of all, "incentive loans" would be offered to inner city blacks to get the "riffraff" out of urban areas from Boston down to Atlanta, and to strategically relocate "the ghetto masses" in warm states like Florida, Texas, Arizona, New Mexico, and California. As Samuel Wilkes aptly described it to his CRL comrades, "This much-needed purging of the thirteen Atlantic Coast states will be similar to the old nineteenth century adage of 'forty acres and a mule'. I'm certain that our monetary fifty-thousand-dollar bribes will easily accomplish *our* purpose. Once our military allies take over the East Coast, soon the state militias will become stronger than the regular Army, Navy, Air Force and Marines. Thank you, 'Article 2' of the U.S. Constitution for your benign assistance, ha, ha, ha!"

Then, Richard Adams added to Samuel Wilkes' observations and predictions. "Yes, Sam; and then the Harlem Project will be initiated where those urban blacks that didn't cooperate with our sugar-coated money compensation incentive offers will be biologically and chemically 'exterminated' by General Townsend's very competent New York Militia, or to use more benign nomenclature, the obstacle known as 'the ghetto dwellers' will be effectively and permanently 'eliminated'. And then the Newark, Jersey City, Philadelphia, Washington DC, Baltimore and Boston 'Sister Projects' will be swiftly implemented. In many respects, my fine Gentlemen," the wealthy importer/exporter gloated, "Hitler had the right idea attempting to make Germany exclusively Nordic Aryan. But in our case here in America, the burden-to-society blacks, gays, atheists, Mexicans, drug addicts, and chronic alcoholics will be systematically dispensed with. Our vigilant State Militias will handle *that* essential responsibility. Just think Gentlemen," Adams proceeded with his profound propaganda. "All of the ugly sinfulness that the present United States indifferently tolerates will be effectively eradicated so that our 'New National Order' can rise to power and begin flourishing. All of the corrupt symbols of our parasitic, wasteful, politically correct government must be quickly erased," the famous importer/exporter maintained as if Richard Adams was Patrick Henry reincarnated. "And when the Capitol Building, the Supreme Court Building, and the White House are proudly burned just like the German Reichstag had been set ablaze in 1933, then…"

"Then, true measured freedom, responsible liberty, and a new rigid, inflexible justice system will become reality once more; and

America will again be able to lead the world in triumphing over evil by becoming a worthy model for every sinful European country to imitate," Minister Roger Williams pontificated. "America will once again be the true leader of the Free World."

"Excellent point! Great speech!" Richard Adams exclaimed and praised the venerable man of the cloth. "Just look at Japan and China, for instance! Those Oriental countries have no so-called sanctuary cities to accommodate illegal immigrants! They're all basically exclusionary; thus, allowing their own gene pools to prosper. Those self-protecting countries are not interested in mongrelizing *their* cultures and *their* civilizations by allowing too many outsiders to contaminate their populations' gene pools by *liberally* allowing natives of their lands to intermarry with foreigners," Richard Adams persuasively elucidated. "Tokyo and Beijing have been achieving right along what Adolph Hitler had failed to accomplish in Nazi Germany. In order to compete with the proliferating Chinese and the ambitious Japanese on a worldwide scale, *we* must first..."

"Cleanse our fifty-states of all harmful, deleterious non-Christian, unproductive, and evil elements so that WASP America can be both revived and rejuvenated; therefore, giving *us* an even playing field on which to compete with our Japanese and Chinese economic and military rivals," Samuel Wilkes firmly indicated to his political soul-mates. "We'll scrupulously transport the Mexican and other dark-skinned Hispanic infections to the warm states to join the blacks, gays, drug addicts, atheists, criminals and other malignant sub-cultures. As much as I hate to admit it, the Nazis had the right idea! We must purify America by first purifying our mongrel gene pool. We've reached a stage in *our* historical evolution where our country's laws are contaminating our basic moral principles. Laws should be absolute, and not arbitrary. God's laws should always prevail over man's defilement of it!"

"Agreed! Bravo! Bravo!" Richard Adams praised his banker colleague's rambling, extemporaneous oration. "Within a year our marvelous plan will go into effect. We'll save America from itself if it's the last thing we'll ever do! And if our critics vociferously balk and claim that *our* adopted methods are 'discrimination', let it be said and known that throughout history good has always discriminated against evil. When things are black and white with little gray area in between," Adams pompously resumed his garrulous discourse, "then nothing is subject to interpretation, and everything is completely understood by the general populace. But please remember, Gentlemen; all black officers are to be excised from the State Militias within the next year, and when the thirteen separate rebellions occur all at the same time, the whites in the regular Armed Services will also rebel and chase-out blacks and Hispanics, and gays from *their* infected ranks. If all goes according to the prescribed script," Adams hypothesized and concluded, "then Friends, I predict that the much-warranted takeover of the United States of America should occur in less than two months of ongoing internal strife and intense conflict."

"Plato was absolutely right in what he had so eloquently expressed in his *Republic!"* William Rogers sagely concluded and shared. "Only honorable and moral people should be eligible for citizenship, which should, in the final analysis, be an earned *privilege* based on individual performance and good reputation, and not be predicated on an automatic *right* conferred upon a person at birth. And the major difference between a republic and a democracy is that in a republic there is respect for law, organization and tradition," the renowned televangelist communicated. "That's exactly the kind of patriotism that conservatives do best, Gentlemen! We patriotically *conserve* our revered American way of life! Too much democracy will ultimately only lead to open anarchy! American Democracy has really become wicked socialism in disguise!"

* * * * * * * * * * * * *

In mid-September, Samuel Wilkes and Richard Adams delegated the talented William Rogers to author the "New American Manifesto" that would represent the official blueprint outlining the future direction and function of the United States of America. "You'll be like *our* own Thomas Jefferson; wonderfully organizing the requisite ideas we've been diligently discussing over the past five years," Wilkes congratulated the thoroughly elated Episcopalian preacher. "You'll give much-needed definition and meaning to our presently fragmented CRL *revolutionary* ideas. You're a born wordsmith; Bill!"

"We'll meet again a week from today at eight p.m. sharp for dinner and a detailed progress report at the Embers Restaurant on 24th Street and Philadelphia Avenue down in Ocean City, Maryland!" Richard Adams suggested to William Rogers and Samuel Wilkes. "The resort city will be virtually devoid of the annoying tourist crowd, and we'll have the entire place to ourselves to review last minute details to the essential document that *you,* dear William, will be assiduously drafting. What do you think Reverend Bill?"

"I do believe that the thoroughfare Philadelphia Avenue in Ocean City, Maryland above 17th Street is called Coastal Highway," the always precise William Rogers respectfully corrected his less meticulous CRL ally. "17th Street marks the boundary between old Ocean City and New Ocean City, which as *you* know, had been annexed into the ten-mile-long stretch of beach way back in the 1960s, if my nebulous memory still accurately serves me. And conversely," the acclaimed minister proceeded, "the New American Manifesto will clearly mark the boundary between the old dysfunctional America, and the new necessary and vibrant Christian Republican Left America, that's impatiently waiting on the horizon to happen."

"Yes, Reverend Rogers," Samuel Wilkes readily conceded to the minister while simultaneously endorsing Richard Adams' proposal about the next scheduled meeting of the CRL intelligence committee. "I'll get a room at the newly renovated Holiday Inn up near the 62nd Street Bridge; you know, the *Route 90 Expressway* into north Ocean City. Reverend Bill; you're welcomed to join me and stay in my suite," the pompous banker invited the appointed wordsmith. "The food in the Reflections Restaurant at the Holiday is gourmet to say the least, and I promise that the treat will be on me. Or Bill; we could dine at Phillips Seafood Restaurant instead if that's what you'd prefer."

"No thanks!" the highly focused church minister William Rogers politely declined. "When visiting Ocean City, my wife and I usually stay at the old Atlantic Hotel; four blocks up from the inlet on the boardwalk between Wicomico and Somerset Streets. It's a quaint, old-fashioned, casual hotel featuring Tiffany lamps in the lobby, and it's located just north of the town's only amusement pier," the preacher further elaborated. "The Atlantic's reduced fall room rates are much more reasonable than the ones at the much more exorbitant Holiday Inn!" the frugal and thrifty minister added. "My dear wife's wild spending habits, and her frequent mall excursions keep me operating on a rather strict budget. My spendthrift spouse is far from being parsimonious!"

"After you finish writing the New American Manifesto," Samuel Wilkes remarked to Puritanical William Rogers, "then you could put together the Second Constitution of the United States! You certainly have the fine language and grammatical acumen to do precisely that, you know!"

* * * * * * * * * * * * *

In mid-September, the Reverend William Rogers occupied the desk inside his modest third-floor room at the landmark Atlantic Hotel, while his extravagant wife Esther was out shopping looking for season closeout bargains in souvenir and casual apparel shops situated along the popular Ocean City, Maryland boardwalk. The televangelist meticulously organized his random ideas, and then laboriously commenced incorporating them into his 'highly focused principles' that would constitute the first draft of "The New American Manifesto".

'Let's see now,' Rogers imagined while looking out the window overlooking Somerset Street. 'Freedom of speech; freedom of press, and freedom of religion will be limited only to white European ancestry Christian Republican Lefts. As an exception, Italians (and Sicilians) are to be accepted as part of the standard 'Occidental Christian heritage'. And *those* specially described and listed *privileges* must be earned and maintained, all according to one's accomplishments and one's contributions to the general society. They are not *unalienable rights* as is currently believed and practiced. Citizenship will not be automatically conferred at birth! And I must remember to include the statement that two felony convictions will result in the immediate loss of citizenship and prestige. Yes, *that* specific condition must be a veritable reality not subject to either debate or change!'

According to the particulars of the "breakthrough document" being developed by William Rogers, certain *revolutionary* elements were essentially introduced into and defined in the New American Manifesto. 'Radicals and anti-government Arabs, along with Hindus and Buddhists, will either be deported from the country or be conveniently transported to Florida, Texas, New Mexico, Arizona and California,' William conscientiously contemplated. 'After the apathetic urban dwellers from the original thirteen states have been removed from their all-too-comfortable slums, and sent to the warm climate states, then the 'Red States' family-oriented areas in the former 'Bible Belt' are to be rid of welfare recipients, atheists, gays and lesbians, felons, blacks, drug addicts, dope distributors, Hispanics, and also of indolent Indians parasitically living on reservations. Those disposable, welfare-dependent individuals will then be immediately transported to New Texas, which would ultimately become the new 'American Reservation' reserved for all of the formerly undesirable elements of society. I must make certain that in the New America, law and order, and family values, must take precedence and prevail over all else.'

William Rogers next concentrated his cerebral activity on other articles to be neatly synthesized into the New American Manifesto. 'The 'undesirable elements' living in Florida, New Mexico, Arizona and California will be conveyed under military and police supervision to myriad security barracks in New Texas. When all of the 'non-productive individuals' living off the welfare of the productive white citizens of America have been herded and corralled into New Texas, then the central 'Red States', and also Florida, New Mexico, Arizona, and California could then smoothly join the thirteen original states, and be efficiently absorbed into the new United States of America, which would ultimately consist of fifty prosperous and indigenous Christian Republican Left districts. The country will finally be ethnically and ethically cleansed, and we'll let the exiled lawyers down in New Texas figure-out how *that* deliberately isolated mass of wasteland will be able to survive on its own productivity with its millions of new imported, worthless residents no longer being a perpetual burden and drain on the incomes and lives of productive and conservative, God-fearing white Christian Republican citizens.'

On September 23rd at precisely 8 p.m., the three Christian right-wing confederates met at the aforementioned Embers Restaurant to orally review the articles that were to be included in William Rogers' initial draft of the "New American Manifesto".

"The spirit of the Louisiana Purchase and the pursuit of our enterprising pioneers' most august Western Movement, Manifest Destiny, must be re-captured, identified, and expressed in the 'New American Manifesto," Samuel Wilkes firmly instructed the greatly inspired and highly motivated William Rogers and Richard Adams. "Two years from now, our great New America will be born! It'll rise like the proverbial Phoenix from the ashes of despair! Yes, sir, Gentlemen, Darwin was positively right in making his extraordinary assumption! Everything must have renewal in order to adapt, endure, and survive. But first," Samuel Wilkes prefaced while switching to a more sociable subject of conversation. "Let's enjoy our succulent surf and turf dinners before our New World patriot seated next to me returns to the Atlantic Hotel and continues authoring his immortal document. I predict that someday, the old wood-framed Atlantic Hotel will be revered in public school classroom textbooks throughout America as being the new Independence Hall!"

"I'll drink to that!" importer/exporter Richard Adams echoed his political sentiments and religious convictions as the investor slowly raised his stemmed glass of Merlot wine. "Here's a toast to the ascension of the CRL to political and military prominence," the adamant co-founder proposed inside the nearly empty Embers main dining room. Then Adams addressed Samuel Wilkes in a low soft voice. "And I trust that you, Mr. Wilkes, have orchestrated the Second Great Depression stock market crash while secretly collaborating with your trustworthy Wall Street cohorts."

"Yes Richard, that'll be the first operational phase of our nice grandiose scheme," the influential banking tycoon smiled and lowly answered before sipping down a mouthful of red wine. "Once the stock market fails, everyone will be out of work; cash flows will cease; bills won't be paid; people will lose their mortgages, abandon their houses and their properties; and poverty will become rampant and on such a widespread scale that anarchy throughout the land will prevail. Consequently," Samuel Wilkes uttered and paused to gauge the impact of his words on his perceptive audience of two; "yes consequently, Gentlemen; the average starving American will gladly be willing to be transported at *our* expense under military and police supervision to warm climates states in the south and southwest. Then our little Christian coup can be satisfactorily put into motion with little political opposition.

"How could you be so sure?" asked wealthy importer Richard Adams. "You make it all sound too easy."

"Since the designated scum won't have any money to live, and since we'll promise them food, shelter, and welfare in the warmer states," Samuel Wilkes chuckled, "they'll wholeheartedly cooperate with our foolproof plan. And then, several months after the other states are cleansed of their heavy scum burdens, namely sin, crime and government waste, and after all of the social deviates have finally been transferred from Florida, New Mexico, Arizona and California to New Texas," the banker specified, "*we'll* promptly and gladly shut-off the welfare and funding valves. And soon, the disgusting vermin and their exploitative lawyers will start killing one another in New Texas, once the old economic system is no longer working in *their* favor. What poetic irony! Parasites will be killing parasites! Ha, ha, ha!"

"I have to get back to the Atlantic Hotel and finish-up my all-important first draft," William Rogers ambitiously disclosed, just as the Embers' waiter brought the three extra-large cherries' jubilee desserts to the table. "The sacred words 'In God We Trust' will have a much more tangible meaning, once I get through with modifying and refining the Manifesto's exact language. I just can't wait to finish-up the masterpiece!"

* * * * * * * * * * * * *

Reverend William Rogers had driven across Delmarva from Ocean City, Maryland to Baltimore to conduct some personal business. Before departing from the "Eastern Shore" beach town, the televangelist had promised his wife Esther that he would be returning to the resort early the following morning. But the famous minister's meeting with an Episcopal Church Council wound-up ending early, so the TV preacher decided to return to the Atlantic Hotel and finish-up his New American Manifesto in order to show copies of the completed manuscript to Samuel Wilkes and to Richard Adams the following afternoon.

'I'll coordinate the last seven paragraphs, and have the language typed-up on my laptop computer by noon tomorrow morning!' the anxious minister thought. 'I'm slated to meet again with Sam and with Rich at Phillip's Seafood Restaurant tomorrow evening at 8 p.m. to give them copies of the final draft. I hope that Esther hasn't spent a small fortune gallivanting around the myriad Ocean City malls and various shopping emporiums.'

Upon entering his third-floor Atlantic Hotel room, the nationally acclaimed televangelist was speechless when his arrival had barged-in on discovering his unfaithful wife in bed with the notorious importer/exporter tycoon, rich importer Richard Adams. Immediately, the dumbfounded intruder interrupting the romantic interlude, garnered his courage, and had the wherewithal to demand an immediate explanation from his cheating wife.

"Esther! How could you do this vile wicked betrayal to me! You're a Jezebel! A sinful Delilah! What has happened to your sacred wedding vows?" the jilted preacher vehemently accused and ranted. "Where is your loyalty to our marital relationship?"

"Never mind the meaningless small-talk!" Richard Adams answered as the discovered paramour slowly climbed out of the ancient bed in his boxer shorts, and next pointed and waved a handgun at his new protesting enemy. "You bungling Idiot! You would have to come back to your room early and spoil everything you had going for yourself!"

"What do you mean Richard?" the still-shocked Reverend William Rogers nervously asked as his emotions-in-turmoil did a complete vacillation from anger to fear. "Now don't do anything drastic or rash that you might regret! Please put the gun down!"

"Well now, my dear Reverend William, or should I call you Father Billy Boy," Adams condescendingly proceeded with his derision. "For your information, I've already shot and killed Sam Wilkes this morning when I accidentally discovered him lying in the sack with my wife in my condo' up in Bethany Beach. His body's already been disposed of, dropped off twenty miles at sea into the deep Baltimore Canyon between Rehoboth Beach and Cape May; his corpse was chained to a heavy slab of utilitarian concrete. The ocean predators will have a nice little surprise feast, that's for damned sure! Now unfortunately, for your ignorant, naïve sake, sanctimonious Reverend Bill, it looks like you're gonna' have to be my second shooting victim of the day!"

"Now Richard, please control your fierce temper and calm-down a bit! Don't get yourself into a dangerous rage and throw a tantrum!" Reverend William Rogers futilely pleaded. "Things can be worked out. An amicable solution can be arranged! Isn't that right, Esther? You don't even have to apologize to me!"

"That's what the hell you think!" an incensed, livid Richard Adams snidely returned. "Why do you suppose your adorable wife always wanted to go out shopping? Certainly not to spend *your* petty cash all over the Delmarva Peninsula! Wake up Billy Boy!" the man holding the revolver chided and admonished. "Esther desired to escape your lunatic, sanctimonious sermons and your irrelevant gospel ranting because your charming wife preferred being in bed with me!" Adams vehemently remarked and then snickered.

"I can't believe all of this is happening!" appalled and confused Reverend Rogers cried.

"It's *my* damned money Esther has been spending at the area malls all these years. And when I caught Sharon in bed with that nefarious skunk Sam Wilkes," Adams angrily confessed to Rogers, "I felt that I had to instantly eliminate the amorous impostor out of sheer jealousy and spite. It was without a doubt a strange double love triangle going on, with Wilkes hitting on Sharon; and with me hitting on Esther; and with *you* not suspecting *my* secret activity one second, simply because you were too foolishly trusting and unassuming about human nature, and you were too involved in your televangelism. and too engrossed in *your* propagation of the Christian Republican Left campaign to ever notice that your wife absolutely hates you!"

"Spare my life, and I'll forget that this regretful incident ever happened!" the TV preacher begged on his knees like as ancient Greek suppliant. "Have clemency! Please show me some generous Christian mercy!"

"You gullible, idealistic, quixotic Ignoramus!" Adams hollered across the hotel room. "You're just a dogmatic, religious Zealot; a clueless, moralistic, self-righteous Ideologue! True; the melting pot concept has been a two-century-old American façade; a national canard; a lousy ongoing myth!" Adams bellowed to Rogers. "And you're quite right in thinking that republics last over centuries but democracies flare-up, but then predictably soon die out. Republics breed cultural unity and democracies die because of cultural *diversity,* which is obviously the complete opposite of *unity!"* the irate madman rambled through several standard CRL talking points. "Plato be damned, along with all his confounded academic, Greek philosophical rhetoric!"

"What are you trying to say?" William Rogers jealously stammered. "You're speaking wild gibberish! Your jargon is too vague, too nebulous for me to comprehend! Now Richard, at least I have a clear conscience and am not a contemptible hypocrite like someone I know. Don't I always speak the truth?"

"You petty, inconsequential demagogue! Soon you'll be joining our old pal Samuel Wilkes in Davy Jones' very wet nautical locker. You'll also be fish chum at the bottom of the Baltimore Canyon," Adams augured. "Don't you get it Billy Boy? You're now the second disposable man being routed-out of *our* convoluted triumvirate! I'll soon have full control of the entire CRL! You're to me Billy Boy, exactly what Leon Trotsky had been to Vladimir Lenin and to Joseph Stalin! You're the jackass author of the movement, who incidentally is now considered expendable! You contemptible Dupe! Ha, ha, ha! And Esther here loves and honors me, and your fun-loving wife totally despises you! And all the while, you were too blinded by your impractical dreams and aspirations to ever fathom *that* salient truth!"

"I'll do anything that's feasible to appease you, but please don't pull the trigger!" the now paranoid minister implored the wanton murderer. Have mercy; please Richard, have mercy!"

"Your desperate cowardly pleas are all cried in vain, you repulsive craven Puritan; you deplorable, straightlaced, idiotic Prude! But face reality and experience your impending fate, Billy Boy!" Richard Adams imperatively dictated to his next murder victim. "I'm going to first tie you to that wooden chair, and next I'll shove a gag down your throat, and then you're gonna' emotionally suffer watching me making mad passionate love to your attractive wife!"

"No, Richard! Stop it! Stop it!"

"And then my fine-feathered, holier-than-thou Mr. Preacher Man; after you've agonized through witnessing *that* very special debauchery," the power-hungry tormentor arrogantly bragged, "you'll finally realize the vast discrepancy that's wholly existing between academic/political/religious philosophy and real-life biological gratification!" Richard Adams loudly articulated.

"What are you saying Richard? I don't fathom the meaning of your nebulous words?"

"It's your final chance to get real before you die, Reverend Billy Boy! But your great agony and anguish will all be done in vain! Yes, Reverend Bill!" the power-hungry narcissist indulgently laughed. "What a marvelous reversal! The shrimp and the lobsters will be having *you* for supper! Say your final prayers, Father Bill! Soon your soul will be fully prepared to meet your Maker! Get ready for your Last Supper, but *you* are going to be the food!"

About the Author

Jay Dubya is author John Wiessner's initials (J.W.) and also his pen name. John is a retired New Jersey public school English teacher and he had taught the subject for thirty-four years. John lives in southern New Jersey with wife Joanne and the couple has three grown sons.

Jay Dubya has written other adult literature besides *One Baker's Dozen. Fractured Frazzled Folk Fables and Fairy Farces* and *FFFF and FF, Part II*, are satires. *Black Leather and Blue Denim, A '50s Novel* and its sequel, *The Great Teen Fruit War, A 1960' Novel* and *Frat' Brats, A '60s Novel* are adult-oriented literary endeavors constituting a trilogy. *Pieces of Eight*, *Pieces of Eight, Part II, Pieces of Eight Part III and Pieces of Eight, Part IV* are short story/novella collections featuring science fiction, paranormal and humorous plots and themes. *Nine New Novellas* is the companion book to *Nine New Novellas, Part II*, *Nine New Novellas, Part III* and *Nine New Novellas, Part IV*. And *So Ya' Wanna' Be A Teacher* is a satirical autobiography describing the author's thirty-four-year educational career in American public schools.

Ron Coyote, Man of La Mangia is adult humor and the work is an imaginative satire/parody on Miguel Cervantes' *Don Quixote*, published in 1605. *Mauled Maimed Mangled Mutilated Mythology* is a work that satirizes twenty-one famous ancient Greek tales. *The Wholly Book of Genesis* and *The Wholly Book of Exodus* are also adult satirical humor works. *Thirteen Sick Tasteless Classics*, *Thirteen Sick Tasteless Classics, Part II*, *Thirteen Sick Tasteless Classics, Part III and Thirteen Sick Tasteless Classics, Part IV* are adult satirical rewrites of famous short fiction.

John has also authored a trilogy of young adult fantasy novels, *Enchanta*, *Pot of Gold* and *Space Bugs, Earth Invasion. The Eighteen Story Gingerbread House* is a new collection of eighteen diverse and creative children's stories.

Jay Dubya likes '50s rock and roll music and he also enjoys pop' songs by the Beach Boys, Fleetwood Mac, the Eagles, the Rolling Stones, *ELO*, John Mellencamp and by John Fogerty. When not writing or listening to music, Jay Dubya likes watching *76ers* basketball and *Phillies* and *Yankees* television baseball games.

Author Biography

Born in Hammonton, NJ in 1942, John Wiessner had attended St. Joseph School up to and including Grade 5. After his family moved from Hammonton to Levittown, PA in 1954, John attended St. Mark School in Bristol, PA for Grade 6, St. Michael the Archangel School in Levittown for Grades 7 and 8, and then Immaculate Conception School, Levittown, PA for Grade 9. Bishop Egan High School, Levittown PA, was John's educational base for Grades 10 and 11, and later in 1960, the aspiring author graduated from Edgewood Regional High, Tansboro, NJ. John then next attended Glassboro State College, where he was an announcer for the school's baseball games and also read the nightly news and sports over WGLS, GSC's radio station.

John Wiessner had been primarily an English teacher in the Hammonton Public School System for 34 years, specializing in the instruction of middle school language arts. Mr. Wiessner was quite active in the Hammonton Education Association, loyally serving in the capacities of Vice-President, then building representative, and finally, teachers' head negotiator for a period of 7 years. During his lengthy teaching career, John had been nominated into "Who's Who among American Teachers" three times. He also was quite active giving professional workshops at schools around South Jersey on the subjects of creative writing and the use of movie videos to motivate students to organize their classroom theme compositions.

In addition, John Wiessner was very active in community service, being a past President of the Hammonton Lions Club, where he also functioned for many years as the club's Tail-Twister, Vice-President and Liontamer. John had been named Hammonton Lion of the Year in 1979 and in 2009 received the prestigious Melvin Jones Fellow Award, the highest honor a Lion can receive.

John also was a successful businessman, starting with being a Philadelphia Bulletin newspaper delivery boy for two-years in the late 1950s in Levittown, Pennsylvania. After his family moved back to New Jersey in 1959, John worked at his grandparents and his parents' farm markets, Square Deal Farm (now Ron's Gardens in Hammonton) and Pete's Farm Market in Elm, respectively. He later managed his wife's parents' farm market, White Horse Farms in Elm for three summers.

Also, in a business capacity, for 16 summers starting in 1967 John Wiessner had co-owned Dealers Choice Amusement Arcade on the Ocean City, Maryland boardwalk and also co-owned the New

Horizon Tee-Shirt Store for eight summers (1973-'81) on the Rehoboth Beach, Delaware boardwalk. In addition, "Jay Dubya" was a co-owner of Wheel and Deal Amusement Arcade, Missouri Avenue and Boardwalk, Atlantic City. And then, for 18 summers beginning in 1986, John had been the Field Manager in charge of crew-leaders for Atlantic Blueberry Company (the world's largest cultivated blueberry farm), both the Weymouth and Mays Landing Divisions.

After retiring from teaching in 1999, writing under the pen name Jay Dubya (his initials), John Wiessner became the author of 75 books in the genre Action/Adventure Novels, Sci-Fi/Paranormal Story Collections, Adult Satire, Young Adult Fantasy Novels and also Non-Fiction Books. His books exist in hardcover, in paperback and in popular Kindle and Nook e-book formats.

In January of 2022, John Wiessner (Jay Dubya) was nominated into Marquis Who's Who in America, and in April of that same year, was one of nine distinguished Who's Who in America members honored with receiving Lifetime Achievement Awards, all nine sharing a news article of recognition appearing in the Wall Street Journal.

Google: Jay Dubya books
Google: Walmart, Jay Dubya

www.ingramcontent.com/pod-product-compliance
Lightning Source LLC
Chambersburg PA
CBHW020557310726
48979CB00008B/1252/J